D1523725

DEADLY DREAMS

KYLIE HATFIELD SERIES: BOOK FOUR

MARY STONE
BELLA CROSS

DESCRIPTION

Sometimes the rescuers need to be saved...

Search and rescue responders are going missing one by one. A predator is on the hunt, an aggressive monster out for revenge, and he's preying on those who risk their lives to save others.

Meanwhile, Kylie Hatfield has a wedding to plan. She and her search-and-rescue boyfriend, Linc Coulter, are finally getting married. If only they could skip the entire ceremony part and go straight to the honeymoon, she would be thrilled.

When her boss throws the case of a missing SAR from Georgia down on her desk, she jumps on it. It'll be just the thing to keep her and Linc busy, so Kylie can put off having to fret about invitations, DJs, napkin colors...

But little does Kylie know that, by taking this case, she's putting Linc in the path of a dangerous killer. A killer who has a score to settle with Asheville's top SAR guy—and who will not stop until Linc Coulter is dead.

Deadly Dreams is the fourth book in the Kylie Hatfield

Series and will take readers on a white-knuckled journey with memorable characters and a few good dogs.

1

Keep your head about you, Beez. Just a little longer.

As Beatrice Crosby admonished herself, she put money on her little lost lamb being around the next bend.

It was a gorgeous fall morning, with a sun-dappled canvas of bright autumn leaves overhead. Cool air braced her skin, and the sounds of birds chirping and insects buzzing their summer goodbye were like a symphony. Everything was in place for this to be a nice autumn stroll through Tallulah Gorge Park in Northeastern Georgia.

Except for that damn missing person.

Sighing, Beatrice berated herself. She didn't mean that. Missing people were her lifeblood and had kept her and her husband, Ollie, "in the lifestyle they'd grown accustomed to" ever since he'd been placed on disability a few years ago.

Still, Beatrice knew she wouldn't be able to fully enjoy the day until she'd safely returned the subject—another lost and hopeless—back to headquarters, whether he wanted to be there or not.

This particular little lost lamb was a sad case. Well, they

were all sad cases. But from what she'd heard, this was especially heart-wrenching. A young man, just twenty-two, had gone off after penning a farewell note to his sweetheart, explaining how his life just wasn't worth living anymore.

After being out on the trail for an hour, she lifted a hand to her chest, as she had for most of her nearly sixty years, picking up her worn Saint Anthony medal and kissing it. As she did, she said a prayer, "Anthony, patron saint of lost things and missing people, please deliver this lost lamb to us and ensure no harm comes to him."

She'd recited those same words thousands of times, but it never got any easier. She especially hated the young ones, giving up hope while still in the prime of their lives. Beez looked up at the glorious autumn day, blinking against the rain that was just beginning to fall again. Even on a cloudy day, the scenery all around her was glorious. How could one possibly witness such splendor of nature and think that life wasn't worth living?

Poor lamb.

In her three-plus decades of SAR work, she'd learned to have just as much of a nose for the way these things would go as the dogs she minded. They'd likely find him, sitting alone on a ledge, having determined not to make the jump after all. Then she'd have to employ her sense of diplomacy and a soft, encouraging voice to lure him back from the edge.

At least, that was what she was hoping for. The alternative was so much worse.

Her companion on this particular jaunt was Tiger, a brindle pit bull only a couple months into his SAR career. A tiny thing in stature, still a little skittish, the dog was coming along nicely. Beatrice'd trained hundreds of SAR dogs over the years, and three-year-old Tiger was shaping up to be one of her favorites.

They walked along a steep, narrow path astride the gorge that, in this spot, featured a three-hundred-yard drop to the river below. Tiger was careful about where he stepped, hugging the side of the mountain, and she liked that about him. So many dogs were just too eager, especially at the very start, and they'd make dangerous moves even with the proper training.

But Tiger was instinctively wary. There were quite a lot of fallen leaves on the ground, which could be slippery. The last thing Beez needed was to have him take the path too quickly and slip, sending both of them toppling over and hurtling to the jagged rocks on the gorge floor. Beez had found more than a few hikers at the bottom of the gorge, the victims of such a fall, too late to be rescued.

It wasn't pretty.

Tiger stopped at a rocky outcropping that jutted out into the gorge, letting out a small whimper. He looked up at Beez to make sure he was doing it right. When she nodded her approval, he ducked his head around the stone blockade, measured, and stepped himself over the obstacle with relative ease.

Not bad, little guy. That was one of the tougher maneuvers in old Tallulah.

Beez often told the other rescuers she trained—and she'd trained dozens of them—that she could walk the gorge blindfolded. She'd grown up in this area, first fishing with her father down on the river and then spending most of her summers as a teenager camping out here, so she knew it like the back of her hand. But that didn't mean the park was safe, even for her.

There were constant rockslides, especially after rainstorms, and it often seemed as though the terrain was always changing. Plus, many of the rocky trails were perilously narrow, barely enough for one person to walk, and high on a cliff's edge.

This obstacle, though, posed no trouble for Beez. Though her advancing age meant she wasn't in the greatest shape of her life, she did keep active. She practically vaulted over the rocky ledge to meet with Tiger on the other side.

She could give those cocky SARs half her age a run for their money, she wagered.

She ruffled his ears. "Good boy. Very good boy. Just a little more. I bet we find our missing man over here."

The Heights Trail was the only trail rated *extremely difficult* in the park's guide map, with the warning: *Only experienced hikers and those with proper equipment should attempt.* That was two years ago, before three people died on it in one awful summer.

For the next printing of the guide map, online and off, the Heights Trail had been removed, as well as all signage pointing it out from the main road. The only thing that remained was a bright-yellow sign at the very entrance to the trail, only visible to those attempting it. It read:

WARNING: DANGEROUS HIKE AHEAD

THE HEIGHTS TRAIL is not for those with physical limitations. Attempt this route only if you are physically fit, wearing proper footwear, and have experience in climbing near exposed cliffs and heights. Be prepared for high winds and allow three hours for a round-trip climb. Avoid this route during inclement weather or darkness. Stay on trail, and do not throw or dislodge rocks onto hikers below.

Permits required; all laws and regulations strictly enforced.

Persons have received serious injuries, and others have died on this mountainside! Do not be one of them!

. . .

THE SIGN WAS USUALLY ENOUGH to keep any day-hikers away.

But not always.

There were always several yahoos attempting it, which meant Beez and the others would be called in for a rescue. Most were fine. And then there were people who, either overestimating their abilities or underestimating the dangers the sign warned of, ended up in trouble.

And then there were those who just came here to end their lives.

This poor lost lamb hadn't said what trail he planned to go to in the suicide letter his girlfriend found. They never did; never made it easy. No, it was usually more like, *Goodbye cruel world* and *I can't be a burden to you any longer.* No specifics on location.

But the call had come in over the police radio at close to the same time that a hiker arrived at park headquarters, breathless and worried. She said she'd been on the Heights Trail and heard someone weeping, and when she'd looked over, she'd seen what looked like a glimpse of an orange parka through the trees.

She'd tried to call out to the person to see if he or she needed help but hadn't received any answer. It seemed as though the individual was on the very edge of a cliffside, and it had worried the hiker enough that she'd run all the way back to a ranger. Putting two and two together, the rangers had called in the nearest SARs available. Beez was one of them.

She was always one of them. She was proud that she was damn good at what she did. Proud that she was high on the call list.

Sweet of them, really, to leave the strenuous Heights Trail to her, the oldest one in the group.

She didn't mind, though. She was the most experienced, after all. The climb didn't bother Tiger or her. She felt more at home on this mountain than she did anywhere else in the world. In fact, her husband had proposed to her at the pinnacle of the trail thirty years ago.

She smiled at the thought of Ollie down on one knee, then helped Tiger up onto a waist-high step in the trail, just as the sun broke through the clouds. It was still raining a bit, so she stopped and looked for the rainbow she knew she would find.

There it was. A perfect arch of vibrant color, appearing like a blessing from the heavens.

Beez smiled again, allowing herself another minute to admire the meteorological phenomenon before taking hold of the metal spike lodged in the rocky ledge and hoisting herself up after the dog, huffing and puffing in a way she never had when she was younger.

Got to lay off those Oreos, she thought as she climbed the last few steps to the very end of the trail, a place overlooking the falls, where the trail opened up. Edging forward and shielding her eyes from the dappled sun with her hand, she looked over the cliffside, trying to spy that bit of orange the hiker had seen.

Nothing.

She looked again, straining her eyes, which also weren't what they used to be. She pulled out her binoculars and studied the area below more closely. Nothing.

Beez felt sure this was the place the worried hiker had been speaking of and scanned the area again. She could hear the falls from here, along with the swish of the breeze through the trees. But no one calling for help. No sign of life anywhere.

Well, so much for that. Lady must've been hallucinating.

That was the problem. Anytime someone reported a

missing person, the rescuers took directions from whoever reported it with a grain of salt. It was easy to get turned around or panic in the heat of the moment and forget what you'd seen or where you'd seen it. Often these things were like wild-goose chases.

But knowing that, Beez had kept her eyes peeled for that glimpse of orange the whole way up. She hadn't seen a thing. She also hadn't heard a peep from the tracker below, who'd been assigned to scour the base of the cliffs with his cadaver dog.

She'd have to hold off on praising God for his glory on this beautiful day just a little bit longer.

She turned to head to her right, around a bend, where the little-known trail met with the more popular and heavily traveled North Rim Trail. This trail was deemed *moderate* in the guidebooks. It had its steep drop-offs, but it wasn't nearly as perilous as the one she'd been on.

She relaxed a little, then picked up her radio. "Come in, headquarters."

"Hey, Beez, what's up?"

"Just finished up on the Heights Trail. No sign of him or anyone else yet. I'm alone out here. Anyone else see anything?"

"Negative."

"The woman give you any more details?"

"Nothing other than what you were told in the briefing. You looking for an orange jacket?"

"Yep. There's nothing that can possibly be construed to be an orange jacket out here on Heights. Trust me."

"All right. Keep at it. Come back along the North Rim. You shouldn't be going back the way you came. Too dangerous."

She opened her mouth to say that he was wrong. Nothing was too dangerous out here for her. She'd told headquarters that, time and time again. But the ranger beat her to it as the radio crackled and came back with, "For Tiger, I mean."

She smiled, hitched her walkie-talkie to her belt, wiped a honey-colored curl from her forehead, and adjusted her grip on Tiger's leash. "Poor lost lamb," she muttered, still listening for any signs of distress.

Nothing.

Great.

She hated to think what that might mean. That this particular lost and hopeless had finally decided to take the life-ending plunge.

From here, the tree-cover was too much to see the bottom of the gorge. However, if that was the case, someone at the bottom would've seen it by now. There were always fishermen down there, and hikers enjoying the falls. Plus, she'd sent Kevin and Molly down Sliding Rock to the gorge floor. If he hadn't radioed in by now, it was a good sign.

That meant there was still hope.

Noticing Tiger was starting to hang his head and pant a little more than usual, she ruffled his ears. "You thirsty, boy?"

He licked her hand. Aw, of course he was. That'd been some workout. The Heights Trail was not for babies.

The dog was a peach. Ollie'd gotten him for her on her fifty-seventh birthday, from the pound. They'd become the best of friends. Beez had been around dogs all her life, but Tiger was like her second self. Her children were grown and out of the house now, scattered across the United States. She had grandchildren but only got to see them once in a blue moon. So, Tiger was her baby. She doted on him, pouring all the love and attention she had for her six grandchildren on that pup.

Beez glanced up when she heard the noise of footsteps coming close. Heavily traveled was right—it seemed like everyone was off on the North Rim Trail today. She figured she'd probably meet up with a couple of the other rescuers from her SAR team, probably by the Pulpit, but she was high above it. Devil's Pulpit, a large, very popular rocky outcropping at the bottom of the gorge was probably hopping with people, even on this rainy day. Lonnie had been sent to the South Rim, and Crystal the North.

Beez was familiar with all the roads less traveled, the hidden gems. She knew there was a nice spot to rest only a quarter-mile down the trail, just above the Pulpit, that would be less populated and have more shade for her tired pup. She led Tiger to it, stepping aside on the trail every so often to let more hikers pass her by.

The resting spot was just an area with a nice, scenic view overlooking the falls. There were a couple of picnic benches, but nothing more. She looped Tiger's leash around the branch of a sapling and dropped her heavy pack, then pulled out his collapsible water dish.

Filling it from a bottle of water, she sat down on one gnarled plank of the picnic table, lowering the water bowl for him to drink before pouring him some kibble into another collapsible dish. He slurped it up in great, thirsty licks, splashing more water out of the dish than swallowing it. She petted his brindled coat and smiled at him with all the love in her being.

"That's it," she said soothingly, surveying the area. "Take it easy, boy. Not too fast."

As she was stretching, she heard it.

She paused to listen, but the sound didn't come again. It could have been a child, shrieking in glee.

Or a person, screaming in agony.

Beez stood, her knees popping at the movement, and pulled a few treats from her pack. Leaving them on the ground beside the bowl, she headed in the direction of the noise, holding on to the trees for balance.

The skeletal branches of smaller brush clawed at her red L.L.Bean jacket as she took another few steps into the woods, toward the ledge. She crunched over a blanket of newly fallen leaves, pushing aside branches that threatened to poke her eyes. When she reached the ledge, she looked over but saw nothing but some scrubby pine. No flashes of orange. Nothing that she was looking for.

Although…

Wait. There was something.

Nothing obvious, but still, something that didn't quite fit in.

It looked like there was a bit of something glinting on the side of a faraway ridge just a bit below them, across the gorge. She craned her neck, unable to make it out, and pissed that she'd left her binoculars back in her pack with Tiger.

Beez grabbed instinctively for her St. Anthony medal, praying for some sign.

Whatever the sound was, it hadn't come from there. That was too far away. The sound was probably just a child having fun on the trail. Sounds always seemed to echo around this gorge. It was all the rocks surrounding them. It was impossible to tell what noise came from where.

Shaking her head, she'd just begun to turn when Tiger barked, the sound like a bullet in the quiet environment.

Tiger was a good watchdog. Almost too good. He barked whenever he saw another human anywhere. Ones he disliked. Ones he liked. Mailmen. Babies. Old men with canes. Birds. Squirrels. And he had a sharp, ear-splitting bark that clawed at her nerves. It was his only flaw.

A gust of wind blew the hood off her head, just as the sun slid behind a fat, gray cloud. Cold raindrops struck her face, and she quickly pulled her hood back up, tightening the drawstrings under her chin.

Tiger barked again. Louder. Sharper. More urgent.

"What is it, boy?" she called, then startled as a form appeared among the dark branches, adorned in a thick cover of sunshine-yellow leaves.

She squinted, blinking away the rain caught in her lashes. Her eyes certainly weren't what they were. "Jaxon? Is that you?"

No answer.

As the figure drew closer, she recognized the jacket. She'd poured compliments on it back at headquarters, because her L.L.Bean jobbie was fraying at the sleeves and she needed a new one. She'd asked where she could get herself some fancy duds like that. It was from the newest line by North Face.

She had to remember that. She had a birthday coming up, and Ollie, bless his poor, shopping-challenged heart, was always wondering what to get her.

Money was tight, though, with him on disability. She could probably stick with her L.L.Bean jacket for another season or two. She hated to be a fuss.

"Hey, North Face," she said, pointing over toward the thing glistening in the sunlight across the ridge. "What do you think that is?"

She was joined at the edge. "Where?"

She squinted again, but with the sun behind the cloud, the reflection had disappeared. She shook her head. "I don't see it now. Looked like a reflection, swinging back and forth like a pendulum."

Then it hit her, and she actually laughed out loud.

"What are you laughing about?"

"I think what I saw was a wristwatch on a hiker or some-thing like that. My eyes just aren't what they—"

She never had a chance to finish her sentence as strong hands pressed against her back and pushed.

Beatrice Crosby tried to right herself, tried to reach out and grab something…anything.

But her hands closed around nothing but air as she fell, face-first, into the gorge she'd practically been raised in. She didn't have time to fight, but she had time to scream.

And scream she did. For as long as it took to fall hundreds of feet to the shallow Tallulah River below.

2

Kylie Hatfield turned the radio up loud and danced around the office of Starr Investigations. As she did, she opened the "A" drawer and dropped a paper into a file folder under the October tab.

Goodbye, October. Don't let the door hit you in the ass, she thought, even though there were a couple days still left in the month. She might be leaving for Georgia soon, so October and all its Halloween fun would probably be gone before she walked into this building again.

Lifting her long brown hair up off her shoulders and gathering it into a messy bun on top of her head, she started to pump her legs as she shuffled to the next pile of papers, most of them boring surveillance bills for Starr Investigations' biggest client, Impact Insurance. They might have been snooze worthy, but they made up a good portion of her paycheck.

It had been starting to get cooler, so she'd broken out a cardigan for the first time since spring. Bad choice. Thanks to Mother Nature's bipolar personality, today was hotter than previous days. The soft cashmere fabric clung to her body with sweat, so she pulled it off and threw it on her chair, then did a series of squats.

As she transitioned to lunges, Greg walked in and grimaced at her.

He didn't say a word.

"Hey you," she said, turning to lunge in his direction. "I'm just a steel town mountain girl. On a Saturday night."

He harrumphed and stalked to his desk. "I bet you are."

She sashayed up to him, taking his hand, doing a twirl. "What up, boss?" she sang in time with the music.

He stared at her, then flipped on his computer. "Someone's happy," he grumbled. "I hate happy."

Ah, Greg Starr, the owner of Starr Investigations, the place where Kylie had been working since spring. He had the most successful private investigations firm in the whole city, and he acted like it was a noose around his neck. Kylie had to wonder, if she had been in the private investigations business for that long, would *she* be just as bitter?

"I'm not happy," she said, doing a Kick ball change dance move back to the file cabinets. "I'm exercising."

He looked over his monitor at her. "And...you can't go to a gym, why?"

She deposited another paper in the proper place and gave him jazz hands. "Because I have so much filing to do," she sang, drawing out every syllable in as close to a Celine Dion version as she could manage. "I've been putting it off for weeks. And not only that, I have a wedding dress to fit into...*someday*." She drew the last part out long and loud, channeling the singer's performance at the climax of "My Heart Will Go On."

Greg covered his ears. "Fine. Whatever it takes to get it done, but can you dial it down a bit? My ears and eyes are bleeding. I'd give anything to unsee and unhear right now."

Kylie grinned, genuine affection for the grump making

the smile grow wider. They'd been working together so long that, by now, he had to know that she ranked filing and straightening the office, two of the things she'd originally been hired for, somewhere among root canal work. She knew he'd be okay with anything she did to spice up the monotonous grind of her daily grunt work. He just lived to grumble. About pretty much everything.

Plus, this was killing two birds with one stone. She didn't exercise, but one of these days she and her mom were going to go out dress shopping. They had to. Her fiancé—she held up her left hand, admiring the sparks of light coming off the beautiful diamond Linc Coulter put on her hand not long ago—had hinted about them setting a date for Christmas, which was only a couple short months away. The last thing she wanted to do when she put on her dress was look like a ghost whale.

That took her happiness down a notch or two. The dress. Even the thought of finding *the* outfit for *the* day when she was supposed to look her *absolute* best…gave her hives.

Talk about pressure.

Actually, everything about planning a wedding made her want to go bury her head in the sand somewhere, ostrich-style.

She'd much rather just flashdance her woes away.

"Did they ever call you with more info on the missing SAR woman?" she asked, bumping the filing cabinet closed with her hip. Greg had gotten a call earlier that day, telling her that he had a new case for her, but wanted to sort through additional details before he sent her packing to Georgia. That had been hours ago, and she was itching to know more.

"Yeah," he said, lacing his hands in front of him. "That's what I need to talk to you about, kid. I'm sorry for putting this case in your lap so soon after your…adventure."

She sat down, breathing hard, wiping sweat from her brow. It was so unusually warm for the end of October that it felt like summer, and they didn't have the AC on. It'd have been a little sticky, even without the dance break.

"Are you kidding me? Bring it," she said excitedly, grabbing her trusty notepad and pencil. "I'm on the case, boss!"

Kylie never backed down from a challenge. Even though she'd just gotten done with an "adventure," as Greg called it, that involved learning who her real father was and dealing with a mafia madwoman he'd married after disappearing on Kylie's mother, she was up for anything. She hated sitting around, waiting for work to fall in her lap. She loved action, loved being in the thick of things.

He lifted a paper from his beaten old briefcase and stared at it, and Kylie's bit of patience snapped. She turned the music down and leaned forward. "Come on, spill."

He stared at her through his bifocals, the crotchety look back on his face. "What are you, three?"

"I'm excited! Enthusiasm is a good thing, boss. You should try it." She stared at the back of the paper he was reading, trying to make out the words. "Come on. I need to get the details to Linc. He's been doing an online seminar all day, so I haven't been able to talk about going to Georgia with him yet."

Linc Coulter, her fiancé.

She never got tired of hearing the word, even as that same word still scared her more than just a little. But she was getting used to it, having someone to lean on, someone she could trust. Someone besides her mother to have her back and love her unconditionally, zany personality and all.

Not only that, she thrilled at the prospect that the two of them could work together, solving missing persons crimes. Since she was training to be a private investigator, and he was a search and rescue guy, they complimented each other so well. In many other ways too.

Where she was a risk-taker, he was the voice of reason. Where she had the brains—when she deigned to use them—he had the brawn. She invited trouble, he deflected it. They'd kick ass together as a team of crime-fighters, like Batman and Batgirl, if only given the chance.

Greg nodded. "Yeah. It's for a friend of mine from high school."

She stared at him, her mouth an O of mock-surprise. He hadn't told her about the close connection when he mentioned the missing SAR woman earlier that day. "Wait. Really? They had high schools when you were young?"

"Haha," he said, studying the paper. "Most of my class-mates are dinosaurs, but Ollie is an actual human being. And he's in trouble. I think you can help him, you and that ever-so-dreamy fiancé of yours."

Kylie felt bad for joking about it, even though with Greg, it was just too easy. They could usually go back and forth, mildly insulting each other all day. It made the boring days a lot more interesting, trying to think of ways to get Greg's proverbial goat since the seasoned PI didn't get upset by much. But with this, she thought she detected more than a bit of concern in Greg's voice.

"What do you need us to do?"

Greg let out a breath that smelled of the cigarettes he smoked whenever he wasn't in the office. "Well, as I told you, he called me, very distraught after his wife went missing in Tallulah Gorge. They still haven't found her. You know the gorge?"

She shook her head. When it came to state parks, Linc was the expert. "I don't."

"Well, it's on the border between Georgia and South

Carolina, only a hundred miles or so from Asheville. Nice scenery, so I hear."

In Kylie's mind, anything called a gorge couldn't be very beautiful at all, but she didn't say a word. As much as she wasn't a fan of any outdoor activity, she knew it was right up Linc's alley. He was the best search and rescue guy in the state, and Linc and his German Shepherd, Storm, made a really unstoppable duo. They'd handled thousands of cases in the area. But this was North Carolina. That was Georgia. A little out of his jurisdiction. "Why us? Why isn't the Georgia SAR looking for her?"

Greg snorted. "Beez *was* SAR. She and her dog were on the trails looking for a missing hiker. They found the hiker at the bottom of the gorge, dead from an apparent fall. But Ollie's wife and her dog just disappeared during the search. Ollie's heartbroken. Been married over thirty years. He sounds like he doesn't know what to do, he's so beside himself."

"That's terrible," Kylie murmured.

"I was going to take a ride down there, just to pay him a visit, but you two would be more help than I could be."

Kylie nodded. So what if the case involved tromping around in the wilderness? So what if she didn't know Ollie? She already felt terrible for the poor man and wanted to help. And Greg looked so distraught…

"Yes. Of course."

The relief that flooded Greg's features made Kylie even more intent on helping her boss, no matter how much of her comfort zone got destroyed out in the wilderness.

"Woman's name is Beatrice Crosby, known as Beez to her friends, and the dog is a pit bull named Tiger. She radioed in from the North Rim Trail to tell headquarters that she hadn't found anything of the missing hiker. That was the last anyone ever heard from her." Greg looked like he was aging right in front of her eyes. "It's been raining like hell, slowing everything down, and because of the uptick in visitors wanting to see the fall leaves, there has also been an uptick in missing persons, so the local SAR is being stretched thin."

"That's awful," Kylie said. She couldn't imagine what Ollie was going through, waiting and wondering for news of his spouse like that. She could only imagine he must be frantic. "Poor guy. And this happened yesterday? Does he think she'll be found alive?"

He shook his head. "Let's just say that he's very worried. Ollie knows that if Beez could have made it out, she would be out by now. Or she would have radioed for help. Something. Ollie's a good guy. Pretty easygoing. And he's not quite right with the way things have been playing out, or so he tells me."

Kylie's ears perked up. "What do you mean?"

"Well, he thinks that the local authorities aren't doing enough. He told me he thinks there might be something shady going on. That's why he was really hoping someone outside of the force would come in and give him an outside assessment."

There was nothing she liked better than shady goings-on. "Something shady...like what?"

Greg wagged a finger in her direction. "That's what you're going to find out."

Kylie nodded solemnly. "I will do my best."

Greg rolled his eyes. "Yeah. He tells me his wife was brought up on that mountain and that she can find her way around there in the dark. And she's had decades of experience as a tracker and outdoorswoman, so it just doesn't add up in his book. He suspects foul play. Plus, her body not being found is more than a little suspicious."

"Hmm," Kylie said, unsure of how quickly a body should

be found under those circumstances. "Does seem a little suspicious."

"Right. So, you on it?"

"Yes!" Kylie shuffled to the edge of her seat. As if there was any other answer.

Then she looked at the last pile of paper on her desk and frowned. The case of her father hadn't been an official case, but Greg had wanted her to do all the paperwork as if it was. She'd been avoiding it, some because she'd taken time off to tend to the gunshot wound Linc had sustained during the struggle with her father's crazy mafia-princess wife. But mostly, she just didn't want to relive how disappointed she was in the man who'd abandoned her as a baby.

"But…can I?" She waved a hand at the folder titled William Adam Hatfield. "You're okay with me leaving you alone?"

He snorted. "You think I can't handle this place without you?"

Well, he'd managed this as a one-person office for thirty years, so she suspected he'd be fine. But upon her recommendation, he'd begun some sorely needed technological upgrades. He'd recently gotten them used computers, and she'd switched out the old fire hazard of a coffee maker for a Keurig. But after she'd brought in all this new-ish technology —it wasn't really new, considering that most people had been using the things for decades—she realized precisely why Greg was averse to it. Technology hated him. And he hated it right back. If it had more than one button, he wasn't interested.

She motioned to the Keurig. "You and that coffee maker have daily fights. If it weren't for me, you probably would've died from caffeine deprivation."

"True, the thing is ridiculous. But there's a coffee shop

down the street, and I kept the old one under the sink, just in case. I'll live."

"And the computers?"

"I have that help desk you fixed me up with. I'll handle it." He shrugged. "Besides, you're the one who uses the computer. Most of what I do is still manual. Except email. And what can happen with email?"

She gnawed on her lip doubtfully. "But you're barely ever around this place to begin with. You're always so busy." Though she wasn't sure about that. Most of the time when he was gone, she wasn't sure if he was out on a case or just galli-vanting. "Don't you need me to help with—"

He waved his hand toward the door. "Get out of here. I've been thinking about reducing my caseload anyway."

She blinked. *Thinking* about reducing his caseload? She'd noticed that the paperwork had been growing slimmer, and she wondered if he'd started that reduction already. "Why?"

"I'm too old for a lot of this shit, kid. What can I say? I'm not a Hardy Boy anymore. The thrill is gone."

Her eyes widened. What did that mean? Did that mean he was going to close up shop soon? Retire? After she'd finally found a job she was good at, a job that made her want to wake up in the morning. And she still had over a year before she could get her own PI license. If she was ever going to do this permanently one day, did that mean she needed to start working with another PI before Greg retired? "But wait, what does that—"

"Short stuff. This ain't like you."

She stopped short, worry and confusion crashing together. "What do you mean?"

"You're always chomping at the bit for juicy cases. Now I give you one, and you're dragging your feet. Why?"

Right. She was known for diving into things headfirst. Kylie studied the piles of paper on her desk. No, that wasn't the real reason she was hesitant. And she definitely knew Greg would be fine without her.

As much as she wanted to jump at the idea, it wasn't just herself that she had to think of now.

She was part of a couple. Successful couples took each other's feelings into consideration. If she was going to get married, she knew she'd have to start doing that, sooner rather than later.

And though juicy cases were all she ever thought of…Linc had quite a different opinion of them. Especially where Kylie was concerned.

She thought of where he probably was right at that moment—in his office, dealing with an online seminar because his injury was still healing, and he'd had to take some time off from physical training. He was still recuperating from the gunshot wound from Kylie's last case, which had started as a personal search for her father and had ended up…

She shivered, not wanting to think about that.

Kylie looked at her boss's forlorn face, then thought of her handsome husband to be.

They could think of it as a little vacation away from Asheville, especially since their last "vacation" up to New York had been cut short when they realized the mafia was after them. She really loved the idea of working with Linc, as a team.

But she couldn't answer for him. He'd had a rough year, dealing with resurfacing memories from his time in Syria. He'd been working through his PTSD, but the last thing she wanted to do was push him.

"I know I should be jumping on it, but I have to ask Linc first. I think his expertise is just what this case needs, but I'm not sure he's up for it yet, considering his shoulder is still bothering him."

"Is it?"

"Yeah. He's frustrated."

Greg nodded. "Then, by all means, talk it over with him. But let me know tonight. I don't want to leave Ollie hanging. He's in enough pain as it is."

"Okay," Kylie said, jabbing in a text to Linc.

He was normally a very calm, stoic man, but this injury was pushing him to the limit. She wondered if he'd resorted to throwing things and hurling curses into the air yet. Upkeep at the farm had all but gone to pot since he'd been injured. She'd tried to keep up, but she hadn't had much luck mucking stalls and brushing llamas. She wasn't a farm boy, like Linc. He lived for that stuff, almost as much as he lived for nature and tromping through the wilderness.

Kylie sighed. They were supposed to be planning that wedding too. Linc seemed to be pressing her, albeit gently, to get her shit together where that was concerned. But in the weeks since he proposed, she hadn't done a single thing.

The truth of it was, though the idea of getting married to Linc thrilled her, putting together all the details of the party? Hives. Massive hives. That was her job, though, as bride, wasn't it? The bride was supposed to love the idea of planning a wedding. But even her mother seemed more excited about the details than she did. She wondered what she could do to psych herself up for it.

Maybe she was still suffering from leftover daddy issues. Even though she felt like she'd resolved most everything with her father and decided that Linc was nothing like him, the concept of forever?

It was a scary thing.

Whenever anyone brought up setting a date, she felt like she was part of a snowball about to be pushed down a hill. Once the planning began, she knew it would pick up momentum, and nothing would be able to stop it until she crashed.

No. She had no doubts about Linc. He was everything to her.

It was really just...the wedding. That was the problem. The whole *"make this the best day of your life OR ELSE!"* thing that always seemed to haunt her every time she thought of the details.

What if she did it wrong and ruined the best day of their lives? Wouldn't that mean their marriage was doomed before it even started?

She forced herself to stop thinking about it before that sick feeling started to bloom in the pit of her stomach again. "I'll definitely ask him as soon as I get home. Things have just been crazy. You know, with Linc being down and out. It's been a whirlwind couple weeks."

"Gotcha. If it's easier, short stuff, you can work the job from home. That way you can help Linc out at the farm too."

She smiled at him. As grumpy as he was, he really was the best boss. "Thank you. I might just. He's kind of at the end of his rope."

"All right, kid. Maybe you should give me another tutorial on this space-age coffee machine, just in case."

She laughed. She'd already given him three, but she figured one more wouldn't hurt.

3

A nother red-letter day of getting not enough done. Damn shoulder.

He'd tried. It ached. Dully now. Was it that he was getting older? He didn't remember his last gunshot wound hurting this much.

Today had definitely been Farm 1, Linc 0.

Now, exhausted and beaten, Linc sat on the porch of his farmhouse as the sun set behind him, waiting for Kylie to pull up the driveway. It was a good thing that he'd been tied up with the online seminar most of the day because the few chores he'd gotten done had been a struggle. It pissed him off.

Flanked by Storm, his trusty German Shepherd, and Vader, Kylie's Newf, he stroked their ears and studied the phone on his knee, which contained a text from Kylie. *Love you. Have something to ask you.*

He wondered what hare-brained thing his fiancée had gotten into her head today.

She was excited about getting married. At least she

seemed so, since she kept talking about everything they could do as "man and wife."

She didn't seem quite so excited about the actual wedding, though. He'd had to reel her back from some of her craziest ideas, most of which involved jetting off, just the two of them, and tying the knot at some exotic locale.

Yesterday, she'd read an article about a couple who'd exchanged vows on the rim of a dormant volcano in Maui. Linc had seen that look in her eye and talked her down real fast. With Kylie's sometimes scattered personality, he couldn't put it past her not to fall in.

He smiled, thinking of it. He was excited too—but about all of it. The wedding, especially. He was trying to steer her toward a small wedding at the farmhouse this Christmas. By then, hopefully, his shoulder would be back to normal. Tent, white lights, big cake, and all of their closest friends. So far, she hadn't bitten. He'd figured it was because she was distracted by all the bright, shiny options available, but part of him had begun to wonder if it was cold feet.

No. They'd gotten over her issues with her dad. She was all in. They were deliriously in love.

Christmas. The farmhouse. He'd nail her down for that tonight.

The dogs' ears perked up, and he straightened as he heard her Jeep pinging gravel as it made its way up the drive. He moved, and pain shot up his arm. The shot he'd sustained from Kylie's father's wife was the second bullet wound in his shoulder, but this one definitely hurt a hell of a lot more than the first. He'd been able to get back into the swing of things fairly quickly after the last one, but the doctors said there was more musculature involved in this one. He still wasn't able to lift much of anything with the arm.

Taking care of the farm one-handed had proven all but impossible. Kylie'd helped as much as she could, but she worked in downtown Asheville and had her own things to worry about. He couldn't rely on her to do everything.

He stood up and walked toward her vehicle as it appeared from behind the trees. The evening sun illuminated the bright smile on her face. He grinned back.

Hell, he loved her. More and more every day. He'd never had a woman make him so happy just by showing up. And clearly, by that smile she was sporting, she felt the same way.

He walked around to the driver's side of her car as she stepped out and pulled her into a one-armed embrace. She wrapped her arms tight around him and kissed him, long and slow. When he pulled his lips from her, he took a good look at her lovely face. "Hi."

"Hi," she said back, grinning.

The dogs circled around them, wanting to get in on the lovefest. Linc took Vader's collar and led him toward the house as he wagged his tail happily.

Kylie bent down and ruffled his ears. "Hi, baby! Hi, boy! You miss me?"

He licked her face in response, his tail wagging against her side like a beating drum.

She looked over at the front of the house, where the bulbs Linc was trying to plant for spring blooming were still in their containers. "Have trouble?"

He shrugged, immediately wincing at the movement. "A little," he confessed when she gave him a pointed look. "I dragged the food for the dogs out of the back of my truck, but I might've pulled something."

Her eyes widened as they went to his shoulder. "You shouldn't have! I told you I would—"

"Seventy-five-pound bags?" he countered with a scoff. "I don't think so."

"I can do it!" she insisted, flexing her nonexistent muscles. "You shouldn't be! You know what the doc said."

"I'm not having my fiancée lugging around something I should easily do. It nearly weighs more than you. I'm taking care of it. But..." he looked down at the bulbs, "it's just going to take a little longer than usual."

Hopefully, he'd get them in before it got too cold, rendering them useless.

She shook her head and looked at the thriving mums and other fall flowers he'd planted before he was injured. "You always make this place look so beautiful, but you don't have to. It's more important that you get better."

His mouth twisted as he considered it. The place had been his grandparents', and since he inherited it, he'd always felt a certain burden to keep it up in the way that his grandparents once had. That meant always having the lawn out front trimmed, keeping the inside clean, and putting flowers in all the window boxes and in the flower bed outside the porch. He hadn't changed a single thing in the years since he'd taken ownership, and he liked that. He liked keeping it as a tribute to them.

Until now.

Until Kylie came into his life, and he started thinking about renovations and updates that would work better for a wife, and hopefully, a child. Some day. Maybe a couple of them.

"I am taking care of myself," he said, rubbing the back of his neck.

"I *know*," she said, her eyes filled with compassion as they walked up the steps to the porch. "I'll plant the rest of the bulbs after dinner. That way you can just take it easy and relax, like you're supposed to be doing. What do you want?"

He opened the screen door. "I made spaghetti."

She sniffed and threw her purse on the little bench in the mudroom, then walked to the island, which he'd already set for two. "You shouldn't have! What happened to resting?"

She made a fuss, but he could tell she was glad. She hated cooking. "I knew I loved you for a reason."

He went to the cabinet and pulled out a bottle of red, pouring her a big glass. "I'm not letting you go out and plant after dinner. It'll be dark by then."

She laughed. "We have lights out there. And news flash... I'm an adult, Linc. I'm not afraid of the dark."

"Screw that. You've been working all day."

"Sitting on my butt most of the time. I need the exercise. Trust me," she said, leaning over and kissing his cheek. "It's fine. Besides, you cooked for me. I feel free as a bird. I have absolutely nothing to do for the rest of the day."

He grinned at her, reaching under the table to tweak her ass. "We could screw."

She rolled her eyes. Yes, he'd become such a horndog since he proposed. Now that he had the ring on her finger, he wanted to make love to her all the time. He wasn't sure what it was, but he couldn't get enough of her.

"Really? You're so romantic. We're not even married yet, and that's what it is?"

"I'm sorry. Making love." He said it in a very flowery and grandiose way as he brought the pot to her plate and gave her a heaping helping of pasta carbonara.

"Actually, when you say it that way, I prefer *dirty.* Oh, my gosh," she said, sniffing the pile of creamy pasta with cheese and ham he'd placed in front of her. "I'm definitely going to need exercise after this."

He sat down and winked at her. "Like I said. I have no objections to helping you with that, you know. Upstairs."

"Screwing?"

"Yes, ma'am."

She laughed and tangled her feet with his as they sat together. "I'm not averse to that, but let me get the bulbs taken care of first. Then I'll have a double dose of exercise, which I think I might need because..." she shoved a forkful into her mouth, "this is indescribably delicious. I'm going to lick the plate."

He sighed. "If you must."

She polished off the food in record time, and all the while, he kept smiling like a sex-starved teenager at his pretty fiancée and thinking dirty thoughts.

Yes, he was a horndog. But weren't they supposed to be? They were engaged.

"Don't say it," she said to him, not looking up.

He had to laugh. He liked that she got him. That he didn't have to say a word, and she knew what was going through his mind. That was the way it should be, with husbands and wives. He knew her best too.

Her eyes trailed over to the pile of mail propped up against the wall. She lifted a brochure out from it and opened it. Linc noticed it said something about *Fairy Tale Weddings*. She wrinkled her nose as she read it. "Gosh. Two-hundred dollars a plate. That's ridiculous."

"Right. That's why I think we should have the wedding up here. We can rent a tent for a couple thousand."

She nodded. "Yes, I guess," she said absently, still studying the brochure.

Linc eyed her curiously. She didn't seem enthused about that. Was she not into the idea of having the wedding at the farmhouse, or not into the idea of a wedding at all? "Did you send away for that?"

She closed the brochure, checked the postmark, and shook her head. "No. I really haven't had time to think about it. I wonder how they knew?"

"The jewelry store where I got your ring downtown probably shares info with them."

"Oh." She stared at her ring and smiled. "I guess we should start getting serious about it, huh?"

Linc nodded. "Yeah. I'm still thinking a Christmas wedding would be perfect."

She stuffed a mouthful of pasta in. "That feels so soon."

He shrugged. "It's not soon. That's two months away."

"Yes, but..." Her expression was that of a trapped animal. "What if it rains? Or snows?"

"That's why we'll have tents, with heaters in case there's a cold snap."

She still seemed doubtful. Okay, there was definitely something holding her back. As close as they'd become since they met, he had no clue what was going through her mind, and he didn't like it.

"Hey. Kylie. Level with me." He took her hand and stroked her palm. "What is it?"

She sighed. "I know I'm being stupid. It's just that forever is a long time. And this day is supposed to be the first day of our forever."

She'd always been insecure when it came to men. It'd taken months for her to finally make the jump from casual hook-up to exclusivity, and even after they started dating, she was always suspicious he'd run off with no explanation, the way her father had. He'd gradually earned her trust, though, and after the issues with her father were behind them, and she finally had the ring on her hand, he'd hoped those days were gone.

Apparently not.

"You trust me, though, right?" he asked, kissing her hand.

She nodded and met his eyes, giving him a solemn look. "Yes...I do. I just..." She looked lost, unsure how to complete the sentence.

"Don't trust yourself," Linc finished. They'd been over this before. She'd told him she was afraid that she had her father's blood in her, and that she'd let her ambitions get the best of her and make stupid decisions. "I told you. You're not like him. You just worrying about this shows me that you're not. And even if it turns out that you are, that's a chance I'm willing to take."

She smiled a watery-looking smile. "I know, I know. But, it's...nothing. Forget it. I really do want to marry you. I have no reservations about that. Honestly."

"So...Christmas? Or if you want, we can wait until spring. Or next fall. Right now, having a date will ease some of the worry I'm feeling, but I don't want to pressure you if you want to wait."

As relief flooded her features, he smiled. He would give her time. There was really no rush, after all. His ring was on her finger and she slept in his bed each night. That was enough.

She leaned in to kiss him. "I love you, and I promise that we will pick a date. Soon." She grinned and ran her fingers through his short hair. "Maybe on our way to Georgia?"

"Um...what? Georgia?" Linc knew he looked as confused as he felt. "Why are we going to Georgia?"

"Greg has a case for us."

Linc wiped his mouth with a napkin. "For *us*?"

"Yes. For a friend of his."

"A friend of his?" He sounded like a damn parrot. "Why would he give it to us? Why wouldn't he want to help his friend himself?"

"I don't know. He's been acting weird. Maybe it's just me, but he's been getting more and more removed as the months go on."

"Well, it's been unseasonably warm. No one wants to work in the heat."

"Yeah, but now it's the end of October, and he's still slowing down. He talks about getting too old for this shit, and today he told me he's thinking of limiting the number of cases he takes on. And he's just…I don't know. Giving off weird vibes."

"Weird vibes?"

"Yeah. Retirement vibes. Like he may be thinking of closing up shop."

Linc gave her a sympathetic look. He knew how much she loved the job. And he also knew she was still at least a year off from getting her official PI license. But he knew exactly what she'd have said to him in this situation.

"Hey. What is it you're always telling me? Don't worry until there's something to worry about?"

She twirled her fork in the pasta. "You're right. It's stupid to get all worked up about it."

He waited for her to say more, but it was clear she'd forgotten where she'd been headed when she'd said she had something to tell him. "So…this case?" he prompted, nudging her back on track as he often did.

"Oh! Right! It's for one of his friends from high school. Poor guy. I really feel sorry for him, so I want to help, but it's down in Georgia. We have no idea how long the case will take, so if we're staying there, it might be difficult for us to get all the planning done for the wedding in two months. I checked it on the map, and it's about two hours away, and even if we were driving back and forth that would be four hours a day, and—"

She was rambling, leaving him no choice but to cut her off. "What kind of case? I'm curious…why's he giving it to *us*? Where do I come in?"

"Sorry." Her face went a pretty pink. "The man is Ollie Crosby. His wife is search and rescue in Georgia and was conducting a search for a missing hiker when she and her dog just vanished. They've been missing since yesterday, but the husband thinks something is suspicious."

Linc searched his brain for a Crosby, cursing himself for

taking a pain pill earlier as it slowed his thinking more than he liked. As one of the state's most experienced rescuers, Linc was pretty well-known along the SAR circuit and had given dog obedience and SAR classes throughout the east. He'd also worked with dozens of SAR people over the years, and the community wasn't all that big. The name Crosby definitely struck a bell.

At once, it came to him. An older woman with sandy hair. He'd first met her at a conference down in Atlanta. Since then, they'd been on a few cases together, whenever he got called to that neck of the woods. She'd had more experience than most everyone. A lot more. Hell, she was a fixture in the close-knit SAR community. "You mean Beez?"

When Kylie's jaw dropped, he knew he'd hit the nail on the head. "Yes! You know her?"

"Yeah. Not well, but I first met her at a conference in Atlanta. We've been on a few searches before because it's not uncommon for them to call in neighboring SAR teams for large-area searches. She's missing?"

Kylie nodded. "Her husband is Greg's friend, and he seems convinced that there's foul play involved."

Linc rubbed his jaw. "Being missing for only a day isn't rare in that neck of the woods, but Beez was definitely experienced. I'm not sure how suspicious it is, but it is very concerning that someone like her hasn't been found. She knows her shit, especially concerning the parks in Northeastern Georgia. Whereabouts was she lost?"

"Um…" Kylie thought for a second. "I can't remember. A gorge, I think, on the South Carolina/Georgia border."

"Tallulah Gorge," he said, leaning back in his seat. That was Beez's old haunt, if he remembered correctly. He'd been there before, years before, right when he'd gotten out of the service. He recalled the waterfalls and the steep drop-offs.

Most of the pathways weren't difficult while some of the trails were bitches.

One thing that Linc remembered from their time together was Beez telling him that she was queen around those parts. She'd boasted that no one knew that gorge better than she did. He'd liked her confidence and spunk.

Foul play? Could be. Could be not. The weather in Georgia had sucked the past couple weeks.

"Her dog is missing too?"

Kylie reached down and put her hand on Vader's big head. "He could've just run off or something."

"Not a SAR dog. SAR dogs know better than to just go off. They're trained to find their way back to civilization if their handler's in danger. To summon help. For him to disappear too...it's not good for either of them."

Kylie's brow knitted. "That's what I'm afraid of. But I really do want to help Greg...and Ollie. He must be at his wit's end."

"Yeah. We should get down there tomorrow."

She seemed relieved. "Are you sure it's a good idea, considering your shoul—?"

"Storm's the best search *and* cadaver dog around. She'll come in real handy during this job. And my shoulder's fine. I just need to keep icing it and take it easy now and then."

"Yes, but..." She gnawed on her bottom lip.

What? First, she'd seemed gung-ho about this job, and now she was holding back? It didn't make sense. As he studied her, a thought struck him, and he understood what her reluctance was about. If it wasn't the shoulder, it had to be his PTSD.

Not that he could blame her for being worried about that.

He'd scared the shit out of her enough with that. Last month, when he'd been having unchecked memories resurfacing from his harrowing days in Syria, he'd gone into a garage collapse and had a panic attack when he'd uncovered a dead woman. Since then, therapy had helped him come to terms with his anxiety upon seeing dead bodies, but there were still bumps in the road. The gunshot hadn't helped things, but it was good to see Kylie worried about something instead of diving headfirst without looking, which she'd been prone to do.

He stood up and wrapped his good arm around her. "I get it. But this is what Storm is good at."

"I'm not worried about Storm so much as you." She didn't meet his eyes.

"Well, it's what *I'm* good at too, you know. Or at least I used to be, and I hope to be again. I'm getting better, Kylie. Honestly, I am."

She exhaled deeply. "But with your arm? You usually control her with your right arm. You'll need someone to help with her, won't you?"

He bristled. "I can handle it."

"No, you can't...yet." She placed a hand on his arm. "I can, though. Storm trusts me too. And I've been around you two enough to know how you handle her."

Linc knew enough not to argue with his fiancée. When it came to these things, she carried on until she got her way. "Fine. I'll let you tag along."

She returned his smug smile and slapped his good shoulder lightly. "Ha-ha. You'd better. Since it's *my* case, buster, you'd do well not to forget that. But..." the worried expression returned, "are you sure you'll be okay? She is a friend, not a complete stranger, after all. And the dog..."

He knew that look in her eyes too. He hadn't gone on many cadaver searches since the one at the collapsed parking garage, when he'd thought his heart was giving out. Since then, he hadn't had much contact with dead bodies. But he was good. Mentally, he felt stronger than he had in a long time.

"The counseling has helped, sweetheart. And I've been strict about taking the meds too. I'm good."

She nodded, and her eyes lit up like they did whenever she had a juicy lead to follow. She was pleased. "Okay. Then…tomorrow?"

"Yeah. Sounds good."

She finished up her plate, stacked it on top of his, and took it to the sink. "I'll make a deal with you. You get the dishes, and I'll handle planting the bulbs?"

He shook her hand. "Deal. And then…screwing?" He gave her a hopeful look.

She smacked his good arm. "Absolutely."

He reached for the dish soap and saw her staring at the wedding brochure. On the cover was an elegantly dressed couple, staring into each other's eyes. It was a nice sight, one that would make even the most hardened non-romantic smile.

But Kylie was frowning.

Frowning like she wanted to kill that happy couple.

That was interesting.

"It looks like our wedding planning will have to be put on hold, I guess," he added, opening up the dishwasher.

She clicked her tongue in what he thought was probably fake disappointment. "I suppose. But that's okay. We have time."

He couldn't be sure, but as she turned away, he thought he might have seen the smile come back.

4

In the midmorning, in a driving rain, Kylie and Linc took off in Linc's truck toward the little town the Crosbys called home. As they drove, with Storm and Vader in the back seat, Kylie kept trying to feed Linc his breakfast—handfuls of Cheerios— without the dogs getting there first.

"We probably should've eaten breakfast before we left," she said as the dogs snapped at her hands. Mostly Vader, since Storm was too dignified and well-behaved for that, but Kylie had the distinct feeling that being around her unruly pup had changed Storm's normally ladylike ways.

Vader—her rescue pup and the reason she'd met Linc in the first place—had always been the wild one, as much as she loved him. Storm had always been militantly precise, just like her handler, but one had to be so in order to work for the Army's Military Police in Syria. Once so different, they were now like two peas in a pod.

Just like their owners, Kylie thought with a smile, holding out another handful to him, dodging the heads of her pups.

He took it and shoved them into his mouth. "Nah. I like you feeding me. Have any grapes?"

"Har-dee-ha-ha. You're funny," she deadpanned, looking at the raindrops marching across her window. "It's been raining every other day for the past three weeks. I think we're going to wash away one of these days."

Linc shrugged. "What've you got against rain?"

Sure, *he* didn't care. He was the manly man, the type who loved tromping around in the great outdoors no matter how cold or miserable it was, no matter how much mud he sunk into. She imagined him on the side of a mountain, beating his chest. Oh, the great outdoors! How glorious! Meh.

Kylie much preferred indoor activities. But whenever "foul play" was at hand, she found it within herself to deal with even the things she loathed. Still, she would've preferred dryness, especially knowing they'd probably walk the trails in the gorge later that day. Everything felt so damp and dreary.

And mud? She hated mud. She looked down at her hiking boots and grimaced. She might have been dressed the part, but that was about it. "I despise it. And the dampness. And mud. And cold."

"And everything about nature in general. I got it."

"Why do you like the rain so much?" She was genuinely curious, hoping that his outlook about bad weather might change hers.

He looked up at it, considering. "Rain makes things new again. If you didn't have rainy days, you'd never appreciate the sun."

She wrinkled her nose at him. "What, are you auditioning for a job at Hallmark?"

He laughed. "Life is short. Smile while you still have teeth."

She couldn't help it, she giggled. "You're like a Sharpie. Super fine."

"We've found our new career move if investigations and

SAR don't pan out," Linc said, a big smile still on his face. She could look at that smile all day. "But back to the rain…one thing that does suck is that it'll make finding any traces of Beez a lot harder."

The smile slid from Kylie's face as it did his. That wasn't what she wanted to hear.

Not to mention, the damp weather was obviously seeping into Linc's limbs. She watched as he massaged his shoulder, wincing. "How's the arm?"

He put both hands back on the wheel. "Fine. Like I told you the first twelve times you asked today."

"Would you rather me be a total bitch and not care?" she asked, tilting her phone to look at the display. "Oh, you're supposed to take this exit." She pointed, raising her voice. "Now!"

He veered off onto the striped V separating the highway from the exit road, tires squealing, gritting his teeth.

He'd asked her why she didn't just plug the address into the truck's navigation system, but she hated that disembodied voice breaking into their conversation, so she'd kept her phone on mute and was giving him the directions. The problem was, she kept forgetting that he had no clue where he was going. Which wasn't exactly making this easy for him, she realized.

"Sorry," she said when she realized his knuckles, wrapped around the steering wheel, were white. He was all about preparing, planning, and she…simply wasn't.

"It's okay," he said, letting out a breath. "Just next time… give me a little bit of notice, okay? Last thing we need out here is to be driving into a tree. We're the rescuers. Don't want to have to be the rescued."

She sighed. "Notice" always kind of ruined the fun where she was concerned. She loved flying by the seat of her pants, letting life take her wherever it wanted to go. Sometimes she'd ask him to go for a drive, hoping to find a romantic spot, someplace neither of them had ever visited. When she had, he'd brought his maps and his emergency car kit and even a flame-retardant blanket, should the truck spontaneously burst into flames. He was famously prepared for every what-if.

He should be the one planning the wedding, she thought as they found themselves on a narrow country road. He'd make sure every angle was covered. Heck, he'd probably even have a contingency plan for an alien invasion. If she did it, it would probably be a disaster.

Pines crowded in on them, and trees provided a canopy overhead, making it even darker, almost like night. They'd been in the middle of nowhere for the past hour, and now, they *really* were. It felt suffocating, ominous, like they were headed toward certain doom.

Or maybe that was just the rain. If it'd been sunny and she had the rays of light to warm her, she probably would've felt fine.

She looked up at the sky—it was clouds on top of clouds, no sign of a break. Then she studied the map closely. "Just five more miles on this road, I guess," she said, moving the display a little so she could anticipate the next move for him.

"You guess?" He gave her a doubtful look.

"Whatever. We'll get there," she said, reaching over to massage his arm. She tapped his shoulder lightly in the places she knew grew too tight. "What are you worried about? What could possibly happen to us out here?"

He snorted. "You haven't seen *Deliverance,* have you?"

"No," she said, wrinkling her nose. "What's it about?"

He shook his head and looked out the window, into the woods. "It was filmed around here, I think."

She looked at him, waiting for more. "*And?* What's it about?"

"Some city morons who go out into the wilderness like this and get their asses handed to them by the locals."

She picked a lone Cheerio off her shirt, unsure as to how the dogs hadn't noticed it. Popping it into her mouth, she looked into the dark woods. "And so you're saying I'm the city moron in this scenario?"

His thumbs tapped on the steering wheel as he grinned. "If you don't pay attention to the directions your GPS is telling you and end up leading us into the gorge, you are."

She frowned but kept an extra-close eye on her phone from then on out, to make sure she didn't prove him right. Within ten minutes, they'd pulled down a long driveway with a rusty mailbox out front that said CROSBY.

"See?" she said triumphantly as they emerged from the thick pine trees and a small, tiny ranch came into view. "No problem. We shall not meet our deliverance today, Mr. Coulter."

At least, she hoped not.

Though, as she looked at the place, half-swallowed by overgrown landscaping, its roof bleeding with brown stains, windows covered with dusty screens, she had to admit it looked like the scene of a horror movie. Was *Deliverance* a horror movie? She couldn't be sure from Linc's description.

There was a long dog run alongside the drive, and an empty garbage can was overturned near the house. Linc wouldn't be so inconsiderate as to drive on someone's lawn, no matter how unkempt it was, so they stopped there, still far from the door.

That meant walking a long way in the rain, without an umbrella. She pulled her jacket's hood up over her head and slid out of the truck as Linc cracked the windows. "Stay, boy," she said to Vader, who was already trying to poke his head out. He whimpered and laid beside Storm, looking beaten.

She walked closer to the house, noticing different things

buried in the greenery; a ceramic toad by a toadstool, a couple of gnomes, a one-eyed copper bunny with a carrot. She had a strange feeling, the same kind she got whenever something in one of her cases was about to go awry. Her spidey sense, she called it.

She glanced at Linc, who was eyeing the place warily. He felt it too. As she expected, he rushed ahead of her on the path to the front porch, as if to put himself between her and the danger. She nudged him aside. He was a gentleman, but sometimes he took his "duty" of protecting her a little too far.

Before she could climb the crumbling step and ring the old doorbell, the door opened just a crack. First, a suspicious eye, then a wide, doughy face appeared.

Standing behind the dirty screen was a semi-bald man. What hair he did have was pure white and stood up like a koala's. He was wearing thick glasses but still squinted down the end of his nose to look at them. "You selling something?" he muttered.

"No," Kylie said, proudly producing a business card and holding it up to him. With the dirty screen, he probably couldn't read it, so she added, "I'm Kylie Hatfield from Starr Investigations."

"Who?"

Oh no, Kylie thought. *This is starting off just great.*

"Greg sent me. Greg Starr? Your friend from high school. You told him about your wife's disappearance, and he asked me to take a look into it for him. I'm his…partner."

She gave Linc a sideways glance as she said it, and he just shook his head. No, she wasn't technically Greg's partner, but she was constantly lying about her position when the situation called for it. And this situation…called for it. She couldn't put it past the man to not be holding a shotgun behind the door, ready to run them off his property.

Instead, his eyes lit up. "Oh. Right. Sorry." He thunked his head and opened the screen door for them.

Kylie breathed a sigh of relief, then realized the man was now regarding Linc with suspicion.

Hmm. No wonder he thought there was foul play in his wife's disappearance if he was this wary about everyone.

"This is Linc Coulter," Kylie quickly explained as she went past him, taking a short whiff and noticing he smelled heavily like body odor, like he hadn't showered in a while. *Guess losing the person you love the most'll do that to you*, she thought, then reached for Linc's hand. "He's one of the best SAR guys in North Carolina."

"That so?" he said, regarding him through his thick glasses. "Well, Beez was the best SAR in the whole dang country."

He said it like it was a challenge, and they were trying to one-up each other. *Well, Linc is the best SAR in the whole universe!* Yeah. That would probably get her seeing the butt of his shotgun all too soon.

Before she could think of how to best handle this man, Linc extended his hand. "Yes, sir. I worked with Beez a few times. She's truly a gifted woman. I was honored to learn quite a bit from her."

Ollie Crosby shook the hand, still wary. "Well, good to meet you," he said, closing the door and ushering the couple to a room cluttered with old flowered couches and Hummel figurines. The man walked, creaky and bow-legged, his baggy jeans dragging on the floor, to a vinyl recliner and threw himself down on it.

He certainly wasn't the model of fitness his wife must have been, Kylie observed as she followed, trying not to breathe in too much. The air was hot and stuffy and smelled like bacon grease and the aforementioned body odor. Kylie fought to keep a straight face as she sat on one of the mismatched chairs near the upright piano. Linc sat next to her, on a spindly piano bench that creaked under his substantial weight.

"I'd get you something to drink, but…" He looked regretfully at the kitchen, and Kylie understood. The poor man was lost without his wife, his other half. The half that clearly kept his world glued tightly together.

"It's fine," she said, reaching out and touching his hand. "I know this must be hard for you. We don't want to disturb you, but we do want to help you as much as possible. That's why we're here."

"I appreciate that," he said, gruff and unsmiling. His manner reminded her of how Greg spoke to her, but the difference was that this poor man had a reason for being grumpy. "I called Greg because I get the distinct feeling I'm being hoodwinked by the police. They ain't doing all they can to find her. Jockeying me around and giving me the runaround. You know?"

"That's what we want to get to the bottom of, Mr. Crosby," Kylie said. "We'll do all we can to locate your wife."

He nodded, his jowls flapping, reminding Kylie not so much of a koala now than a sad St. Bernard. "What can I do to help you?"

"Well," Kylie reached into her bag and pulled out a pad and pen, "you can start by telling me a little about Beatrice. Linc was telling me she was quite a good tracker and outdoorswoman?"

He scoffed. "She wasn't good. She was the best." He motioned with his chin to Linc and rubbed his whiskered jowl. "Am I right? Been doing it for going on three decades. Ain't no one ever been as good as Beez. Bet kids like you could've learned a thing or two from her."

Kylie looked at Linc, who nodded, though she had a good feeling Linc could've given any SAR tracker a run for their money. He was just being humble, as usual. As far as Kylie was concerned, if Linc couldn't find it, it didn't want to be found.

"Yes, sir," Linc told the man, using a respectful tone. "Like I said, she was a fixture in our community. I'm sorry you're going through this."

"And that's what I don't get," Crosby said, waving his hands in agitation. "She was exactly that. A fixture at that park. Born on that mountain. More at home there than the rocks and the trees. She knew it like the back of her hand. I proposed to her there 'cause ain't nowhere else she'd rather be. She'd be the last person I'd expect to go off and get lost there. So I've been tellin' the police that there's some serious shit going down in those hills. Something bad. Something real bad."

Kylie looked up from her scrawlings. "By the mountain, you mean—"

"The gorge. She done rescues in Tallulah Gorge all her life. That's where she was headed when she disappeared. After some crazy lunatic with a death wish."

"Death wish? Oh," Kylie said, scribbling again. "Why do you say that?"

Ollie immediately looked ashamed, but only for a moment. "Because the man was suicidal, left a note."

Kylie swallowed, her heart breaking for anyone who had lost hope that their life could get any better. "And when was the last time you saw her?"

"Well, I was reading..." He scratched his nose, looking a little embarrassed. "You see, I'm retired on disability, and Beez is ten years younger than me, and they couldn't make her retire if she was a hundred." He cleared his throat. He rambled more than Kylie. "Anyway, she stood right there..." he pointed at the door, "and she told me she'd got a call about some missing suicide at Tallulah Gorge, and she was gonna take Tiger and hoped she'd be back by dinner."

"Tiger? Your pit bull, correct?"

He nodded. "Sweet dog. I looked out the window, saw her get into her pickup with the dog, and that was the last I ever saw of her or the pup."

Kylie dropped her head when she noticed the man's eyes were brimming with tears. She looked at Linc, who said, "Do you know anything about the missing hiker she was going after? Was he familiar with the area?"

"Hiker?" The man looked appalled. "He ain't no hiker. Just a poor dumb sap with nothin' to live for. I don't know nothin' more than what I heard on the news. Some jumper that didn't wanna live. Left a note at his apartment for his girlfriend to find, about how he wanted to end it all and didn't want to be found."

Kylie nodded, flipping through her pad. "I saw it mentioned on the news. A Craig Silva, is that right?"

Ollie grumbled under his breath. "Yeah, that's him. And the irony of it is, he was found. Dead at the bottom of the gorge. But my wife, she's gone. My poor wife died looking after some idiot who didn't even wanna live. What a waste."

"Hold on a minute," Kylie said, reaching over to place her hand on the older man's. "Beez hasn't been found yet. Don't assume the worst. You have to have hope."

Linc looked at her, and she got the feeling, in all her incurable optimism, that she'd said something wrong. Maybe it was too foolish even to have optimism now. Maybe it was good to strive for acceptance.

Ollie let out a long breath. "Nah. She's dead. Ain't no way she wouldn't have come back to me if she were alive. I can feel it."

Kylie's heart twisted. She wanted to go to the poor man

and hug him. She felt tears fighting their way out of her eyes, and her throat started to close up.

Thankfully, Linc picked up where she'd left off. "It's been rainy in these parts the past few weeks. Makes the trails hard to handle. She could've run into trouble because of that."

"I don't buy it," Crosby grumbled.

"She was on the North Rim Trail when she disappeared?"

Crosby shrugged. "I don't know those trails like she does. I'm not SAR. We gone up there a few times, but I'm not much of a hiker myself. I know all the people she works with 'cause she's worked with a lot of them a long time. But I don't know which trail she was on. She said something before she left that the guy didn't get a permit to be on any of the trails, so they had no idea where to search. And yeah, it'd been raining, but she was used to that."

Kylie flipped through her pad. "Craig Silva was found off the North Rim Trail."

Crosby rubbed at his whiskered jaw. "That's right. They found him, and a few hours later, they realized Beez hadn't reported back and wasn't responding on her radio."

Kylie scanned the room for any sort of identification she could find, to put a face with the name of Beatrice Crosby. She'd gone through some news articles online, but none had shown the woman's recent photograph. She noticed a lot of crosses on the walls and religious figurines on the surfaces. Spotting a frame in a shabby glass and metal cabinet in the corner that was littered with many religious sculptures, she walked over to it.

It was a picture of a dog, possibly Tiger. No Beatrice. "Do you happen to have a picture of her?"

He scratched the pockmarked side of his face, then held up a finger. He picked up the book laying by his feet, an old Louis L'Amour, and pulled out what he'd been using as the bookmark. He glanced at the crumpled item for a second before passing it off to her.

Kylie swallowed as she looked into the sweet face of a spry, fit woman in a baseball cap. She was wearing sunglasses, had sunburned, chipmunk cheeks, and a bright, open-mouthed smile. In the picture, she wore a bright red windbreaker, holding a walking stick, her other hand clasping the strap of a heavy backpack. As much as Kylie disliked the outdoors, she had to admit, the scenery around Beez was breathtaking.

"Where was this taken?" she asked.

"At the gorge," Crosby replied. "She never wanted to hike anywhere else. That was her place."

"Okay. And what was she wearing when she went out?"

His eyes fell to the photograph. "That red jacket. Turtle-neck. Jeans. Just like the picture. She didn't wear anything else this time of year. I don't think she was wearing the ball cap. If she doesn't wear that, she puts her hair in one of those scarf things." He motioned to his head, then nodded at Kylie. "You know, right? Like a wrap thing women wear. Keeps bugs out, I guess."

"Right." Kylie stared hard at the picture, then lifted her phone to take a photo of it. After making sure it wasn't blurry, she handed the original back to him. "When she went out, was she with anyone? I mean, other than Tiger? Were there other people on the search with her?"

Crosby tucked the photo back into the book and hitched a shoulder. "I don't know. Knowing how much ground they had to cover, she was probably by herself. They'd put the other SARs on other trails. Beez couldn't stand being told what to do." He laughed a little, but the sound was so sad Kylie's heart squeezed. "Stubborn ol' girl."

He hung his head low, staring at the dirty shag carpeting

between his legs. His heavy, flannel-shirt-clad shoulders heaved.

He was crying.

"I don't know," the man said, not looking up. "I can't help thinkin' the worst. If she's dead, I just need to know it, and I need to know how it happened. She told me that if she ever died, she wanted me to scatter her ashes over the gorge. If the worst has happened, I want to do that for her. If her body's in the gorge, it's where she wants to be, but not *how* she wants to be there. I want to put her to rest. She deserves that."

Kylie looked at the man's long face, then at Linc, and her heart started to thump painfully.

Before she realized she was crying, a tear slipped from her cheek and landed on the pad.

She tried to be the hardnosed PI, but that wasn't her. And it seemed that the more experience she got in investigations, the worse she got. She hated to see people suffering. Always would.

Linc reached over and squeezed her hand. *It's okay,* he mouthed to her.

Kylie wanted to believe that was true. But she knew that for Ollie Crosby, if the worst had indeed happened, life would never be okay again. The man would be forever altered, and Kylie felt like it was up to her to make whatever amends she could to give him back some semblance of a normal life. She wanted it so badly, it hurt.

5

They didn't find a huge number of pet-friendly lodging choices once they got to the small town of Tallulah Falls. Actually, they didn't find a huge number of lodging choices at all. Or restaurants. Or much of anything besides scenery. Lots and lots of beautiful, breathtaking scenery.

If it hadn't been for Kylie and her nature hating ways, Linc would have been happy to pitch a tent under one of the gold and burgundy trees but knew better than to introduce camping to his fiancée just yet.

One day, maybe.

With it being in the middle of autumn foliage season, the area was enjoying an uptick in visitors, although peak leaf viewing was still a week or two away. They ended up driving to another town just outside their destination to find lodging and settled on a no-tell motel called the Twin Pines, a place that Linc couldn't help thinking looked like the motel from *Psycho*, only a lot older and more broken down. Like Janet Leigh, they wound up having the only car in the lot.

Inside, Linc had to get Kylie to stop from tossing her stuff on the furniture before he had a chance to check the place for bed bugs and other equally disgusting hazards. He had a special black light that he carried to make sure the sheets were reasonably clean, and he made sure they didn't use the blanket, since even good hotels rarely washed that bedding.

Once that was done, Kylie curled up under the clean blanket he'd brought and looked at a brochure for a restaurant. "So, in this horror movie you were talking about, where they all got picked off by the locals...did it have anything to do with there not being suitable human food to eat?"

He looked up from giving the dogs bowls of water. "Are you talking about *Deliverance*?"

She made an uh-huh noise deep in her throat.

"Well, in the movie, these men decide to escape life for a week, leaving their jobs, wives, and kids behind. They—"

Hmm...maybe it was better that he not tell her all the details.

Kylie blinked innocently at him. "They what?"

He cleared his throat and fudged the plotline a bit. "They went kayaking and ended up fighting for survival. The end."

She narrowed her eyes at him. "Sounds...fascinating." She looked back down at the brochure. "About as fascinating as the dining choices around here. Is Frank's Chicken Hut seriously our best choice?"

"Frank's is delicious." He bent down to retie the laces on his hiking boots. "We can think food later. We need to head over to the park to meet with Dina. We're meeting her at headquarters in a half hour, remember?"

She burrowed under the covers and let out a long grumble. "Can I have five more minutes? Cold. Mud. Outdoors. Maybe I can find a bootleg of *Deliverance* on YouTube. Never mind. There's shitty cell phone service here."

He sat down next to her and patted her hip through the blanket. "This is the job from hell for you, isn't it?"

"Yes and no," she answered, sitting up and wrapping her

arms around her legs. "I wish there was bigger hope in finding Beatrice alive, and that would certainly make me happier. But since it's probably too late for that, I want to help that poor man. I just feel so terrible for him. I want to bring her back," tears brimmed in her eyes and she blinked them away, "but I'm afraid there won't be a happy ending."

He rubbed her shoulder gently. "I'm not totally counting Beez out yet. Sure, the odds are stacked against her, but she might just surprise us. And if not, we can bring her body home to her husband. Give him that bit of comfort. That would be a good thing."

She stared off into space. "Yes. I suppose. I don't know, though. It doesn't feel good enough."

He moved his hand to her back, gently massaging the muscles around her shoulder blades. That was Kylie. She sometimes got so wrapped up in other people's emotions that these things got hard for her. She cried for a week when she learned that the missing person she'd searched for in her first big case had been killed, and she hadn't even known the young woman.

Such a quality probably wasn't the best to have as a private investigator, but Linc wouldn't have changed it for the world. He loved all the things that made Kylie, Kylie. Even the things that made him want to bash his head into a wall.

She leaned onto his good shoulder and looked up at him. "How do you stand it?"

He took in a deep breath, knowing she meant the cadaver hunting. It wasn't his favorite thing, no. Obviously, the garage collapse had proven that.

"You don't think of what you're looking for. You just think of the search. And you think of, like what Ollie said, bringing people peace by answering those what-ifs. It does mean a lot, and sometimes, it's the most we can do, sweetheart."

She brushed away the tear that had made it past all the blinking. "Okay."

"Come on," he said, standing up and pushing back the curtain to peer outside. The rain was still falling in sheets, unfortunately, drumming on the roof in a way he normally found soothing. "Looks like there's a break in the clouds over there."

She stood up reluctantly, strapped on her hiking boots, and shrugged into her jacket. "All right. Lead the way."

She was soaked by the ten-yard dash to the truck. They got in with the dogs, and after he pulled out, he glanced over at her, with her hood pulled so tight it only bared a tiny circle of Kylie's face. She looked pathetic and waterlogged, and they hadn't even gotten out on the trail yet.

"If you want, I can go on the trail by myself while you meet with Dina and the others," he said, patting her knee, and he was glad he'd forced her into waterproof pants.

There was supposed to be a two-hour window of clear skies that afternoon, and Linc wanted to get Storm's nose on the ground while Kylie conducted her interviews. His shoulder wasn't quite ready for an advanced missing persons hunt, but a cadaver hunt, he could handle on his own.

Kylie's phone rang. Frowning at the screen, she shot a glance to Linc. "It's Dina, the SAR woman I'm supposed to interview first. Hope she isn't cancelling on me." She took the call. "Hello?"

Linc could hear the other woman talking but couldn't understand the words.

Kylie covered the mouthpiece. "They have another missing hiker, and they are all gathering to get ready to search."

"At headquarters?" he asked.

Kylie repeated the question into the phone, but Linc had already made his decision by the time Kylie nodded her response. He had everything he needed for a search in his truck. He could help. He needed to help.

"Tell Dina that I'm on my way," he said to Kylie. "Storm and I can help."

Kylie raised an eyebrow and spoke into the phone. "Linc, Storm, Vader, and I can help. We'll be there soon."

After she disconnected the call, Linc reached over and squeezed her knee. "You don't have to go out. It will be miserable and treacherous in this—"

"No. You need someone to help control Storm because of your shoulder." She smiled and rubbed her hands together then lifted a finger in an eureka gesture. "Oh. Dina mentioned that a drone they'd been using to assist with the search picked up a flash of something, but it hasn't been able to get close enough to identify what it is for some reason or other. Also, the rain has caused a small rockslide, which has hindered the search. The bad weather is forecasted to stop within the hour, and the search will renew while they catch that bit of a break."

He squeezed her knee again. "Are you sure you want to do this?"

She turned toward him as much as she could while buckled up. "I want to do this. I just need to...you know. Psych myself up."

"Okay. Can I help?"

A small smile played on her lips. "You could sing 'Eye of the Tiger' for me or something."

He laughed but played along, humming a few bars of it for her, grinning as she started to move her upper body around like a fighter, throwing air-punches, getting into it. By the time they reached headquarters, they were full-on singing the verses as loud as they could, and she looked more relaxed.

"Okay. I'm better. Let's do this thing."

The psych-up had worked. By the time they stepped out of the truck, Kylie was smiling. After tossing the dogs a few treats to keep them happy, she grabbed onto Linc's hand as they dodged more raindrops on the walk to headquarters and whispered to him, "I'm sorry for being a brat."

Linc laughed. She was often a bit of a brat, but this was the first time she'd recognized and apologized for it. But she hadn't been nearly so bad...yet. Maybe she was apologizing in advance for all the complaining that would likely be coming when they set out on the trail? Probably.

Linc opened the door and let Kylie in, then found himself in a small, crowded room. He wasn't a fan of crowds, especially people he didn't know. He was a leader, but only on the trail or while training dogs—places he felt comfortable.

Groups didn't normally qualify, which Kylie knew. It warmed his heart to see her take the lead. Not only because it was her nature to be outgoing, but because, in her own way, she thought she was protecting him.

They made a good team.

"Hi," she said in her normal bright, loud voice. "Is this the SAR group?"

A basketball-player-tall man near the door looked down at them. Linc knew him. It was Kevin. Kevin and his dog... Molly. They'd worked together a few times at least. The man spoke in a deep voice. "It is. And who are you?"

All heads swiveled toward them, and Linc lifted a hand, recognizing many of the faces.

"I'm Kylie Hatfield, a private investigator, and this is Linc Coulter, a fellow SAR. We're investigating the disappearance of Beez Crosby at the request of her hus—"

"Linc!" everyone shouted, almost in unison. They seemed genuinely glad to see him.

He momentarily hoped that maybe his panic attack in the parking garage collapse hadn't made the gossip rounds to Georgia, even though he was slowly learning not to be embarrassed by his temporary meltdown. He was currently dealing with those emotions, those fears, and to hell with anyone who would judge him.

The people who mattered most understood.

Kylie looked back at him, eyes wide. "I guess introductions aren't necessary," she said with a smile.

He shook the first hand that stuck out at him. "Hey, everyone. Nice to see you all."

After a round of handshakes, Linc knelt to pet a pretty Golden Retriever that had been giving him eyes and wagging his tail, hoping for attention. As he did, a couple of other dogs noticed and came forward.

"Is Dina here?" Kylie asked after everyone had gone back to their seats.

"Present."

Linc grinned as the rough female voice replied and the stout woman with a short blonde buzz cut approached, shaking Kylie's hand. "Good to meet you, Kylie. We were just about to set out." Linc got the strong handshake next. "Linc and I go way back. It's an honor to have your help out here in my neck of the woods. We don't usually get much action like this. Although I'm no stranger to action. I was in the army too. Afghanistan."

Linc couldn't stop his surprise. Not at her admission but at the number of words the seasoned SAR had strung together. Dina was usually the strong, silent type. That she'd said more than two words to Kylie was interesting.

"Great to help out," he said from a crouch, petting a white

German Shepherd that had nosed his way into the crowd of dogs competing for his attention.

Kylie leaned over and petted the dog as Dina took the animal by his collar. "This is Ghost. She's my baby."

"Hey, Ghost," Kylie said, ruffling her ears. She let her lick her face. "She's so pretty. Did she serve overseas with you?"

Dina nodded proudly. "Yep. Been with me for six years. I live right here in Tallulah Falls, so this is a little close to home. I'm glad you could come up here, Kylie. You too, Abraham Lincoln."

Kylie raised an eyebrow at him.

Fondness for that odd nickname aside, Linc liked Dina, who essentially had so much in common with him, it was a little bizarre. She introduced Kylie around to the rest of the SAR team.

"This is Kevin and Molly," Dina said, pointing at the Golden. "And this is Forrest and his German Shepherd, Shep." Kylie shook hands until they came to the last one, a skinny man standing with his black lab. "This is Lonnie and Dozer. They just joined the team last year."

Dina, who had the most experience, had been the leader of this group. Linc had more seniority but didn't know the trails the way Dina did, so he let her take the lead. When everyone was organized, she explained to Linc and Kylie that they had twenty miles of trails and about 2,700 acres of the Tallulah Gorge State Park to cover, although the drone had narrowed that expanse considerably.

"Listen, guys," she said, sipping her coffee. "It's too wet out there, so that's going to leave us off most of the permit trails. But when you get to the nearest station, just check in with the ranger there to let them know you're out and searching with dogs. No one is allowed to go missing." She gave them each a pointed look. "Understood?"

Good-natured chuckling went around the room before

Kevin held up his hand. "Molly and I will take Lonnie and Dozer and cover the North Rim Trail, though I have a feeling the rangers are going to keep us off most of the trails. Hear there's been even more rockslides all over the park because of the rain."

Forrest rubbed his thick double chin as he studied the map on the wall. "Shep and I'll go along the Shortline and head on off there to see what I can see."

Kylie had her nose in the trail map. She nudged Linc. "We should take this trail," she said, pointing it out on the map.

He followed her finger. It was definitely the shortest line on the map, which would explain why she wanted to take it. "That one?" He laughed. "No. You don't want to take that one. Trust me."

She scrunched her nose. "Why? It's quick. And we're not experts in this park, so we should take the easiest one."

"Lee, let me explain something to you," he said, taking the map from her as she struggled to fold it. "In hiking, shortest doesn't always mean easiest. There are other things to take in consideration. Elevation, for one. Plus, it's called Sliding Rock for a reason."

He pointed to the elevation map for the trail she'd pointed out. It went straight down at a forty-five-degree angle and had staircases heading down to the gorge floor. Normally, it'd only be difficult going back up, but with this rain it'd be slippery as hell. He could bet money the rangers would be keeping people off it until it dried up. If Kylie was already thinking this was a nightmare, she'd rue the day she was born if he let her take that trail.

Kylie grimaced as she realized what he was saying. "Oh."

"I've been on that trail. A lot of this park is for experienced hikers only, because there are some seriously steep drops. That trail is a permit trail, and the rangers won't give out permits during weather like this," he explained, pointing to the South Rim Trail. "Why don't we try this one? Easy elevation. Only three miles. Should be pretty good."

Kylie looked appalled. "Three miles?"

"That's a walk in the park, Lee."

Literally. He grinned at her and received an elbow in the ribs in return. "You're hilarious."

Dina poked her head in, handing him a walkie-talkie before addressing the entire group. "Good news, folks. Our missing hiker from today has just been found, so we can put all our focus on Beez. We'll report back here at five, okay?" She turned her attention back to Linc. "Did you say you're taking South Rim?" Before he could nod, she clapped her hands together. "Okay, great."

Kylie's eyes followed the woman and then snapped back to Linc. She frowned and whispered to him, "That woman is the female version of you."

He looked after her and laughed. "Not nearly as attractive and charming, though, you have to admit." He gave her a wink, trying to keep her spirits up. "Come on."

They went outside, where it had actually started raining *harder*—was that even possible? As they climbed into the truck, Linc noticed that Kylie had gotten her pout back. She stared out at the rain like it'd murdered her family.

"Come on," he said to her. He started to hum "Eye of the Tiger" again. "Tell you what. After all this is over, I'll treat you to a nice meal somewhere."

She snorted. "The only place near our motel is Frank's Chicken Hut. It looks like they kill cats out back."

"Just chicken looking ones," Linc joked and tossed Storm and Vader another treat. "Keep an open mind. Okay, Lee?"

She gave him a doubtful look as he drove toward the trail. When they got to the lot, it was empty. Most people had the sense not to go out and seek invigorating nature experiences in such awful weather. Linc pulled up in the spot closest to the ranger's station, and they got out. As the rain poured down on them, Linc fixed on the dogs' SAR vests and clipped on their leashes. Meanwhile, Kylie stood there, staring forlornly into the distance. She really did look like she was about to melt away.

He followed her line of sight to a sign that read:

> WELCOME TO TALLULAH GORGE
> *Over 900 Feet Deep, the Deepest*
> *Canyon East of the Mississippi.*
> BEAUTIFUL <u>BUT</u> DANGEROUS!

HE SNAPPED his fingers at her. "It's just water."

"And danger.".

"Okay. Water and danger. No big deal. And beauty. Don't forget the beauty."

She meandered like a lost puppy toward the sign as a gust of wind blew her hood clean off. She growled and flipped it back again, tightening the strings. "But you should know better than anyone. Isn't it impossible to scent anything in this deluge?" she asked, blinking raindrops out of her eyes.

"Hard. Not impossible," he said, walking toward the ranger's station. "Let's check in here and let them know we're going to be on the trail with dogs. Sometimes they don't allow them. Dina's orders."

Kylie rolled her eyes. "I wish they wouldn't allow humans, either. Is that a possibility?"

He figured she'd say that. Honestly, as much as he liked the outdoors, he had to admit this was the pits. It was one thing if the victim had just gone missing, but after fifty-one hours, the chances of finding a survivor dropped to one percent. Worse if that person was over sixty years old. Beez was almost sixty. Still, he wouldn't count her out.

But why hadn't she radioed in for help?

Where was her dog?

Shaking off the negative thoughts, Linc tried to focus on that slim one percent. Beez's radio could be broken or lost in some fall. There was a chance...

Right then, he was looking forward to spending tonight snuggling in bed with a warm, dry Kylie. If only their hotel room didn't look like Serial Killer Central.

"Maybe they won't allow humans on the trail today," he said, opening the door for her to let her pass first. "That's why we're going to talk to the ranger."

As he did, he smiled when she crossed her fingers.

The ranger's office was barely big enough to fit a desk, a water cooler, and a brochure rack filled with Tallulah Gorge State Park guides, as well as a bunch of coupons for area attractions. Linc noticed one for Frank's Chicken Hut and stuffed it in his pocket.

Kylie flipped down her hood and shook out her wet jacket as Linc went back out and tied the dogs up to a post under the eaves outside. When he followed her in, she was already talking to the park guide. "Awful!" he heard her say, and assumed she was talking about the weather.

"Tell me about it," the ranger said, leaning on the counter. He probably wasn't much older than legal drinking age, his thin face marred with acne scars. "What are you two doing out in it?"

Linc read the placard on the kid's thin chest. His name was Tanner Peck. "Ranger Peck, we're part of the SAR team searching for Beatrice Crosby."

The kid studied Linc's ID and pushed his glasses up on the bridge of his nose. "Oh, yeah. I heard about that. The SAR needing a rescue of her own. Kind of ironic, huh? I thought you guys were supposed to be good at finding stuff."

Linc bristled, and Kylie, clearly sensing his irritation, moved to stand between the two men. "Did you know her?"

The kid came out from behind the desk. He was all lines and angles, like a teenager who hadn't filled out and become a man yet. He shook his head. "Nah. But..." He pointed behind them to a bulletin board. They swung their heads in unison, and Linc caught sight of a small MISSING sign pinned to the corner of it. "I've seen her around, of course. We've had a lot of missing people lately, but she's the only one not accounted for."

True to his word, there was only one picture still pinned to the board.

Beatrice Crosby, in all her smiling glory.

Linc studied the flyer closer. It had a different photo of Beatrice than they'd seen at the Crosby house. In this one, her light, curly hair and big, dark eyes were visible.

Kylie stared at the picture. Then she reached out and smoothed a curled edge of it back. Was she going to cry again?

Linc scanned the rest of the board. It was empty except for a bunch of thumbtacks, an advertisement for firewood with half of the numbers ripped off the bottom, and a flyer for BINGO happening at the First Baptist Church of Tallulah Falls.

"Sorry, guys. I'm still getting the hang of things around here. Started this job a couple months ago," Tanner Peck was saying. He tilted the blinds and looked outside. "Hell of a day to be performing a search and rescue. Can your dogs find a scent with the weather like this?"

"I guess we'll see," Linc said, scanning the rest of the small space. "Can we head out on the South Rim Trail with the dogs? Storm is experienced in SAR, but our other dog is in training."

"Yeah. Sure. That trail's pretty easy to navigate," he said, reaching for a map. "You two familiar with the trail?"

Linc held his hand in front of him and tilted it back and forth in a "somewhat" gesture. "Haven't been here in a couple years, though."

Tanner spread out the map on the counter, and the three of them huddled over it. The ranger pointed out the trail, then ran a yellow highlighter over it to make sure it was clearly seen.

"You might have a little trouble with puddles. A few slippery rocks and stuff. That's about it. Kind of level. Trail's pretty wide. You won't have to worry about the dogs slipping or anything. Just be sure to get back here before five. You have plenty of time, but that's when it starts getting dark, and you want to give yourself plenty of time to make it back to the gate." He gave them a serious look. "You don't want to get caught out here in the dark, especially if you don't know the trail very well."

"Sounds good," Linc said, folding the map and zipping it in one of the waterproof pockets of his jacket. "Thanks for all your help."

He turned to leave and saw Kylie leaning against the counter, still shaking the raindrops from her hood. He realized she was leaning into a little space heater that the ranger had set up. When she saw that he was ready to go, she sighed. "All ready? I'm still wet."

"Yep. The sooner we start, the sooner we get it over with, and you can be nice and dry in the hotel room."

Kylie lifted her hood reluctantly and tucked her dark hair in. She tied the drawcord tight around her neck so that only her nose and eyes were visible. "Fine."

Tanner Peck waved at them. "Good luck, guys. Thanks for all your help. Let me know if you need anything."

They walked outside, where the dogs were waiting, and they each took a leash. "Come on, Lee," he said to her, stepping out into the driving rain. It bounced off his face, not unpleasantly, but Kylie looked like she was undergoing Chinese Water Torture, blinking like she was on the verge of madness. "Think of it as an adventure."

She followed him toward the trailhead. "I can't believe that I've fallen so far that I'm actually looking forward to eating at Frank's Chicken Hut."

"Hey, me too," he said, taking the lead. "Stay close to me and watch where you step. This may be a safe trail, but you can still get in trouble. And I don't want you falling, because with my shoulder like it is, I'm not sure I'll be able to handle you and the dog."

The fat-lower-lip pout was back. Oh, this would be a joy.

6

Kylie's nose had quickly started running something awful, even before they reached the trailhead. She had a tissue buried in her pocket, but what difference would that make? It was soaked. She was soaked. Rain kept pelting her face, mixing with the snot, slinking down her face and off the edge of her chin. Not to mention that her cheeks were probably bright red and her hair was now matted around her face, giving her the impression of a drowned rat. Lovely.

The air was so damp and about ten degrees colder than it was supposed to be for this time of year. She grabbed Vader's leash tightly and hurried into the woods, hoping that the tree cover might provide a little protection. It didn't. She shivered, shifting her sweatshirt under her jacket a little, only to find that near her neck it was wet and ice-cold against her bare skin.

This was her worst nightmare come true.

Not to mention that she'd stepped in a puddle deeper than her boot was high, and now she felt mud congealing around her ankle. She needed better gear.

Linc walked ahead of her, as he usually did on the rare

occasion they went on hikes together, just because he knew the terrain better than she did, and his step was surer. He spoke, his words mostly getting drowned out by the thundering downpour around them. Something about how it's probably safe to assume that the human scent has been washed away by the downpour, but it was better to do something than nothing, but that dogs only needed a minute amount of scent to find someone.

Really? She wasn't sure. It was bad enough that she was shivering like crazy, but going through all this for no reason? That made it cruel and unusual. And he'd said it himself—this was dangerous. What if someone got hurt on this useless mission?

Then she thought of Greg. Of Ollie. Of the poor missing woman and her dog.

She needed to get over herself, embrace the situation and be okay with being uncomfortable. No more pouting, she scolded herself. No more complaining. Just help.

After a few minutes, Linc stopped and pulled out Beatrice Crosby's headscarf, which Ollie had given them with hopes of the dogs catching her scent. He brought it down to Storm's level, keeping it in the dry, and Vader eagerly nosed his way in there to have a sniff too.

"We'll keep them on the leashes for this," Linc said, wiping his face with the sleeve of his jacket and staring out into the dreary woods. "Vader's too unpredictable, and if I let Storm off, he's likely to go berserk, wanting to be let off too. We can't risk it."

Kylie nodded, knowing he was exactly right. She wanted to help, but she also knew that she and Vader were a liability.

"Just let me know what you need me to do," Kylie said, and wiped at her face with her hand. Sure enough, it was slimy with water and snot. She was glad she already had the ring because she doubted she looked like marriage material right now. Right now, she was a stark contrast to Linc, who only happened to look more hot and rugged and manly, the dirtier and wetter he got. Right now, he looked like a freaking cover model for *Outdoors Magazine*, all muscled and beautiful. It really wasn't fair.

They walked on, and after a few more steps, Kylie felt her jeans, wet and stiff beneath the rainproof pants, chafing her nether regions. Great. She'd get back to the hotel with a massive rash between her thighs. That would be an attractive way to initiate foreplay, asking him to rub Vaseline on her crotch.

She wiped her face again, hardly listening to Linc as he spoke in a soothing voice. When she tuned-in, he was saying something about how pretty it was there.

"Yes, it might be rainy, but it's actually kind of nice and peaceful, when everything's wet like this, don't you think?" He looked around, and she could tell he was in his element. "Usually, this path is crawling with people. It's nice that it's just us."

She could think of many things to call this hike, but *nice* wasn't one of them. She tried to concentrate on her hot fiancé instead of the rain, the beauty of nature instead of her raw fingers turning numb from the damp chill, the bracing fresh air instead of the icy water dripping down her collar... but it wasn't happening.

She gritted her teeth. If she'd been watching this on television, she'd admit it was lovely scenery. The path was dotted with charming stone steps every so often, and as they went up, Linc traversed the obstacle, then turned to help her over it. That was nice. He looked after her better than she could look after herself. She reminded herself for the thousandth time to use the "glass half full" outlook, which she usually applied to most things.

"It is pretty here," she admitted through her chattering teeth.

He looked back at her, just as she was sure a droplet of slimy snot was escaping her nostril. "You're just saying that."

"Okay. Yes. I am," she agreed, swiping at her face again. "I mean, it would be pretty if I weren't a part of it. I'd love a postcard of this exact view."

He laughed. "You're an odd woman, Kylie Hatfield. Why a postcard when you can actually experience the real thing? Have it wrapped around you, a three-sixty-degree view?"

"Because I can't feel my fingertips," she admitted. "I *like* my fingertips."

He stopped, then took both leashes and tied them to a branch. He lifted both of her hands and looked at them. It wasn't really all that cold, probably in the fifties, but her extremities never did well in lower temperatures. The tips of her fingers were all bright red. He held her hands between his big, warm ones—how was it possible he was so warm? "Where are your gloves?"

She could see them, nice and warm in her suitcase. "I left them at the hotel."

He reached into his bag and pulled out something black. As he unfolded it, she realized what it was. His own gloves. Of course. Even though it was unseasonably cold in Georgia and had probably never been so frigid here in a decade, he'd brought gloves. He was such a boy scout. He fixed them onto her hands. "Better?"

She nodded as she looked up into his warm brown eyes, his handsome face. Her mother was right—he was a total hunk. A gem. She told herself—again—to suck it up and quit complaining. "Yes. Thank you."

Then he reached over, and with his bare hand, wiped the end of her nose with his finger.

She smiled. That was real love.

From that moment on, she vowed not to complain again. She'd just do what she always did to take the things she didn't want to think of off her mind: Talk.

Kylie was a champion talker. Where some people found that excessive talking irritated them—Linc included—Kylie was energized by chatter. There was nothing she liked better than shooting the shit with people. She could go on and on for hours, just talking about absolutely nothing. She decided to use it to her advantage.

Linc lifted the leashes of the dogs up and handed one to her. Feeling better, she walked along with him. He said, "You okay?"

"Yeah. I am. I've just been thinking about Greg and Starr Investigations."

"Oh yeah?" Linc cocked an eyebrow at her. "What about him?"

"Oh, you know. That it'll be a real shame if Asheville loses his business. His private investigations firm is the best one in town. He might not be fancy or high-profile, but he's a fixture downtown."

Linc stepped over a fallen log, then held out his hand for her. "You don't know he's closing shop yet, Kylie, remember? Don't worry until there's something to—"

"Well, he's going to eventually. He's nearing retirement age, anyway. And it just sucks, doesn't it? I've finally found something I love to do, for a man I love to work with, and... it'll be just my luck if he decides to close up and leave me..." She stopped and swallowed hard, emotion burning in her face.

No. This was not about being abandoned.

Greg had worked hard all his life and deserved to enjoy a life of retirement.

But still...she felt the future loss of Greg as if it was already happening.

Linc's eyes softened, as if he understood exactly what she was thinking.

"There are other firms in town, right? With your success rate, I'm sure one of them would snap you up in a second, letting you finish your license requirements with them."

She nodded. She knew it was true. But she'd miss Greg so much.

"I suppose."

From behind him, she watched his shoulders go up and down. "Well, if nothing else, it was a good run."

Vader stopped to sniff something, and Kylie tugged on the leash, unable to believe her ears.

A good run?

What did he mean by that?

Linc hadn't known her before she started working at Starr Investigations. If he thought she was a flake now, that was nothing compared to how directionless she'd been before she stumbled into Greg's office, looking for some job, any job, to bide her time while deciding what to change her college major to. She'd gone through precisely seven majors.

It was hard to believe that was just six months ago. So much had changed the moment Greg decided to take a chance on her. She'd gotten the best little doggie in the world as a pet, moved on from her seemingly endless college days, fallen in love with Linc, started actually adulting and taking responsibility for herself, and now she was engaged.

In short, she'd grown up. And it was all because of that grumpy old man she called her boss. "Don't be so blasé about it. This career means everything to me. You know that?"

He raised an eyebrow at her. "Everything?"

"Well, of course you mean even more," she said, elbowing him. "You know I love you, but what'll I do if I'm suddenly out of a job? Go back and finish my criminal justice degree? I only have a couple semesters left."

"That depends. Do you want to?"

She wrinkled her nose. She couldn't imagine, after all she'd seen and done since taking the job with Starr, going back to the classroom. It would be like shoving a butterfly back into its cocoon.

"If I did, what would I do when I graduated? I'd still have the same questions I'm facing now. I don't know. It'll only be a year or so apprenticing until I can get my license. Should I try to find another PI to work under? Even if it's in another town?"

"Um, yeah. If you want. You have to decide what's best for you."

"But it's *us* now. Best for *us*. If I decided to do that, then *we* might have to move. And I don't want to leave Asheville. I know you don't, either." She sighed, giving him a sideways glance. "And I know you've never been too happy about me taking on this career because I've had one or two brushes with danger, but—"

"Try half a dozen."

"Whatever." She waved her hand dismissively. "That copperhead did not even count. You were in more danger than I was." She realized she was off track. "The point is, this is the only job that I really ever felt like I was doing well. You know? Like, you get excited, working with dogs. I get excited, going into work every day, not knowing exactly what I'll be up against."

"Yeah. Okay. But," he said softly, "how are you going to feel in a couple years, when there's a little Kylie or Linc to think about? Excitement is fun, but there's something to be said for sameness. Stability."

She hesitated, missing everything he said after the "little Kylie or Linc" part. They'd never seriously talked about kids before. Sure, she figured that would happen, eventually, but it always seemed so far in the future. Other than the fact that whenever they went to family gatherings he gravitated to the children before he went to talk to the adults, he hadn't given her any indication that he even wanted to start a family right away.

"Is having kids important to you?"

She held her breath, knowing this was a question she should have asked before accepting his ring.

"Well...yeah." He chuckled. "I mean, not tomorrow. But yeah. I'd love a little girl to spoil."

She smiled, relieved. She could just see him coddling a little baby, and it was nearly enough to make her ovaries burst. "I'd love a little boy, just like his daddy."

"Great. So, how are you going to feel, flinging yourself into the unknown with them to think about? Stability's the best thing you can give to your kids, I promise you that."

And with that line, they'd circled back to the original problem. He hated when she put herself in danger. No one ever said that to Linc, even though his job was dangerous too. She resented the double standard and scowled at him.

"But I love the work."

"Is that the only thing you love?"

"No," she snapped at him, getting annoyed. "Obviously not. Except maybe, when you act like this."

"Like what?"

She pointed to the gorge hundreds of feet below them. "Like your work is more important than mine. Why don't you give up your dangerous job to watch the kids?" Her voice had been steadily rising. She put her hand to her ear to listen for his response, but he was silent, staring at her, point taken. "No? Why not? Because you love it? Well, I love my job as—"

She stopped as Storm's ears perked up, and the German Shepherd pulled on the leash, letting out a sharp bark.

Linc grimaced as his leash was pulled. He reached for his

shoulder and massaged it, gnashing his teeth. Had he hurt himself again?

"Did you—"

"Shh." He raised his head and let Storm take the lead, walking off the path somewhat.

She started to speak again, but he held up a finger.

"What is it?" she said after a moment, watching the dog's skittish behavior. Storm was rarely skittish, so when she acted this way, it was hard not to take notice. Kylie peered at Linc's face, which was etched with concern, and suddenly, she started shivering again.

Linc crouched beside the dog. "What is it, girl? Okay. Lead the way. Nice and slow."

They headed off toward a rocky outcropping as Kylie followed close behind with Vader. They passed close by cliff ledges with steep drop-offs into the gorge. The sound of raindrops gave way to rushing water—a waterfall?

The forest of trees opened up to a large, flat area. Nearby, there was a sad looking old picnic bench. Linc held out his arm, urging them back. Kylie squinted at a sign in the distance.

Overlook for Devil's Pulpit.

Oh, that just gave out the warm fuzzies.

"Stay back," Linc warned her. "It's at least a five-hundred foot drop-off from here."

Kylie wasn't fond of heights, so she did as she was told. She craned her neck to the sound of rushing water to see the top of a gorgeous waterfall. Linc was right. Even if it was raining, even if the place was named after a devil, it was beautiful here.

Beautiful and...somewhat spooky. Why was it called Devil's Pulpit? She shivered again.

Out of the tree cover, the rain pelted her face as she watched Linc step surely to the edge of the cliff, taking it entirely too casually. As experienced as he was, Kylie still held her breath. It was slippery, and Beez had been doing this type of work for thirty years, and now she was missing.

Linc took something out of his pack. A bit of blue ribbon to mark the area, which she knew was something he did to track any spots Storm found of interest. He turned around and crouched in the mud, near a tree. He'd found something of interest there, but Kylie squinted, trying to make it out.

She couldn't see anything. "What?"

"Kibble," he said, gathering it, lifting it up and giving it a long sniff. "Surprised it hasn't washed away, but it's under this pine. There's a possibility that Beez might have stopped here with her dog to rest."

"Couldn't it belong to another dog?" Kylie asked.

Linc lifted a shoulder. "Another SAR dog, yes, but other dogs aren't permitted on this trail. Too dangerous."

"Oh." Kylie looked around, and it suddenly occurred to her that it wasn't the cold that had her shivering. It was her spidey sense. Vader looked up at her curiously. He could feel it too.

While Linc was crouched with his back to her, Kylie took a step toward the edge of the cliff. Then another, her instincts whispering at her to look.

Soon, she was right at the edge of the smooth, slippery rock, the traction on her boots the only thing keeping her from a five-hundred-foot fall. But she couldn't help it. It was like something had pulled her there.

A gust of wind picked up, knocking her off-balance, and she immediately went to her hands and knees to keep from falling.

"Hey!" Linc called behind her, but her body was already on high alert, so she didn't even startle. "Get back!"

But she couldn't. She just couldn't turn back now.

Lowering herself to her belly, she snake-crawled to the edge again, her hands curled around the rain-slicked rocks.

All the while, she kept hearing Ollie's voice as he'd described the last thing he'd seen his wife wearing. *A red jacket.*

The hair raised on the back of her neck as she focused her vision, forcing her eyes to examine each and every crevasse far below, one by one.

When she caught sight of it, the smallest of flashes, her heart began to beat in double-time.

"Linc!" Her voice cracked from a mixture of excitement and dread and sorrow. "Linc, I see it! There's something red down there!"

7

Linc massaged the pain from his shoulder as he peered over the edge of the gorge for the hundredth time that day.

Stupid really. Storm had yanked the leash just once, but that was all it needed. He'd felt the muscles in his shoulder tearing, as if whatever healing they'd been doing in the past few weeks had been undone in the space of a couple seconds.

Dammit.

In the distant sky, he heard the helicopter drawing near. More emergency personnel arrived via ambulance, and he lowered his rope with an orange flag attached until it hovered just above the flash of red, giving the rescuers a more accurate place to search.

Recovery of whatever was down there was proving to be no easy feat. It hadn't fallen to the bottom of the ravine, instead landing in a crevasse with some sparse vegetation partially covering it. That was why it hadn't been spotted. From where Linc stood, all he could make out was a triangle of red. It could've been anything.

But because Beatrice was missing, and because she'd last

been seen in a cherry-red jacket, most people seemed convinced that it was her body that had finally been found.

In the hour after they made the radio call, madness and a whole hell of a lot of crowds had descended. Funny how, not long ago, Linc had considered this part of the world peaceful. Now, ambulances and police cars were arriving en masse, as well as news reporters and curious onlookers. The place had become a zoo.

Lonnie, the newbie who'd been searching with Dozer, stood next to Kevin and Molly, shaking his head. "She must've slipped on the edge of the overlook. They've got to put up more signs."

Kevin scratched at his jaw. "That doesn't make sense. She loved that vista. I think she told me once that her husband proposed to her up there. Why would she—"

"She didn't fall from the overlook," Linc added, pointing to the less well-traveled area where he thought she'd slipped from as he rested his shoulder. "Under there is where her body was found. I think she stopped to feed her dog and must've seen something, gotten too close to the edge, and fallen."

Or was pushed, a voice in his head said.

They all figurately scratched their heads and nodded. So, it was a hell of a lot of theories, but no one really knew anything.

Other rescuers were showing up now, relating their own theories. Linc excused himself and walked to a weather-worn picnic table in the midst of some scrubby pines, where Kylie was sitting, head down and mostly hidden by her hood. She'd been excited by the find, then immediately sad by what it meant. His fiancée's heart wasn't made out for this type of work.

"Hey, slugger," he said, sitting next to her. "You all right?"

She looked up at him, her eyes rimmed in red. Her face

was already wet from the rain, but he knew she'd been crying. Her nose had started to run again too. She sniffled, but it didn't have much effect. He offered her a mostly clean rag from his pack, and she blew her nose loudly. "I guess. You hurt your shoulder again, didn't you?"

"Nah. Well, a little. It's not so bad." In the distance, the helicopter was descending into the ravine. "Shouldn't be much longer now."

She sniffled again. "Do all the other SAR people know what we found?"

He nodded. Dina radioed she was on her way from the trail she was searching, and Forrest had shown up only a few minutes after he reported what they'd found. After that, the rangers had gotten on the horn and said that an emergency vehicle was being sent in.

Twenty minutes later, they had determined that there was no way to reach the body without the proper climbing equipment. A half hour after that, it was determined that they'd need to bring in a helicopter. It'd been a long, soggy, depressing day.

She looked at him, biting on her lip, which was trembling. "Does her *husband* know?"

Linc put his elbows on his knees and clasped his hands together. "Not yet. We have to make sure it's Beez first."

She hugged herself and shuddered. Linc reached into his bag and pulled out a Mylar blanket, wrapping it around her tightly, cursing himself for not doing it sooner.

"You want to go back to the motel and take the dogs? I'll hang out here and catch a ride back with one of the other rescuers."

She shook her head. "No, I want to stay with you."

He looked up as he heard a commotion coming from the gorge. Just then, Forrest lumbered over to them, clutching his fisherman's hat in his hands. "Dammit," he muttered, sorrow plain on his face. "Just heard from the rescuers. They've got a positive ID. It's Beez."

Linc nodded as the man ran off to spread the news. Kylie hung her head lower. "Now, can we leave?"

"Yeah." He picked up his pack, trying not to grimace as he shouldered it on his back.

Kylie stood up, staring out at the cliff. "But I still wonder how she fell. She should've known all the dangers of this place."

Linc had wondered about that too, but he also knew there were a number of potential dangers in this job. It could've been anything, but he had a good idea.

"Her dog wasn't as experienced as she was. Maybe he took a wrong step and pulled her over. I guess we'll find out what happened later. Or maybe we'll never find out. Sometimes, you just have to go with the best guess. Let's go."

They said goodbye to the others before making their way down the mountain, both of them silent as the dogs trudged along. Back at the truck, they were just getting ready to load the dogs when Dina pulled up in a yellow Jeep very similar to Kylie's.

Linc went to her window as she rolled it down. "Is it true?" she asked, her face a tight mask of concern. "It's Beez?"

Linc nodded.

Dina banged her fist on the steering wheel. "Dammit," she muttered under her breath. She turned down her radio, which was playing "Sweet Home Alabama." "Guess I'd better go and tell Ollie. Dammit."

"You want help?" He wouldn't have wanted that job, but he knew Kylie would want to offer condolences. She didn't shy away from things like that the way he did.

"Nah. I've got this one."

"Anything else we can help with?"

She shook her head. "Not unless you want to give Ghost a bath for me. He's all mud and burrs."

Linc gave her a sympathetic look and motioned to Vader and Storm, who were both covered in mud. He wasn't sure how they'd manage to clean them up in the hotel room. "I think we've got enough on our hands with these two."

"Thank you both for helping out. Couldn't have done it without you. You going back up to Virginia now?"

"North Carolina," he corrected, "and no. It's getting late, and we've already got a hotel. We'll stay here overnight. If there is any info about what happened to her, could you let us know?"

"Sure thing," she said, stepping out of the Jeep and letting a very dirty Ghost out behind her.

Linc looked for Kylie, but she'd already climbed into the truck and turned on the ignition. When he opened the door, it was like a sauna. She had the heat going full blast, but her teeth were still chattering. She held her hands in front of the vent, trying to get them warm. Her cheeks were as red as if they'd been slapped.

"I can't wait to take a hot shower," she sighed wistfully.

She'd taken the words right out of his mouth. He drove out of the state park, still thinking about Beatrice Crosby. Poor lady. To lose her life endeavoring to help others. It was probably the way she would've wanted to go, knowing how he felt about the job. It was a damn good reminder that his job of saving people was a dangerous one. And here he was always telling Kylie that her chosen career was more perilous.

Kylie didn't speak much on the way. He knew she was thinking about it too.

She was suffering. He'd never seen her look so despondent.

"I think I'll drop you off at the motel so you can get

started on that shower," he said. "Then I'll find a place to hose off these dogs and bring us back some takeout. Okay?"

She nodded. "Frank's Chicken Hut?"

He forced himself to grin. "I know how much you want it, so I'll deliver."

She cracked a small smile.

After he dropped her off, he found a gas station with a hose that allowed him to clean off the dogs. Then, he went and got a bucket of wings with some mashed potatoes with gravy and biscuits. When he came back with the clean dogs and the takeout, the shower was still running. Kylie's marathon showers had a way of lasting the better part of an hour. He stripped out of his wet clothes, sat down on the kitchenette chair in his damp boxer briefs, and flipped on the television.

The local news station's top story was the death. The newscaster said that it appeared the death was accidental, and that the woman had slipped. Nothing he didn't already know. When he heard the faucet in the bathroom turn off, he quickly switched to a different channel. He needed to get Kylie's mind off the case. *Iron Man* was playing on TBS. Perfect.

She came out a moment later in a haze of steam, a towel wrapped around her middle and another wrapped in her hair. He'd bet money all that was left was a hand towel for him.

"Yum," she said, sniffing the air. "Frank's Chicken Hut?" She batted her lashes. "How did you know?"

He laughed. At least she still had her sense of humor. Linc brandished the tub in front of her as the dogs yipped at him for a bone. She climbed over their wagging tails and grabbed a drumstick, then took a ravenous bite.

"That Frank sure knows how to make chicken," she said

dreamily, her eyes wandering to the television. She grinned. "*Iron Man*! You, my dear fiancé, are a dream date."

Linc smiled as she climbed to the center of the king bed, still nibbling on the drumstick, and crossed her legs. She looked and sounded more like the old Kylie. That was good. He finished his chicken and headed to the bathroom. "I'll be back."

A ten-minute shower and shave later, he emerged to find Kylie quietly snoozing as Vader gnawed on the discarded drumstick beside her. "Off," he said to the dog, wrestling the bone from him before he pulled out the pillow and made room for himself. As he did, her eyes flickered open.

She looked around and murmured sleepily, "Oh, gosh. How long was I out?"

He smiled. "Not long. Go back to sleep if you want."

She turned to him, a sleepy grin on her face. "You looking for a little something?"

He chuckled softly. "Yeah. For you to go back to sleep. Sorry I woke you."

She shook her head. "No. It's good. Got to dry my hair or I'll regret it tomorrow."

She climbed out of bed, unwrapped the towel from her head, and finger-combed her hair. Then she found an old hairdryer and turned it on, probably trying to get all memory of "wet" away from her body so she wouldn't have nightmares. It did nothing more than purr softly as she ran it over the long strands.

As she was finishing up and grumbling that the dryer had no power, the television station turned to a special report. Linc scrambled for the remote as an announcer said, "New developments in the search for a seasoned rescuer in Tallulah Gorge..."

He held up the remote to snap it off, but it was too late. Kylie'd already turned to look at it. "Wait. Don't," she said and sat on the edge of the bed, rummaging aimlessly through her bag as she stared at the television. She pulled out a toothbrush and paste but otherwise just sat there.

And there it was again. The crinkle in the forehead. Dammit. He'd wanted a nice, relaxing evening. Now, she'd be on edge.

When he flipped it off, she shouted, "Hey!"

He shrugged. "It's nothing we don't already know, Lee. They think it was an accident. Let's just let it go, okay?"

She pressed her lips together, then pulled off her towel and squeezed into her boxers and camisole. As she climbed over the dogs, trying to get close to Linc on the bed, he noticed that worry crinkle was still there.

"I'm just wondering," she said. "Did they find Tiger?"

He stiffened. "What?"

She wrapped her arms around him and laid her head on his chest. "You know. You said that she was experienced, but her dog wasn't, and maybe the dog took the wrong step and they went over. So, did they find Tiger too?"

It was a good point, and he'd been thinking the exact same thing. No one had said anything about the dog. But one thing he was sure of, he wanted Kylie to get some rest right now. "You're tired. You should go to sleep."

Just then, Linc's phone rang, and Dina's name flashed on the screen.

"Hi, Linc," she said when he answered. "Just wanted to let you know that the police have decided Beez died of an accidental fall."

"They've declared it an accident so soon?" he asked, to which Kylie sat up, listening. He motioned for her to go lay back down. She didn't, of course. "You know if they found her dog?"

"That's a negative," she said, sighing. "If you don't mind, I'm going to go and drink heavily. It's been a shitty day. I just got done at Ollie's place. He's obviously not taking it very well."

"Yeah. I understand."

"And no. He does not think it was an accident."

He ran a hand through his hair. "Even after they found the body?"

"Kept fighting me, saying there's no way she could've fallen by accident. 'My wife's like a mountain goat,' he kept saying. 'She sticks to those mountains, and Tiger would never just go off a cliff like that!'" She sighed. "Denial. That's what that stage is."

"Yeah. Sounds like it."

He hung up, and of course, Kylie was staring at him, nowhere close to sleeping. "So, they didn't find the dog, huh?"

His mind whirred through all the options.

"No, but that doesn't mean he wasn't with her. Wild animals could've gotten…"

The wrinkles on her forehead were back. "Yes, but wouldn't they have found the leash or vest or something?"

He scrubbed his face, pissed when his shoulder throbbed with the movement. "Maybe. You have to remember that this is basically a wilderness, and it could've been dragged away by wild animals or something."

She tilted her head, thinking. "But if the dog wasn't with her, then really, it makes no sense how she fell, right? Everyone keeps saying that she wouldn't slide on her own. That she was too seasoned for that. And that's what Ollie thinks too."

Linc pushed a long strand of hair behind her ear. "I'm seasoned too, and it's one of those things you can't put past yourself. Falling could happen. To anyone. No matter how long you've been at it. Pro baseball players still strike out all the time, right?"

She gave him a doubtful look. "I guess." She worried her bottom lip. "And Dina broke the news to Ollie?"

He nodded. "He's a wreck."

The very tip of her nose turned pink, and her eyes grew glassy with tears. "I want to visit him tomorrow," she announced.

Linc had been expecting that. "All right. We can stop there on the way out of town."

"And I have to call Greg, too, just to let him know. I know he's worried." She lay back and stared at the ceiling, then let out a big breath of air. "So, we're going home?"

He rolled onto his side and looked at her. He thought that went without saying. "Right? It was an accident. Case closed. I think our part of the case is over." He stroked a finger down her cheek. "You found her, Lee. We're done."

A tear escaped. "Yeah. I guess," she said and rolled until her face was pressed against his chest. "Let's go home."

8

O ne month later...

AMY COOPER STOPPED at the base of Tallulah Gorge and watched the rushing water from the previous week's rainfall slipping by like whitewater rapids. So fierce and loud and alive.

She had a new perspective now. She'd decided to turn over a new leaf and no longer be a victim. This morning, it was good to be alive. Alive and young and single. And she was happy to be a part of this beautiful world, to acknowledge there was life outside of the microcosm of her college campus.

It was nice out today, especially for late November. Calm and quiet and cool, perfect since it was barely seven in the morning. She'd left her apartment nearby Piedmont College early, leaving her dreary life behind as most of the kids headed to their home for Thanksgiving break.

Not her. She wanted the silence of being alone. Wanted

away from the alcohol-fueled fights that highlighted every family gathering. Wanted away from her thoughts of him.

Lowering her backpack, she pulled out a granola bar and willed away thoughts of the man who she'd thought she would be spending the holiday with. Ted, with his flowing brown hair, melted-chocolate eyes. The way he'd walk to the front of the lecture hall in those jeans that fit just right, pushing his glasses up the end of his thin nose as he recited Keats or Shelley. He'd say a verse in his deep timbre, and all the girls, who always sat in the front row to be close to him, would swoon.

As sexy as he was in front of his British Romantics class, nothing quite beat how he looked reciting those words to her on the bed in her off-campus apartment, the white of the sheet contrasting perfectly with his tan skin.

She shivered a little at the thought. *Ted Merced is good in bed.* That was the refrain among the other female graduate students at Piedmont. She'd thought they were all chomping at the bit to get into his good graces. She'd thought she was lucky. She'd thought that after twenty-three years of not being considered particularly pretty, or thin, or smart, or anything that boys would write home about, she'd finally landed *the one.*

The one who would change her from an ugly duckling to a beautiful butterfly. Or swan. Whatever.

It wasn't until much later, when she'd fallen hopelessly in love with the man, that she found out that those other women who'd recited that rhyme about Dr. Ted Merced— teaching assistant extraordinaire—being good in bed...were actually speaking from experience.

She winced as she realized she was thinking deeply about him again. How she wanted to scrape those thoughts from her head! She walked a little farther down the path abutting the rushing river, cursing herself. So much for a good bit of exercise to clear the mind.

She lifted her sweat-soaked shirt from her chest, letting the cool morning air waft inside. The trail down had been muddy from so much rain over the last several weeks and this particular trail had been closed because of rockslides during much of the fall leaf season. When she read it had recently reopened, she'd decided to be the first to get a permit. It sounded like just the challenge she needed.

Climbing down the Sliding Rock Trail had been difficult, but that's what she wanted. After what she'd been through, she felt like she had something to prove, and the near forty-five-degree incline straight down the gorge had provided that. She'd been uneasy on the walk since she'd always been overweight and never particularly graceful, but she'd made it.

Proud of herself, she walked a little more, heading toward the sound of rushing water, and smiled. She'd never seen it before, but people in her classes had said it was a beautiful sight. It was the gorgeous Bridal Veil Falls. It looked like a long, elegant bridal veil, she supposed, not that she'd ever get a chance to wear one.

No, she'd never seen herself as the marrying type, but when Ted had asked her out for coffee to discuss a poem she was working on, that changed. He had charm. She was a virgin and had believed she'd stay that way forever, but he quickly finessed her out of that idea. She was in his bed in a week, and by midterms, she was already imagining what it would be like to be called Mrs. Merced.

She had a fantasy of how he'd propose to her, on one knee, in a romantic locale such as this one. Of course, after reciting some obscure but irresistibly romantic British sonnet about how her eyes were like stars.

The beginning of the end was when she went down to his basement office during office hours. He spent most of his time in his cluttered, cramped office, he'd said, simply reading the classics and wishing his students needed him more. At least, that's what he'd joked about.

But when Amy went there, wearing a new lace thong that she knew would cheer him up, she found him already occupied. As she listened at the door, she heard a definite moan.

Heartbroken, she'd waited in the shadows to see a lithe, willowy blonde from her class leaving the room, tucking her blouse into her skirt as she left.

After that, there were more. Many more. She counted five, at least. Sometimes subtle things; holding a woman's gaze too long, touching a classmate on the arm, fingers lingering, stroking. But some were egregious. She'd found a woman's red thong panties in the cushions of his sofa, and she never wore red panties.

She looked up at the beautiful falls and realized what she'd done again. Thinking of him. Wasting her time moping over a serial cheater. Or was he even a cheater? He'd never called her a girlfriend. Maybe she was just a notch in his bedpost, like all the others.

Whatever it was, she'd vowed time and time again to forget him. To move on with her life.

Her willpower to do such a thing only lasted a few minutes, at the most. He'd wormed his way so tightly into her brain, she thought she'd never get him out.

Thus, this hike. Something to get away from the campus. To clear her mind. Think. To accomplish something meaningful, for once, that didn't involve Ted Merced. He was an indoor guy, a thinker. He'd never deign to muddy himself on the hike down into this gorge.

Which was why coming here was perfect.

She scraped her hiking boots along a sharp-edged boulder, freeing the mud caked on the soles. Then she moved to the edge of the rock and leaned in, feeling the water with one hand. It was icy cold, for sure, but exhilarating.

She finished her granola bar and walked on a little farther, until she came to a calm pool. Looking around, she realized how beautiful it all was and how lucky she was to be a part of it. A walk in the woods could be so rejuvenating; life changing. She'd studied English writers most of her life, but wasn't that what Thoreau had said? He'd gone to the woods to live deliberately, to suck the marrow out of life.

Ted Merced and his indoor life? He was living aimlessly. She was so much better than him, standing here, sucking on that bone and taking out every last drop that life would offer her.

And staring at the calm water, Amy Cooper decided that was exactly what she wanted to do. Right here, right now.

Peering into the woods behind her, she slipped her back-pack off her shoulders and set it down on a rock. Then she crouched, unlaced her boots, and kicked out of them. She knew this was crazy, but it was also just what she'd come out here to do. To be a little crazy. To empower herself. So what if the water was freezing. She needed to stop sitting on the sidelines and just reading about things. She needed to *do*.

She grabbed the hem of her t-shirt, preparing to lift it over her head as the whole of Thoreau's quote came to her: *I went to the woods because I wished to live deliberately, to front only the essential facts of life, and see if I could not learn what it had to teach, and not, when I came to die, discover that I had not lived.*

Yes, she thought, imagining the feel of the cold water on her skin. *No more hiding. I need to live this life of mine.*

Ripping off her shirt, she unhooked her bra, letting her breasts swing free. She smiled as the first rays of sun broke through the gorge, warming her face and chest. It was like a sign.

She pushed down her pants and slipped them down to

her ankles. This would be it. Her chance to wash him away from her skin for good, to cleanse and baptize herself, and most importantly...move on.

She was so excited. As she raised her arms over her head, worshiping the sun as it shined down on her, she smiled, ready for her future.

The scrape of a shoe on rock caused her to jump as adrenaline and shame swept through her system. But before she could even cover her breasts, bone-jarring pain, deep and exquisite, vibrated from the top of her skull.

No! she mentally screamed as darkness descended on her vision. *I need to live.*

WRONG PLACE. Wrong time.

As I looked down at the naked woman at my feet, I raised my arms to the heavens, just as the girl had done only moments before, thanking God for putting her exactly where I needed her to be.

My right place. My right time.

This was becoming easier and easier.

Practice made perfect, right?

I could almost hear you tell me just that.

I was also learning to take advantage of an opportunity when it presented itself. And present itself, Amy Cooper did.

I wished I knew what she'd been thinking, stripping down to the buff like that. She didn't strike me as a person to do something so daring. But of course, neither did I.

But I dared, didn't I, my little love?

I dared because the time had finally come.

I'd been patient. So very, very patient. I'd bided my time, waiting for the perfect time to strike.

This girl was perfect. She'd come here alone from the

local college. Knew that from the sticker in the corner of her car's back mirror. With Thanksgiving break, it could be days before someone missed her. Weeks even. Months. It didn't matter.

All that mattered was that she'd gotten a permit to come to this part of the gorge, and the station would be the last place she was seen. The park rangers would have to account for her. They'd wonder why her car was still in the lot, and they'd grow concerned.

Then the "professionals" would be coming. Professionals like Beez, the old goat.

And I was ready.

Finally, ready.

I'm so sorry that it's taken me this long to act, sweet darling.

Poor Beez. She hadn't known what hit her, had she? Damn, that little woman could scream. I was afraid someone would hear, especially that close to the Pulpit. That was where all the hikers stopped. Partly because it was a nice view, but mostly, I thought, because of the name. People liked evil things, didn't they?

I did. Hadn't always, but in the past few months, I'd been thinking things I'd never thought before. Which was good. Sometimes, you had to do what's wrong in order to do what's right, didn't you think?

With the way those assholes went out searching for Beez, you'd have thought she was a fucking celebrity. The teams that scoured the mountain were unreal. All that chaos and craziness for a little old biddy who didn't mean shit to anyone.

The rescuer, beyond rescue. How funny was that?

Rolling Amy's naked body over, I examined her face, her tits. She wasn't awful looking, but she was soft. Doughy. She hadn't been taking very good care of herself.

I waited for my dick to stir. It didn't.

Disappointment was bitter on my tongue.

But it was better this way. Because I needed to focus.

Amy…she was different. Much, much different than Beez. This time, I sincerely doubted anyone would care too much about her. Poor, sad nobody. What a waste of a life.

But she would do. The rescuers didn't assign a point value to lives based on their viability—they just went out blindly, like vultures, tearing at bones in the desert. She'd make a nice little fat worm, dangling off that hook.

I dragged Amy Cooper's lifeless body to the edge of the river, then lifted her backpack. I opened it, picked through it. Granola bars, granola bars, granola bars. Obviously, she'd been afraid of going hungry on the trip. Her phone. I tossed that in the river. Extra clothing, goodbye. Car keys, driver's license, and school ID. A photo of her with a guy that was way out of her league.

I tossed all of that in the raging river too.

Found a twenty-dollar bill in one of the pockets of her clothes as I tossed those and her boots in. Kept that. A killer's gotta eat, right? Turns out, murder takes a lot out of you.

I wondered how tiring it would be to die.

You knew the answer to that question, didn't you, my poor sweet darling?

Sadness and anger swept over me as I gathered up rocks, filling the backpack. As I did, Amy Cooper stared at me. Shuffling forward, I kicked her head and made her face the other way. There was blood all over the rocks from where I'd hit her. Head injuries bled the worst, even when they weren't so bad.

"Unfortunately," I said to my dear friend Amy. "Yours is a little bad."

I smiled at my humor, glad to know that I could still joke. I thought the humor had been ripped out of me so long ago.

Clearing my throat, I finished stuffing her backpack with

rocks. Without giving myself more time to think, I lifted her limp form and pushed her arms through the loops, then tied the straps around her body, making sure she wouldn't be separated from her bag any time soon. Amy needed to take a nice long swim.

Then I dragged her toward the river's bank. Holding her up to my chest, I sang one of your favorite songs. *"Just sit right back, and you'll hear a tale. A tale of a fateful trip. That started at the bottom of his gorge, where Amy Cooper flipped..."*

And flip she did, falling from the rock with a splash. I watched her white body rush along with the current a little bit before the weight of the bag pulled her down, and she disappeared from view.

Gilligan's Island. You and I, we loved that show. So funny how they built everything out of palms and communicated with coconut shells and shit like that. You'd gotten a kick of that Gilligan, and how they always wore the same clothes day in and day out. I'd have to go home and binge-watch a little of that. Yeah. In Amy Cooper's honor. That would be nice. A tribute to the big, juicy worm. Maybe tonight, after work.

I turned and took a few deep breaths, preparing for the exertion of climbing up to the top of the gorge. My adrenaline was draining, making me weak.

But there was no time for weakness.

I'd tossed in the bait, and now I just needed to wait patiently for a bite.

9

Kylie walked the dogs out back and shivered in the cool morning air. The temperature had nose-dived in the past couple of days, and here it was, almost Thanksgiving. She sighed as the dogs went around, sniffing and cavorting in the frosty grass, then took a sip of her extra-strong coffee. She smiled. Maybe being out in nature wasn't so bad, after all.

The flowers Linc had planted all summer had shriveled up, looking kind of sad. He would probably want to plant something else, knowing him, although she had no idea what would live through the harsh North Carolina mountain winters.

Maybe she could talk him into waiting until the spring, when they could make the house bright and beautiful for their wedding. That would give his shoulder even more time to fully heal. It was doing much better, and he'd increased his physical therapy visits since he'd reinjured it in Georgia a month ago. Still, she didn't want to take any chances with him exerting himself now. If he insisted on planting something now, she'd just have to help him.

Because they were a team.

The thought made her smile grow wider.

But she couldn't think about that right now.

It was time to start another workday.

She went inside the farmhouse and powered up her work computer, hoping that an exciting case would be sitting in her inbox. After she'd gotten back from Georgia last month, Greg had told her to fill out a report and then head on home. He'd finally come to realize that with computers and all that new-fangled technology he'd resisted for so long, working away from the office was not only a possibility…it actually made sense.

Now, she had started working from home in the morning, then went into the office in the afternoon to deal with the paperwork that seemed to never end. Greg covered the office in the morning and would leave a few minutes after she walked into Starr Investigations, filling her in on any new cases he was working on. Usually cases involving Impact Insurance, their biggest client. He also took on most of the surveillance cases, since Kylie had trouble sitting in one spot for very long.

So far, the new schedule was working well for them both.

Except that she missed Greg.

Missed his crotchety old ways. Missed the moments when he imparted bits of his wisdom that always surprised her coming from his surly mouth.

He was trusting her more and more, giving almost all other cases—besides Impact and surveillance—to her. This would have been fabulous if the cases had been juicy ones. But they were usually boring.

Cheating spouses.

Background checks.

Family law matters that usually involved asset discovery

to make sure cheating spouses weren't hiding their money in divorce or child support court.

People sucked.

When she flipped open the laptop and stared at her email, she sighed. One new case; a background check for a new employee at one of their client companies. Boring. The most fun she ever got from those was finding out the potential employee had a shoplifting charge in the past. Big deal.

Fifteen minutes later, she'd sent out all the "feeler" emails, and an hour after that, she'd finished her report. She emailed it off to the client, went to the fridge, and found last night's leftover pasta.

Throwing it in the microwave to heat it up for lunch, she realized it wasn't even ten o'clock yet.

This was starting to get really old. Her lunches had gradually gotten earlier and earlier, and after a couple of weeks, she was eating second lunches in the midafternoon. It wasn't hunger. It was boredom. Any more of this, and she'd need a forklift to get her down the aisle.

Speaking of which...

The wedding.

They agreed a couple weeks ago that Christmas wasn't a possibility, and she'd been so relieved that she'd pulled out a calendar and flipped to May, tapping her finger on the first Saturday of that month.

And just like that, they had a wedding date.

And just like that, she'd felt frozen with a new wave of fear.

Whenever she and Linc spoke about the plans, he'd told her he was fine with whatever she wanted. He'd given her full reign to make it her wedding. So, this should've been easy.

But it wasn't.

Maybe she just needed to man up and admit to Linc that

she was genuinely terrified to plan such an event. That even though she had his okay to make it as small or casual as she wanted, it still needed to be perfect. After all, it was supposed to be the biggest day in *both* their lives. She just didn't want to mess it up. Mostly for him. Or his perfect family. Or her mom.

She went online and Googled "destination weddings," but after paging through a million search results for Hawaii and Punta Cana and Costa Rica, she nixed them all. One of the things Linc had mentioned—over and over again—was getting married at the farmhouse. He seemed pretty excited about that, and she knew that would make it special for him.

So, they knew two things. The wedding date was the first Saturday in May, and the location would be at the farmhouse.

Kylie should have been cheering at that bit of success, but whenever she did something like search for tent rentals, she wound up going down a giant rabbit hole, wondering how big the tent would have to be. She started to fill out an information request form and realized she had no idea how to answer any of the questions.

Date? She knew that one.

Time? Linc wanted a sunset wedding, but was an eight-p.m. wedding too late? She had no idea.

Size of party? No idea.

Colors? Nope.

When she saw some really cool bouncy houses, Kylie wondered if it would be weird to have a bouncy-house wedding.

Probably.

She scratched at the back of her hand and realized that yep, she had a hive there.

Grimacing, she kicked away from her seat, went to the bathroom mirror, and saw three more sprouting up at her hairline. "Oh, god," she moaned. If she hived up like this just thinking about the wedding, she'd be a walking welt as she walked down the aisle.

Just then, the door opened and Linc walked in. He'd been outside, tending to the animals. The moment he saw her, he froze. "What now?"

"Um. Nothing," she said, arranging her hair to cover the bumps. "You okay?"

She brushed past him, pausing long enough to kiss his cheek before heading back to her makeshift workstation at the kitchen island. It was ten now, prime work hours. If she was going to get emailed new cases, it would happen now.

Or, now.

She stared at her email, willing something to come through.

Now.

But nope. No new emails.

Linc caught her slumping. "Let me guess. No new cases?"

She paged over to Starr Investigations' new website, checking to make sure the online contact form she'd installed hadn't crashed. It hadn't.

Sitting back in her chair, she sighed. "Something is definitely up with that boss of mine. I'm telling you. He doesn't seem the least bit concerned about the business."

He poured himself a cup of coffee and kissed the top of her head. "He trusts you now. You're making money for him with the cases you do take on, so what's the difference? He's happy with you."

"I don't know. It just seems suspicious."

"That's because, in your line of work, it's a good thing to be suspicious. That's what you get paid for," he said, sitting next to her on a stool and squinting at the display. She realized too late that she'd forgotten to close out of the tent company's website.

"Hey." His smile was so wide and filled with hope that it made her heart swell in her chest. "You doing some wedding planning?"

"Yes, I was." *Barely.*

He clicked to another tab and frowned. "Or…are you just looking at bounce castles?"

She stuck out her tongue and ruffed his hair. "Thought you might enjoy a little bouncing fun at the reception."

Her phone rang, making her jump, and she rushed to pick it up. Anything to avoid talking about her nonexistent plans. It was her mom, who she hadn't seen in weeks, though they talked on the phone nearly every day. Rhonda Hatfield had Kylie's effervescent personality, and their phone conversations often went on for the better part of an hour.

Kylie collapsed on the couch and made herself comfortable for another marathon call. "Hello?"

"Oh, my goodness, Kylie," her mother gushed. "You'll never believe what Jerry surprised me with yesterday!"

Kylie smiled. Her mother's new boyfriend, an ear, nose, and throat doctor, was a total dream. Just ask Rhonda, who squealed about Jerry like a teenager every chance she got. Kylie had to admit, it was odd seeing her perpetually single mother in the dating scene again, but it was nice to see her so deliriously happy. And Jerry? He treated her like gold.

"What did that *hunk* do now?" Kylie teased, using the word Rhonda had always used to describe Linc.

"He took me roller-skating last night, and then we went to an old-time diner and had root beer floats. I don't know where he gets his ideas, but he's always thinking of something fun to do."

Roller-skating? Did her mother even know how to do that? "Well, that's good. You didn't break anything?"

"Miraculously, no."

Kylie laughed. It was so strange how one person could

transform another's life so dramatically. All her life, Kylie's mother had been Super Mom, devoting herself fully to Kylie and never thinking of herself. Her husband had disappeared into thin air four days after Kylie had been born, and Rhonda had been forced to raise Kylie as a single mother.

But just recently, and with Kylie's help, Rhonda had discovered William Hatfield's ties to the mafia, and had finally divorced him. Now happily single, she was busy sowing her wild oats and making up for lost time. As odd as it was, Kylie loved seeing her mom so happy.

"Well, that's a good thing."

"So, I was just calling to give you a little kick in the pants," she said.

Uh-oh. Kylie sensed what was coming and cringed. She decided to play innocent. "About what?"

"Your wedding dress shopping, of course!" she said. "You told me over a month ago that we'd go out together and browse. And you haven't said boo to me since then!"

Kylie crossed her fingers. "Well, I've been kind of busy…"

"Honey. This is important. Don't you want to find the perfect dress?"

Kylie chewed on her bottom lip. There was that word again: Perfect. Everything about the day had to be perfect.

She got the feeling her mom's interest was less about finding the perfect dress for her wedding and more about her mother scoping out options for her own possible wedding. No, her mother had never indicated anything about the possibility of marrying Jerry, but with how well they were getting along, it seemed the next logical step. Jerry was a widower, and a traditional guy too.

"Yes, I do, but—"

"So, no dragging your feet. Let's do this. I'll make us an appointment at the boutique in downtown Asheville for tonight. We'll have dinner. Okay?"

Her hive grew a hive, but she tried to ignore it. "Fine," she muttered. "Tonight."

Her mother started to talk about her crazy workweek, but suddenly, Kylie wasn't interested in hearing one of Rhonda's famously long and drawn out yarns. She sat up on the couch and looked over at Linc, who was looking at his phone, pretending he wasn't listening. Which he totally, totally was.

"I've got to go, Mom," she said. "I'm really busy."

"Oh. Okay, honey."

Kylie felt bad for lying, and worse, for cutting her mother off. She threw the phone down in her lap and sighed, deciding she would work on new blog and social media posts to drum up more business.

She caught Linc watching her and smiled. "I'm going dress shopping with my mom tonight. And to dinner. Looks like you're on your own."

"Okay."

She pouted at him. She wanted him to beg her to stay home. Because she'd happily agree. What was wrong with her? Why was this so hard?

He must've read it on her face, because Linc went over to her and sat on the coffee table across from her. "You know what you need?"

"A new, exciting case?"

"No. A massage. You're all tense. Come on up. I'll give you one."

She raised a doubtful eyebrow at him. That was code-word for him wanting a little something-something in the bedroom. Really, as much as she loved him, she would've much preferred a new case, and not just a simple background check. Something meaty, and maybe even a little bit dangerous. It'd been over a month since they went looking for Beez, and that had been short-lived and mostly miserable. She wanted to detect, find clues, get to the bottom of a mystery.

"You're going to screw me, right?" she singsonged as he took her hand and dragged her toward the bedroom.

"No. Massage," he said innocently.

She started to shake her head when her phone began to ring again. It was from a 762 area code. Georgia. She held up a finger and said, "Hello?"

"Is this Kylie Hatfield?" The voice was gruff, familiar.

Her ears pricked up.

"Yes, speaking," she said, looking over at Linc.

"This is Ollie Crosby. You remember me? Greg Starr's friend. You stopped by last month after my wife's death and gave me your card with your number in case I needed anything."

Yes, she'd done that. After calling Greg and reporting the news, they'd stopped at Ollie's house before heading out of town. He'd already known about his beloved wife's demise because Dina had told him, but when he saw Kylie, he burst into tears and cried on her shoulder so long that her sweatshirt was just as wet as if she'd been caught in another torrential downpour.

She'd held him, even though he smelled like sour milk, and let him cry all he wanted as she stroked his back. Linc had watched, stiffly, not used to such displays from another man. Eventually, though, Ollie'd gotten it together long enough to thank her. He'd really seemed appreciative that she'd stopped in.

"Yes, Mr. Crosby," she said, giving Linc a glance. She almost hadn't recognized his name, because his voice sounded much stronger, which was a good sign. "How are you? I've been thinking of you."

"Can't complain. It's been hard without Beez, but I keep on keeping on."

"I understand, Mr. Crosby. It can't be easy. What can I do for you?"

"Well, I just had to tell you. I knew there was something off about my wife's disappearance, and this proves it."

She blinked. Something off? She liked the sound of that. "What do you mean, Mr. Crosby?"

"You ain't heard? Another SAR and his dog are missing. Went missing looking for a hiker a day ago. Vanished without a trace."

Kylie's eyes widened, and she met Linc's gaze before tapping the speaker option on the phone so he could hear too. "Missing? Really? At Tallulah Gorge?"

"Yes, ma'am. And they been searching far and wide and can't find him. Police are sitting around with their thumbs up their asses again. See, I told everyone there was something shady goin' on," he said. "Ain't no way this was natural, two of them going missing so close together."

Kylie's heart began to pound. Linc looked concerned as well. He opened his mouth to say something then frowned and patted his pocket. When he pulled out his phone, Kylie could see the display lit up with a phone call of his own. He walked to the other side of the room and lifted it to his ear as she took her own call off speaker.

"That's really quite extraordinary, Mr. Crosby," she said. "It can't be a coincidence, can it?"

"No, it can not," he said pointedly. "Regardless of what the police think. So, listen here, Miss Hatfield. I want to hire you. Whatever it takes, I want you down here. If my wife's death wasn't accidental, I need to get to the bottom of it and bring whoever did this to justice. It's the least I can do for Beez."

"I understand," she said, nodding fervently. "I want Beez to see justice too."

"Good. You'll take the case?"

"Of course. I need to check some things first, but I'll try to be there tomorrow. I'll call you later to give you a more accurate time."

She finished with him and hung up, rubbing her hands together, brimming with excitement. "That was Ollie Crosby," she said as Linc hung up his phone. "He still thinks there's been foul play, and he wants me to investigate the case of Beez's disappearance some more, along with the disappearance of another SAR."

Linc held up his phone. "That was Dina at Georgia Search and Rescue. She's asked me to come in and help look for the missing SAR. It's Kevin and his dog, Molly. I have to leave now."

Kylie was already heading toward the stairs and their bedroom. "I'm going with you."

Really, there was no decision. It was either stay in Asheville for the night and be subjected to the shopping trip from hell, or else go down to Tallulah Falls and solve a mystery. No contest. Kylie grinned, excited again for the first time in what seemed like weeks.

"Well, look who's happy again," Linc observed, pinching her side. "So, does that mean I'm not getting lucky?"

Grinning, she swatted him away and opened the closet to pull out her suitcase. "You're lucky just being with me."

10

By the time they reached Tallulah Gorge State Park, it was obvious that seeds of doubt had begun to bloom inside Kylie's head.

"Are you sure this is a good idea?" Kylie asked as he drove to the entrance of the park.

He glanced over at her, then reached out to place his hand on her forehead. "Are you sick? I thought you were chomping at the bit for a new case."

She pulled his hand down and held it between hers, watching him closely to see if he winced at the movement. He did, but only a little.

"Your shoulder. I—"

"My shoulder is just fine," he muttered, tilting the visor back now that the trees were overhead, blocking the sun. It was nice to be here in something other than a torrential downpour. At least, he hoped Kylie wouldn't complain as much. "It's been a month since the pull, Lee. Stop worrying so much."

She snorted, but the sound didn't carry any heat. "Famous last words. You thought it was fine last time. You want the doctor yelling at you again? He told you to take it easy for the next couple months, at least."

"I will be taking it easy," Linc insisted. "The doc cleared me, and PT has been going fine."

"Yeah, but he told you to avoid activities that could pull it out of whack again. This qualifies."

"Right. Which is why we left Vader at home. This way, I can concentrate on Storm," he said. "Seriously. I feel good as new. I'm ready for this."

She looked over at him, and her doubt gave way to a smile. "Okay, okay. I'm just worried. Don't want you doing any permanent damage."

"I won't. I'll tell the guys I want to take it as easy as possible this time," he assured her as they pulled into the parking lot by the South Rim Trail, where they'd been just over a month ago. The place was, once again, swarming with people. Not as many as when they'd found Beez's body, but it was crowded. Considering it was a nice day, there were a lot of pleasure hikers about.

But there was nothing pleasurable about this excursion.

Kylie had read him a few news stories on the way down about what had happened. According to the newspapers, a graduate student named Amy Cooper had gone hiking on the Sliding Rock Trail early one morning and hadn't been seen since. The rangers reported her missing after her car was left in the lot, unattended for a couple of days. She was an inexperienced hiker, so the thought was that she might have fallen somewhere on the treacherously steep trail, but no body was found during the initial searches.

A day later, the search had been broadened, and more SAR personnel had been called in. Kevin Friedman, married, father of four girls, gym teacher at the local high school, and all-around beloved citizen of Tallulah Falls, was reported missing that evening. According to the news reports, he'd been partnered with Lonnie, the new kid, who was shadowing him with his pup, Dozer. They separated for a short period, and then Kevin and his dog simply vanished.

At that point, Kylie had looked up from her screen, tears in her eyes. "He was the man we met. Do you remember? The tall one, kind of balding?"

Linc had nodded. Of course he remembered. "I've been on searches with him before," he'd reminded her.

Now, it was clear the man was still on Kylie's mind. She looked out the window and swiped at her eyes. "His poor family. Those poor kids. Four of them! Young ones! They must be so frantic with worry."

"He and the missing college student might be just fine, Lee. It's still early."

"Right. But what if they're not?"

Yeah. He knew that was a possibility, but he was trying not to think about that. That's what he'd learned to compartmentalize and tuck away whenever this work needed to be done: Just finding the victims. Assigning humanity to them only made this stuff tougher.

He'd been learning to do that since the army. Kylie had only been at this kind of stuff for six months. No wonder she'd matured so much since he met her. She'd seen some pretty harrowing shit.

He reached over and squeezed her hand. "Try not to think about it. Remember, concentrate on the search, not on what you're going to find."

She nodded, but he knew her. She'd be thinking about it.

A police officer was posted in front of the entrance to the park, where the gate was. Linc rolled down his window, and the officer said, "Sorry. This area's closed off to the general public."

Linc reached into the cup holder and pulled out his wallet, showing his ID. "I'm part of the search party."

The officer nodded. "Go on ahead, then. They're parked in the South Rim Trail lot."

Linc thanked him. "Any sign of either missing person?"

"Not from what I've heard, sir," he said, waving them forward.

The small lot had no spots left, so Linc parked his truck on the grass. He stepped out of the truck and tilted forward the seat to let Storm hop out, then the three of them walked to where a number of people and search dogs were assembling at the base of the South Rim Trail.

"I need to use the little girl's room," Kylie said, pointing to the shack near the ranger's station. "I'll be right back."

Linc looked around, seeing a few familiar faces among the somber crowd. There was Dina, wearing a baseball cap, who waved at him. He waved back and noticed Lonnie with his black lab, Dozer. The newbie had long, unkempt brown hair and a goatee, and was wearing a t-shirt for some band Linc had never heard of.

Linc was pretty sure that he'd been the one shadowing Kevin the day they'd gone out looking for Beez, so he took Storm by the leash and made his way over to him. The men shook hands.

"Some crazy shit, huh, man?" Lonnie chattered, his eyes darting around nervously as he fisted Dozer's leash in his hands. "That's four in less than two months. The guys I hang out with have been calling this place the Gory Gorge. Not so good for tourism, huh?"

"Yeah. Were you out with Kevin when he disappeared?" Linc asked.

He sucked in a breath, clearly distressed. "I was. Craziest thing, man. I made a rookie mistake, so I kind of feel like it's all my fault."

"Yeah? What happened?"

"There were hunters out in the woods, and Dozer got

skittish from the gunshots." He patted the dog on the head, almost like he was trying to take the sting out of the words. "He got away from me. I ran off to try to get him, got turned around, and when I came back to the place I left him, Kevin was gone. Tried radioing. No answer. Finally found my way back to headquarters 'cause I thought he'd be there, but the guy's been missing ever since."

"Where was that?"

"On the North Rim. Not far from here." He leaned in. "Hell, if anyone was gonna go missing, I'd have bet money on me. Between you and me, I know the guy didn't have as much experience as Beez or you, but he knew his shit. He knew that trail up and down. Something really funky's going on, man. Not legit. Not legit at all."

Dina jogged over to them. "I was really hoping when we saw you again, Linc," she said, shaking his hand, "that it would be under better circumstances. This is not the best thing to be happening to this park."

Storm laid dutifully at his feet, but Linc could tell from the way her ears were cocked that she was eager to get on the trail and do some searching too. "Yeah, I'll say. This happened yesterday, right? How long have you been searching?"

"We're going on our twentieth hour right now. It's been over forty-eight that Amy Cooper's been missing." She reached back and grabbed hold of another man's leather motorcycle jacket sheathed arm. He whirled, along with a platinum blonde with a deep tan. "Jaxon Mott and Crystal Sinclair, meet one of Asheville's best. Linc Coulter."

Linc shook their hands, admiring their dogs. One was a German Shepherd, the other a Boxer. Storm approached the other pups, cautiously getting to know them as she usually did. "Good to be working with you," Linc said to their handlers.

Crystal let out a bubbly hello, but Jaxon just grunted in apparent disinterest.

"That's everyone. Oh!" Dina said, snapping her fingers and looking around the people. "Not everyone. You have to meet Will."

She cupped her hands over her mouth and shouted to a man who was sipping coffee and slouching against a tree trunk, dark sunglasses covering a great deal of his face.

Linc grinned as he walked into the sunlight. He'd bet anything that those sunglasses were there to ward off a hard night of partying. That's just who Will Santos was—the life of the party.

"Well, look who turned up," Linc said with a wry smile, shaking his hand. "Nice to have you gracing us with your royal presence, slick."

"So, you two know each other?" Dina asked, looking back and forth between the two men.

"You could say that," Will Santos said as they separated from the rest of the rescuers. "How the hell you been? Heard you had quite a set-up there in Asheville. You still high in the mountaintops?"

"The highest I could get." Linc crouched to ruffle the fur of Will's golden retriever, Star. If he'd been given the opportunity to hand-pick a search team, Will would've been his first choice. They'd worked together countless times before. "Heard you're not doing so bad yourself. Down South of Atlanta, right?"

"That's right. Things are good. Bought a house. Still living the good life."

Linc grinned. Knowing Will, that meant going to bars every night, picking up hot women. When Linc had been single and just discharged from the army, he'd done his best to keep up with Will at the clubs, but it'd been a stretch. The man liked to have a good time.

"No kidding." He spied Kylie walking through the crowd and motioned her over. "Will, meet Kylie, my fiancée."

Will shook her hand. "What the hell a pretty thing like you doing with this broken thing," he said with a wink, pouring on his Latin charm. Will was like a Hispanic version of Linc's best friend, Jacob. Jacob had loved playing the field; that is, until he reconnected with Linc's ex, Faith. Now, he barely saw Jacob anymore. Knowing how much Kylie loved Jacob, he figured she'd probably get on famously with Will.

Linc nudged him. "Don't give her any ideas. She's already having second thoughts as it is."

He waited for Kylie to object, but she didn't. She just said how lovely it was to meet Will, ignoring Linc's comment. He'd meant it as a joke.

Wait. *Was* she having second thoughts?

They really hadn't been talking about the wedding much, not as much as he'd expected they would be. And Linc had gotten the feeling that when they'd been called down to Georgia, she might have been glad to escape that dress-shopping trip with her mom. He'd have to ask her about it later, because now was not the time.

Dina climbed to the top of a picnic bench and cupped her hands around her mouth. "Okay, guys, thank you for coming out today. We're going to get started."

Will nudged him. "At least we're not on the search for escaped prison inmates this time."

"Yeah," Linc agreed. That had been brutal. Hours on the trail, and the prisoners in question obviously hadn't wanted to be found. He shrugged the hopelessness of that night off and smiled. This was a piece of cake in comparison.

Kylie leaned over, eyes wide. "Prison inmates?"

He whispered, "I'll tell you later," and leaned in to focus on what Dina was saying. The SARs got separated into two teams, with Kylie and Linc part of the team looking for Amy on the Sliding Rock Trail.

Oh, Kylie would really get a kick out of this one. This trail could make even hardcore hikers rethink the hobby.

Well, at least it was sunny.

"Look," he said to her, taking her aside. "This trail is hard-core. It's steep. So stay with me and step where I—"

"I got it, I got it," she said with a smile, tightening the drawcord on the bottom of her jacket. "I don't have Vader pulling me around this time, so it's not a problem. All it is is walking, right? I've been doing that since I was a baby, believe it or not. I'm ready."

He gave her a look. She really had no clue.

"You still have to be careful," he warned.

"I'm always careful!" She looked up from her map, gave him a bright smile, then skipped off toward the trailhead.

Right. He thought about mentioning the serial killer she'd unwittingly gotten herself tangled up with, but she was finally in a good mood on the trail. He didn't know how long that smile of hers would last, but he guessed that if he brought up the Spotlight Killer, it'd probably end a hell of a lot quicker.

Mentally crossing his fingers, he tugged on Storm's leash and followed her quietly to the South Rim Trail.

11

Kylie had never been so unsure as she was in the moment she stood there, fisting a helpless pine tree branch as she contemplated the next step into the abyss.

She dipped a toe down a little, rethought, picked it up, settled it down again, and then stepped.

No, wrong! Danger, danger! She wouldn't have balance if she stepped there. She needed to choose a different spot. Wobbling, she gripped the tree branch harder in a strangling fist, which was now sticky with its sap.

It was a wonder Storm wasn't having more trouble navigating the steep incline. After all, she had four feet and no thumbs to think about, not just two. Kylie hadn't been particularly afraid of heights until this moment, looking down the drop, wondering where to put her foot next.

The guy behind her, Jaxon, a motorcycle dude with a red handkerchief on his head, groaned and said something under his breath. Kylie would've thought he was cute if he hadn't been breathing down her neck the entire walk, all the while talking to the blonde girl he was with as if she was a piece of meat. *Hey, move that hot ass of yours, baby.*

"Hey, sweetheart," he said behind her, louder this time. "You're holding up the line."

Kylie whirled to see him staring at her.

Was he calling *her* sweetheart?

Oh, hell no.

Linc would lay the guy out. Didn't matter how big his biceps and the pecs he was showing off with his insanely tight t-shirt were. Linc's were bigger. She had this thing for looking at men and determining whether her fiancé could kick their asses. Usually, the answer was a resounding yes. But Linc was already several yards ahead on the trail, letting Storm sniff the area.

Kylie fisted her hands on her hips and turned back to Mr. Motorcycle. She said, as sweetly as possible, "If you want, go ahead of me."

He looked back at his blonde girlfriend, who was tottering much the same as Kylie was, except she was only wearing some sneakers. Sneakers...with high heels. Kylie didn't even know they made those. For what purpose? That, and the most obscenely short-shorts Kylie had ever seen, especially in late November.

The woman was somehow managing to guide a rescue dog, a black boxer, down the hill. Her eyes were glued to the ground as she stepped, but she was far enough away to be out of earshot.

Jaxon looked down at Kylie and grinned, slow and easy. "No, thanks. I kind of like the view right here."

Kylie bristled. Was he talking about her ass? Good thing *she* wasn't wearing shorts. Even in jeans, she felt naked.

Linc noticed she'd stopped and began to backtrack toward her. "What's the problem?"

She looked back at Jaxon and scowled. "Nothing."

In front of her, Linc reached the spot she'd been frozen in for the last minute. He patted a stone step at his hip level.

"Step here." Then he pointed to another, a little farther down. "Then here."

She did, her knees wobbling in her sturdy hiking boots. She had to let go of the tree branch in order to make the move, and now she felt like she was flying without a net, and she'd soon go rolling all the way to the bottom of the gorge in a cloud of dust, like a cartoon character.

Too bad she couldn't fall on that idiot Jaxon and flatten his leering face.

When she made it to standing on the landing beside Linc, she let out a breath of relief. "Sweet terra firma. I can't believe there are people who do this for fun."

"Come on," Linc said, letting Storm take the lead.

Actually, she could. People like the man she was about to be eternally wed to did this for fun. Linc wasn't smiling due to the seriousness of their situation, but he was clearly in his element. He kept taking those big, bracing *I love fresh air!* breaths, the ones that moved his whole chest. He might as well have been smiling, he was so *thrilled* by all of this.

Kylie removed her sunglasses and squinted in the sun dappling down through the trees. Supposedly, Amy had been wearing a hunter green windbreaker. She was slightly over-weight, with long, curly strawberry-blonde hair that fell almost to her waist. *A real sensitive child,* Kylie recalled Amy's mother saying in the news clip she'd seen on the ride down. *She was going for her Masters in Literature. She wrote the most beautiful poetry.*

Kylie swallowed, thinking of the lost look in that mother's eyes. She couldn't imagine what that felt like, not knowing where her daughter was. And then Kevin Friedman. He had four young kids. Were they at home right now, crying for their daddy?

She gritted her teeth and tried to remember what Linc had said. *No, don't think of it. Think of the search, not the subject.*

She peeked around, looking for a flash of a green wind-breaker. It should be easier to find now, since most of the leaves had fallen. Then again, the thick layer of leaves could be covering up any signs of the girl.

Craning her neck to see in every direction, Kylie took a step and accidentally stubbed her toe on a rock. She went flying, right into Linc's broad back.

He whirled and caught her by the arm, steadying her. "Watch it."

"Watching it," she mumbled, clinging to his perfectly shaped bicep. Clearly, she could not search for Amy and walk this trail at the same time. She'd have to do one or the other.

"Whoa, sweetheart," Jaxon hissed into her ear as soon as Linc walked away. "You want something to hold on to? I'll give you something *real* hard and sturdy."

If she'd had enough balance, she'd have kicked him in his hard and sturdy nuts. "Funny," she deadpanned.

"You game? It'll feel real good, trust me. Because, if you want, you and I can lose the ball and chains and go off somewhere private. I'll *really* make those knees of yours weak."

She held up a hand. "Seriously. Fuck off."

"Or what?" he taunted, a big, sick smile on his face. "You'll sic your boyfriend on me?"

"No. I'll just knee you in the balls," she told him, turning away to see Linc nearly disappearing from view. He easily traversed the next obstacles, flying down the trail, stepping in all the right places as if he'd practiced this a million times before. Well, he had been to the gorge before, so naturally, he knew it better.

"How many times have you been on this trail?" she asked, calling out to Linc.

"First time," he called back, stopping and waiting for her to catch up.

Hmm. Sometimes he was just so athletically perfect she both wanted to do him and punch him at the same time.

She took a mouse step as she tried to straddle a massive boulder. Her foot slipped and almost got caught, but she managed to drag it out just in time. Once that obstacle was crossed, she jogged the rest of the way to him, out of breath, wayward locks of hair plastered to her forehead with sweat.

After this, they'd get to go back *up* the trail. *Great. What fun.*

She wondered if it was possible to just lay down in the gorge and let it swallow her up. Then she remembered that this gorge practically did swallow people up and decided she'd keep picking her way downward, thanks very much.

A few minutes later, she heard it: the sound of rushing water. Her spirits lifted. Maybe they were almost at the end of the trail.

"We almost there?" she asked Linc hopefully.

"Think so," he said as Storm kept her nose close to the ground, her mind on the job. "Storm hasn't scented a thing, though."

Kylie stopped and looked around, bracing herself against a boulder for balance. After all, it was her eagle eye that had found Beez in the first place. Maybe she could do it again. Though she wasn't sure if she could stomach it. Didn't *want* to stomach it.

Why couldn't these things always have a happy ending? Why couldn't they find Amy, in a grotto somewhere, toasting marshmallows for s'mores over an open fire, completely unaware that she'd been reported missing?

Fat chance.

No wonder Greg was so grim. No wonder Linc hadn't been much better the first time she'd met him. This world could be so awful sometimes.

So so so awful.

She'd always been optimistic, like her mom. Even though her life growing up had been far from perfect, Kylie'd always harbored the belief that everything would work out, that people were mostly good, and that a smile could make all the difference in the world.

Now, she wasn't so sure.

"Hey. You okay?" Linc asked. He was snapping his fingers in front of her.

"Yeah. Just thinking."

He tucked a stray hair behind her ear. "Don't think so much that you forget what you're doing. I don't want them to have to send a rescue crew out for you next."

She rolled her eyes, put a hand on his strong back, and gave him a gentle shove forward. "Ha. Just keep moving, dude. Let's get this over with."

They descended for another ten minutes until the ground finally leveled out, and they found themselves at the bottom of the gorge. Hallelujah.

The river nearby was flowing fairly smoothly, so that hadn't been making the noise that Kylie heard. They walked a little farther, parallel to the riverbank. When they came around a bend, they saw it.

"Now don't tell me nature isn't an absolutely glorious thing," Linc said smugly, staring up at it.

She followed the spray of the waterway, way up, to a beautiful waterfall. It was most definitely majestic, but the fact that so many people had disappeared here recently gave even this beauty a sinister air. She most definitely had the heebie-jeebies, thinking of it. "It's beautiful. What falls are these?"

"Bridal Veil."

She gazed up in awe, until the name hit her, pitting a sick feeling in her stomach. Nature was clearly fond of taunting her. Her mother had definitely *not* been happy when she called to take a raincheck on their dress shopping. She'd explained that it was for a good reason, but she'd been dragging her feet too long. Eventually, people were going to get suspicious.

Linc was already there. He'd tried to ask her about it on the ride down, but she'd changed the subject.

"Oh. It's...lovely," she muttered, kicking a stone at her feet, the sense of awe all but gone.

The rest of the searchers that had accompanied them on the trail began to spread out, walking downriver to search. Now that the terrain was more level, Kylie tried to use her eagle eye to spot something, anything, out of the ordinary. Nothing struck her.

Amy, where are you? she thought in her head, as if she might have a psychic connection to the girl.

She stepped down to the edge of the bank, where there were several flat stones sticking out of the shallow water. Stopping on a wide stone, she crouched, dipping a finger into the water as it swirled around her. It was icy cold. Muddy, but farther along, there was an almost perfectly circular pool of clear water. It looked like a mermaid lagoon.

A sharp bark split the quiet like thunder, and Kylie snapped her head around to see Storm in alert mode.

She'd known the German Shepherd long enough to know the look she got in her eyes when she'd found something. As Kylie watched, Storm jumped and bumped her paws on Linc's chest before focusing again on the river.

Oh, no.

Kylie straightened and backed away as Linc let Storm off the leash. The big dog rushed forward, heading straight into the calm, clear water of the beautiful mermaid lagoon, and began to swim out.

Linc scraped a hand over his face. Kylie knew what *his* grim expression meant too.

"What's happening?" she murmured, backing up toward him, scanning the area. "Can she scent a body in the water?"

"Yes. Bodies release gas, which rise to the surface," he said, exhaling. He lifted up his radio. "This is Linc, at the bottom of Sliding Rock. My dog might have found something."

Kylie stood on the tips of her toes, trying to get a better look. "What do you think she found?"

Linc didn't answer. Was he trying to protect her again? She started to speak louder when Jaxon came closer, a smug grin on his face. "Looks like we might be dealing with a drowning, sweetheart," he hissed in her ear. "Bet the body's bloated beyond recognition. That's what happens. Fish probably ate out the eyeballs."

Kylie's stomach heaved, and she moved away from the loathsome man, not stopping until she reached a rock close to the water. Taking in a deep breath, she bent over, placing her hands on her knees. She blinked rapidly, willing the tears not to fall. When her eyes cleared, she realized she was staring at a large area that looked like the rock had rusted.

She took a step back, her hair raising on the back of her neck.

"Linc?" The word wasn't much more than a whisper.

Taking out her water bottle, she moved to the very edge of the rust-stained area, then poured a tiny capful on a spot. Her stomach heaved again as the rust turned red.

It was blood. Dried blood.

So much of it.

That sick feeling in Kylie's stomach overpowered her. She turned around, bent over with her hands on her knees, and started to gag.

Watching the rescuers fan out, looking for the two

missing people, I leaned back against a tree trunk, polished off another one of Amy Cooper's granola bars, and grinned from ear to ear.

There was something that was just so satisfying about it.

Not the granola bar. The chaos I'd created. God, I loved watching this.

They all looked like ants, scurrying around for bits of food. And they all looked so *sad*. I was surprised they didn't hold out candles for a vigil. Or that they didn't break down in tears over the whole thing.

Fake, fake, fake. They didn't care. Not really.

I mean, a worthless gym teacher and a college student? Who cared whether those people lived or died? What in this world would either of them amount to? The world was better off without them breathing its air. I'd done this planet a favor.

But did these assholes see it that way? No. So fucking concerned about the things that didn't matter. Oblivious to everything else.

If it wasn't for their incompetence, you'd be here with me.

That ear-to-ear grin collapsed when I thought of you, bouncing around the house, doing "exercise" to prepare for your first scouting trip. *Look at me!* you'd chortled, showing me all the colorful badges on your vest. You never could sit still. You'd been so excited that you could finally put all those skills I'd taught you to the test. The knots. The fire-building. All of the shit that really mattered, while your tribemates were probably only thinking about making s'mores and telling scary stories.

I watched the rest of the rescuers disappear from view. Then I pushed off the tree trunk and followed them from a safe distance.

Will Santos was at the rear of this particular expedition. I'd looked him up online. Talk about a waste of a life. Guy spent more time in bars than out of them. He'd had his Facebook page set to public, and every week, his profile picture showed him with another girl. Usually a hot blonde. Probably treated those women like shit. He clearly thought he was God's gift.

People like that didn't deserve to *breathe*, much less breed.

Yeah, he'd be next. Maybe not here, in the park. There were too many rescuers crawling these woods right now, all of them more than a little spooked after two of their own had gone missing, and I couldn't risk being seen. Not yet.

Besides, it'd be more fun to switch things up a little.

Ah, Will. He always looked so cocky. I wondered whether he'd maintain that cocky attitude while staring death in the face.

No. I bet he'd scream like a little girl.

But not a little girl like you, because you were brave. So brave.

The thought made me mad.

Because I felt sure that you'd fought death to the bitter end, and that end wouldn't have ever come if they hadn't given up on you.

But they would pay. All of them.

I swore to you then, and I swear to you now.

After this man-whore, there'd be only two more. That butch, Dina Avery. Fucking disgusting. She was one of those women who thought she knew everything. I'd looked her up too. She'd gone overseas for the army, thinking she was some tough girl, and gotten injured a month later. What a waste of space. I could barely stand to look at her.

And then, for my final act, Linc Coulter.

That one would be fun. A challenge, but fun. Buff and good-looking, and he clearly knew it. He was one of those smart ones—didn't have much of a personal profile online, stayed out of social media. But it was obvious he thought he was something special in the rescuing business. Had his own business training rescue dogs, and his company website said he was "the authority on all things SAR." The internet was practically bursting with articles of his "heroic efforts" and great deeds, first in the army, and then in North Carolina.

It was all a lie.

He was the strong, silent type. The type who never showed fear. It was my mission to see fear in his eyes, right in that split-second when he knew he was going to die.

Damn, it'd be so satisfying. I knew you would approve. After all, all of this was for you. Because all of them, getting their names in the newspaper for this shit time and time again? How was that fair? You deserved to have your name in lights. You're the one who deserved the praise. You're the one who meant more than all of them put together.

So, they'd get what they deserved. I'd make sure of that.

And I couldn't wait.

12

Sitting back to back with Kylie on a large boulder, Linc stroked Storm's ears when she loped up, returning the ball by depositing it into his lap. "Good girl, that's it," he said, tossing it out into the woods again. She eagerly wagged her tail and ran out to fetch it.

Because dogs were sensitive creatures, it was important, especially once a rescue dog made a harrowing discovery, to give the dog plenty of playtime immediately afterward in order to help return it to some sense of normalcy. Storm had withstood all the horror of Syria that Linc had and had seemingly come out of it fine, but one never could tell.

And this discovery? It had definitely been grim.

Linc's hands were still shaking as he wiped Storm's drool onto his pants and looked back toward the river, where the dive teams were working. Then he looked over his shoulder at Kylie, who was staring at the scene, her fingers twisting in her lap. She'd scarcely been able to take her eyes off it. Like she had to bear witness to the discovery to somehow honor the fallen, whether it be the woman or the man.

He waved a hand in front of her face. "Kylie. Hey."

She blinked and looked back at him. "It's one of the bodies, right?"

He nodded. "Yes. Storm doesn't usually make mistakes."

She pressed her lips together, and in the next moments, the divers resurfaced from under the swirling water at the base of Bridal Veil Falls. One waved to the policemen at the bank as something bobbed up to the surface. Linc couldn't see more than a swatch of hunter green, but his mind filled in the rest of the picture.

He jumped from the boulder just as Storm was coming back from her quest. He put the tennis ball in his pocket and clipped on her leash. "Hey," he said, standing purposely in Kylie's line of vision. "Let's go for a walk."

She leaned forward and pushed him to the right. "No, I want to see this."

"Why?" he asked, trying to step in the way again. She stood up and moved around him. When he tried to stop her, she held up a hand.

"For the last time, stop trying to protect me!" she said, fisting her hands on her hips. "I'm fine. In case you've forgotten, I was hired to work on this case. I know it's not pleasant, but it's important I be here."

He threw up his hands. When she got like this, there was no telling her what to do.

Against his better judgment, she watched the whole thing, as the body of the woman was dragged onto the riverbank. Kylie saw it all—the bloated, naked body, the fish-nibbled, blue-tinted skin. It was Amy Cooper.

When they rolled her over, the massive gash on her scalp became visible among her tangle of thick hair. Half of her skull had caved in. She wasn't wearing a stitch of clothing, which led Linc to wonder if she'd been sexually assaulted. The idea of it made Linc sick with anger and sorrow for the young woman.

A backpack strapped to her back had been filled with river stone. Kylie watched all this, and as the crime scene techs did their work, Linc kept an eye on his fiancée. This was upsetting enough to him. They didn't need two people with PTSD in the house.

Once the coroner gave her approval, the body was loaded on a stretcher, and the crowd dispersed. Linc found Kylie nibbling on one of her fingernails, deep in thought. "Hey," he said softly. "You ready to go back yet?"

She didn't answer his question. Instead, she met his gaze with a concerned one of her own. "Well, that confirms it, right?"

"Confirms what?"

"Amy Cooper was murdered, so there's a good chance that Beez was murdered too."

He attempted to follow her line of thought before shaking his head. "There's nothing to say the two are related at all."

"Why do you say that?"

"The deaths are entirely different. The nature of the bodies. Beez was an older woman, who died from the blunt force of a fall. Amy was apparently murdered, but judging by the body, sexual assault may be in play. It's hard to determine."

She gave him a doubtful look. "Give me a break. Add Kevin into the mix, and there are four people who've died of suspicious circumstances."

"Wait, wait, wait. We haven't even found Kevin yet. He could most definitely be alive. Aren't you getting ahead of yourself?"

She took Storm's leash from him and headed toward the trailhead. "My spidey sense is tingling. Ollie Crosby thought something was off, but no one took him seriously. I'm taking it seriously, Linc. Because he knew Beez better than anyone. And if he says she never would've taken a wrong step, I believe him. And even if Kevin is alive and well somewhere, I believe the deaths of Amy and Beez are connected. It can't just be a coincidence."

She started up the trail confidently but flagged after about ten steps. She handed Storm's leash back to him and looked up the forty-five-degree incline toward the top of the trail. "I hate hiking. I really do."

"I gathered that from the first ten-thousand times you told me," he said, motioning her to go up. "Go ahead. I'll stay behind you and make sure you don't fall."

She did. It was slow going because Kylie was overly cautious about where she stepped. As they neared the top, Linc's phone buzzed in the pocket of his windbreaker. He lifted it out and read the text. It was from Will.

"Kevin's been found on the South Rim Trail," he called up to Kylie. Before she could ask the inevitable questions, he added, "Alive, but badly hurt."

"Really?" He realized as she straightened and nearly toppled backward on the rock that he probably should've waited until they were at the top of the trail.

He steadied her and said, "Yeah. He's been shot by an arrow. Hunting accident."

"Hunting accident?" Kylie repeated.

"That's what Will said. Said he must've gone off the trail and gotten pierced by an arrow. It happens." He let out a breath as the sound of sirens echoed through the air. "That's probably the ambulance now, coming for him."

Kylie stopped, standing still as a statue in front of him. He nudged her to keep moving, but she didn't budge. When he looked at her face, she was deep in thought. He snapped his fingers at her. "Hello? I'd like to get up to the top of the trail before the sun sets."

"Right," she said breathlessly before taking another step and tugging on her vest. "But I was thinking. Don't all the rescuers wear these orange safety vests to prevent such a thing?"

Linc sighed. There she went, being all suspicious again. "Yeah. But that doesn't mean everyone is skilled with a bow."

"But aren't there special hunting areas?"

"Maybe. Doesn't mean everyone follows the signs. A thousand things could've happened. I'm not going to speculate until I know all the facts."

"Still," she said, "you have to admit that it's a strange coincidence. *Another* strange coincidence. Don't you think?"

Linc nodded and continued silently on the trail. Yes, it definitely was strange. As much as he wanted to, he couldn't deny that.

13

Kylie could almost hear Vader's pitiful howls ringing in her ears as she and Linc headed home. She'd promised the forlorn dog over and over that they'd be back that night, but the promises hadn't seemed to help. Vader had been simply stricken to be left behind.

To distract herself from the memory of his sad face—and from the worry of what the house would look like when they returned—Kylie fired questions out to Linc. Many of questions were repeats, but that couldn't be helped. She'd learned from her criminal justice classes that it was important to go over and over each case, asking questions in different ways, studying notes repetitively with the hope that something would spark a lightbulb moment that would then move the investigation in a positive direction.

Would Tallulah Gorge State Park be closed, due to four suspicious incidents in only a month? Would they bring in the feds? Why was Amy Cooper on the trail? Had she been she sexually assaulted? Did she have any enemies? Did Kevin Friedman have any enemies? Maybe students at the school where he taught? Was hunting even allowed on the popular South Rim Trail?

And on and on it went. She had so many questions, she felt like her mind was going to explode.

She also listed the individuals she needed to interview, along with the series of questions she needed to ask them. Her notebook was getting full by the time they crossed the state line.

"Poor man," she murmured as she got off the phone with Ollie.

"How's he doing?" Linc asked.

"He's not sad anymore." She pushed her hair back from her face. "More like angry. He's chomping at the bit for me to solve this case."

Linc shot her a cautious glance. "We don't even know if there is a case. We—"

"Stop!" For emphasis, she reached out and pressed a finger to his lips. "Of course there's a case. Amy was murdered."

He let out a long breath, like he was trying to be patient. That exhale simply fanned the fire of her determination that she was right.

He bit her finger, then went on patiently when she pulled it away. "Yes, but there's no saying that any of that has to do with *your case.* Which is related to Beez, remember?"

She ignored him. "We should've gotten a hotel room. I have so much to do. Ollie's depending on me, you know."

"We couldn't. We have Vader at home," he reminded her. Storm's ears pricked up, and she stuck her nose between them at the mention of her best friend. "Remember? I'm still not convinced he didn't tear up the place while we were gone."

She pushed Storm's muzzle back. "I think we should let someone from the vet come tomorrow and watch him while we go back and look into things. There's no sense in commuting back and forth four hours every day."

He didn't speak, just pressed on the gas and passed a slow-moving old pickup.

"There is so much I want to research," she mumbled, reaching into her bag and pulling out her pad and pen again. She opened up her phone and typed a few words in. "And I feel like my hands are tied."

He turned on the radio, twisting the dial for a country station. She knew his nerves were on edge from finding Amy Cooper's body, and from the way he kept massaging his shoulder, it probably still hurt him. "Like what, exactly?"

She'd already begun adding to the scribbled list of questions that was now at least twenty-five lines deep. Her hand couldn't move fast enough to get all of her ideas out. "Like, all those questions I've been asking for the last half hour. Whether I can talk to park management and see what they know. Or Amy Cooper's family and friends to see if she had any jealous boyfriends. What if the suicide of that first victim was staged, and it wasn't really a suicide? And if there was a hunting accident, who'd been granted a permit? Linc, there is so much left for us to find out!"

He nodded, entirely too calmly for her liking. Why didn't he ever get riled up about things?

She scowled in his direction. "You could show a little interest. There is a murderer walking free out there, preying on innocent women."

His mouth curved in amusement. "I get it. Kylie Hatfield doesn't rest when there are injustices that have been done."

"Right!" She didn't like that he was giving her the conde-scending *look-how-cute* face. Whenever she got passionate about something, he had to make fun of her for it. Even after all the cases she'd solved over the past year, he treated her like some dabbling hobbyist instead of a professional investigator. "I'll get to the bottom of it."

"Oh, you will, will you?" His tone was even more condescending now.

She gritted her teeth. "Yes. In fact, why don't you stay up in Asheville next time, and I'll handle it all myself?"

He gave her a cautious look. "No way."

She knew he'd say that. He was her self-appointed protector, after all. "Well, if you aren't interested in helping me, then—"

"Cut it out. I'm interested. But there's only so much you can do in a day. We've been at it since early this morning," he said, lifting his hand and massaging the back of her neck. "Let's just go home, get some dinner, and relax. Okay?"

Kylie's lips twisted. No. She most definitely did not want to relax. Now that she knew that there was weight to Ollie's claims, she needed to see this through. Her entire body itched with the need to get out and do something, but she could see how tired Linc was.

"Fine," she relented. "But let's please call up the vet tomorrow to watch Vader and the other animals for the next few days while we go down and look into this case?"

He was silent for a minute. "All right."

"Is that an 'all right' to get me to shut up, or an 'all right, let's do it?'" she asked, running a suspicious eye over him.

"The last one." He gave her that condescending look again.

"Admit it. You don't think I'm capable."

He shook his head. "That isn't it."

"Then what is it?"

"You're very capable," he said quietly. "But I'm not."

He was trying to be cute again. Of course, he was more than capable in everything he did. "What's that supposed to mean? Of course you are. You're—"

"I'm not capable of losing you."

She stared at him, surprise making her mouth sag open.

"If you think Ollie was bad without Beez, that's nothing compared to what I'd be," he said, staring straight ahead, "without you."

She couldn't speak. She could barely breathe. As she stared at him, her heart flooded with love. "Oh."

"So, fine. We'll spend a few days back at the gorge if it'll make you happy. But if there really is something bad going on around there, I don't want you out of my sight. You've got to be careful. Deal?"

Emotion burned her eyes, clogged her throat. "Deal." Besides, she didn't want Linc out of her sight, either. As much as she wanted his help, he was in more danger than she was. He was the SAR guy, not her, and two SARs falling victim to accidents in such a short time period? *That* was definitely too odd to be a coincidence. "So, we go back? Tomorrow morning?"

"Yeah. Fine." He yawned. "Just…can we not talk about it until tomorrow?"

She sighed. She didn't want to aggravate his PTSD, so she tried her best to screw her mouth shut, as hard as it was. Meanwhile, she scribbled down more and more questions, filling three full sheets of paper with her ramblings.

As the sun finally slipped behind the hills, taking with it the last light of day, she squinted in the dusk to see what she'd written, then stuffed it into her backpack.

Still, her mind kept racing with ideas. She lifted her phone and started to search Amy Cooper's personal information, just as they hit the Asheville exit.

"Any idea about dinner?"

Kylie's mouth watered. They'd had Cheerios for breakfast, watery coffee for lunch, so she had to admit, she was starving. "Something greasy."

Linc didn't like grease, but he humored Kylie because she did, which was probably the reason he'd softened up a little around the gut. He pulled up to the drive-thru of a taco place, and they got home at a little after seven.

As they pulled up the drive, they could already hear Vader yipping his head off, even with all the windows closed.

Storm whimpered in sympathy, then she let out a howl that made both of them look at each other. "What's wrong, girl?" Kylie said, smoothing her ears. She looked at Linc. "Has she ever made a sound like that before?"

"No."

Kylie ran to the door with the tacos and opened it. As she did, Vader came rushing out, not for her, or for Linc. He went right to Storm.

Linc called from the truck, "Jesus. The long-lost lovers reunite."

"Oh, gosh, god forbid you get separated from your best friend," Kylie baby-talked the big dog, batting his tail as the two animals sniffed each other excitedly. "Just remember who feeds you."

Then she turned and looked inside, and her mouth fell open.

It looked like a furniture store had exploded in their living room. Vader had done a number on the sofa. In fact, all of the cushions were bleeding white batting all over the place. Several pillows were shredded to piles of fabric, and there were feathers everywhere. She winced as she put the bag of tacos on the center island.

Linc came in and groaned. "Damn it to all hell."

"See? We can't leave him alone for that long again or we'll wind up sitting on cardboard boxes for the remainder of our lives," Kylie said, reaching for two glasses so she could pour them some drinks. "Can you call someone at the vet to come and watch him tomorrow? Maybe we should just take him there, so he has other dogs to play with."

He lifted the phone to his ear. "Already on it."

After they ate, mostly in silence because Kylie couldn't stop thinking about everything happening in Georgia but knew Linc didn't want to talk about it, they both set to cleaning up the living room. The couch was practically destroyed, so they pushed it out onto the porch so Linc could take it to the dump some other time. Then they swept and vacuumed up all the feathers, and by then, it was late.

They went up to the bedroom, got into bed, and she tried to go to sleep, but Kylie's mind whirled with everything she wanted to do. There was too much to think about. Too much to do.

She looked over at Linc, but he was fast asleep, snoring softly. He didn't seem to think there was anything to worry about, and his meds had knocked him out for the rest of the night. She thought of Ollie, depending on her to get answers. Pressing her lips together, she kicked off the covers and grabbed her laptop.

She opened it up and quickly started to outline all the thoughts in her head. She wrote down the names of the people who'd gone missing, wondering if there was some other connection besides two of them being part of SAR. She'd read somewhere that killers rarely targeted people at random. Was there some deeper connection here?

She glanced over at Linc, sleeping so peacefully, and an uneasy feeling came over her. He dealt with dangerous situations all the time. And in the past six months, she'd dealt with her share of mentally imbalanced people—a jealous wife, a serial killer, a murdering art thief, a deranged mafia princess. What if there really was someone out there who wanted to hurt Linc? What if he ended up on the target list, and by bringing him down there to help her, she was putting him in danger?

She forced the thought out of the way. Like he said, it could just be a coincidence.

Besides, he'd never let her go down there alone. As far as he was concerned, they were a package deal. And looking into this for Ollie was her job. Searching for missing persons was *his* job. They couldn't just give up because of some dangerous possibilities. They needed to see this through.

Dangerous possibilities never had stopped her before. Linc would say that the danger was what spurred her to action. And it was true. She loved this part of the job.

She only wished it didn't involve putting Linc in danger too.

Or…other people. She thought back to what he'd said to her, about having kids. He wanted kids. Would she be able to shelve her love of danger in order to keep their children safe?

She thought about that, long and hard, staring at her computer.

She didn't know. She'd heard that becoming a mom changed a person's whole life. Her mother had told her that. But she'd just found this great career she loved. What if she wasn't ready for her life to change so dramatically?

Blinking away the thought, she forced herself to concentrate on the names she'd typed into her computer. As she was typing out more questions, thinking about how dangerous Linc's job could sometimes be, she remembered him talking with Will Santos about some prison escapees they'd tracked down. That sounded exciting, but in all their conversations about the dangers of his job, Linc had never mentioned it to her.

She wondered why.

She flipped off her laptop and set it on her nightstand, then turned off the light and tried to go to sleep. Instead, she stared at the ceiling, wide-awake. She'd have to ask him about the prison escapees tomorrow morning.

That was just the first of only a thousand questions she couldn't wait to find the answers to.

It was going to be a very long night.

14

At ten o'clock in the evening after the Tallulah Falls search, Will Santos could think of nothing he'd like better than a nice, quality craft beer and maybe a little pussy.

Instead, he was sitting at the bar of the Wagon Wheel Saloon, some backwoods shithole with beer that tasted like ass, women who were old enough to be his mother, and Jaxon Mott chewing his ear off about some shit-stupid sport called extreme ironing.

Not quite a nightmare come true, but not exactly the kind of unwinding he'd been looking for.

He'd desperately needed something to calm him down. When he'd found Kevin far off the trail, covered in freshly fallen leaves, the man wasn't dead, but he'd been damn close. He'd lost a lot of blood from the arrow wound, which had gone straight through his chest. He was pale and barely breathing. The EMT who tended to him said that, if he hadn't found him, he'd have been dead in a matter of hours.

The other team had fared worse, finding Amy Cooper dead, a victim of murder and possible sexual assault.

It was the kind of day that made him wish he'd picked another line of work.

Now he was sitting at the bar, with Jaxon Mott, a talkative fucker who'd been on the search for Amy Cooper. As Jaxon went on, having a conversation with himself, Will popped a handful of peanuts into his mouth and read a text from Sam, his little brother. *We won.*

Will grinned. His brother was a senior at Clemson, and their star running back. He typed in: *Go Tigers.* He was damn proud.

When he looked up, Jaxon hadn't even stopped to take a breath.

Jaxon Mott was a total asshole. Will had known that about three seconds after the guy opened his mouth. He thought he was cool shit, and he wasn't afraid to let everyone know, in the loudest voice possible. Damned if every word out of his mouth wasn't about how wonderful he was or how many chicks he'd banged. He'd strutted into the bar an hour ago, treating every person in the place like they weren't worthy of him. It was a wonder, Will thought, that they hadn't been kicked out yet, or worse.

Jaxon guffawed loudly, drunk already. He was wearing a motorcycle jacket, but Will suspected he didn't own a motorcycle. He was too pretty for that. "Yeah," he said, so loud the voice rattled Will's eardrums. "Extreme ironing is still foreign in a lot of these hillbilly towns. All they're into around here is making moonshine and screwing their sisters."

Will clenched his teeth. *You think you could say that a little louder, dude? A few "hillbillies" on the other side of the state didn't hear you.*

"Hey. Chill out," he said to his idiotic fellow SAR. "I mean, I didn't even know extreme ironing was a thing. What is it again?"

Jaxon sighed and ran a hand down his face. "You take a board to the most ridiculous place you can think of...and then you..."

Will only caught bits of the conversation. As Jaxon went on, he looked furtively around the bar. Three big men in cowboy garb at the other end of the bar tossed back shots and sneered at them. Will had been frequenting bars since he'd come of legal age, but never any place this rough. These "sister-screwing hillbillies" were huge. He'd never been in a bar fight before, and he really didn't want to start with these guys.

Will motioned to the bartender and asked for another as it suddenly hit him, what Jaxon was saying. "Wait. So, it's actual ironing? Like clothes?"

Jaxon shot him a *you've got to be kidding me* look of genuine disgust. "Ain't that what I've been tellin' you?"

Will raised an eyebrow, confused. As he did, he noticed that Jaxon's pants were nicely pressed. "Back up. Ironing. How is that, exactly, a sport again?"

Jaxon blew out a weary-sounding breath, then began to speak slowly, like he would to a small child. "Because you do it someplace really wild. Like on the top of a cliff or something."

Will narrowed his eyes, trying to understand. "But I hate ironing." He looked down at his crumpled t-shirt. "I don't iron. Why would anyone do that for sport?"

"Just something to do, man. It's thrilling, plus nothing beats the satisfaction of a well-pressed shirt," Jaxon said with a grin. He knocked on the bar top to get the bartender's attention. "Give us another round. What's that, rum and coke?"

Will shook his head. This guy was not only a prick, he was completely off his rocker. "I'm good. Got to get back home. Take it easy."

He sucked down the rest of his drink—it *was* a rum and coke, hold the rum. When he discovered they didn't have any good craft beers to tempt him, he'd decided a coke was a better choice, especially since he had to make it all the way back to Atlanta tonight. He hadn't drunk much at all in the last few months. He was tired enough as it was from the search, and the last thing he needed was for his mother to hear about another DUI.

As he reached for his wallet, he thought of Kevin Friedman. Poor guy.

When Will had first spotted him in the forest, he thought the SAR was dead. In fact, he'd been certain of it. Kevin's skin had been covered in dirt and blood, and the hunting arrow sticking out of his chest had looked like a nightmare. Will knew he'd see that imagine for the rest of his life.

It had been cold last night, and it was a miracle that Kevin hadn't succumbed to the elements, and that they'd discovered him when they did. He'd been unconscious, and almost completely covered with leaves.

Next to him, Jaxon did another shot of Jack. "Wooooooooo!" he yelled after he downed it, raising his arms up in victory. "I just wanna get shitfaced."

Looks like you're already there, buddy, Will thought as Jaxon sat down and nearly missed the stool.

He'd come here with Jaxon, hoping they could discuss what had happened because he was still trying to wrap his head around the whole thing…how could a SAR, wearing the orange safety vest, be mistaken for a deer? Especially out on the South Rim, where hunting was prohibited. He'd wanted to unwind, talk a few theories, relax a little before heading home.

Now, though, he felt as tightly wound as an eight-day clock.

He pushed off the stool, more than ready to escape this

place and this man. "Good talking to you. But Star's waiting for me in the car, so I'm gonna—"

"Wait, dude. Just stay a little longer," Jaxon said, nudging his elbow as he spun on the stool. "The night is young, man. Look at that one. I think she wants me."

Will squinted through the smoky haze and spotted a woman who must've been twice Jaxon's age. Surely, he couldn't be talking about her. But there really wasn't anyone else in the vicinity who didn't have either a beard or three chins.

"Wait." Will pointed at the woman, trying not to be too obvious. "Her?"

Jaxon nodded and licked his lips. "Yeah."

The old woman winked, and Will felt vaguely nauseated.

For the second time that night, Will looked at Jaxon as though he was insane. That the hell was the man thinking? He was pretty sure he'd seen Jaxon arrive at the park earlier this morning with a young, hot blonde. "Didn't you come to the search with a blonde woman?" he asked.

Jaxon nodded, not taking his eyes off his prey. "Yeah. My girl Crystal. She's back at the trailer. But…" he punched Will and winked, "what she don't know won't hurt her. Am I right?"

Will edged away from the deranged man. "I guess, but you're on your own. I've really got to go. See you—"

A loud voice boomed across the bar. "Who the fuck do you think you're looking at?"

Will followed the sound to a giant, mean-looking biker. A real one, not just a pretty poser, like his fellow SAR. The man was staring directly at Jaxon.

Oh, shit, Will thought as the man advanced on the kid, hands ready to wrap around his neck. Here it comes.

Jaxon just gave him a surly smile as the guy shouted,

spittle flying everywhere, "You really think you can look at my woman? I'll rip that smug look off your damn—"

Before he could finish, Will jumped in front of him. "Hey. Sorry. My friend didn't know she was your girl. No problem. He didn't even touch her, so no harm done. Why don't I buy you a drink?"

The guy's eyes fell on Will and the heat began to drain from his expression.

Before it could, Jaxon laughed. "Sorry to break it to you, but your girl was making eyes at *me*. She wants to ride me into the sunset." He looked over the guy's shoulder. "Don't you, sweetheart?"

The honky-tonk music wafting from the jukebox seemed to screech off-track, and the silence that pervaded the bar was deafening. Will rolled his eyes, right before the big guy nudged him out of the way and prepared to throw his punch.

Will tried again. This time he stuck up a hand, not sure he wanted to risk a fist to the face. "Whoa. Come on. Nothing happened. Let's just walk away." He motioned to the bartender, who handed him a shot of something he could smell from three feet away. He handed it to the guy. "Here. On me. We were just leaving, anyway."

The guy dropped his fist, grabbed ahold of the shot glass, and downed the fiery liquid, his gaze never breaking from Jaxon's. "You best be going. And don't come back, pansies."

"We won't." Will threw a twenty down on the bar to pay Jaxon's tab.

He grabbed the dumbass by the arm and hoisted him out of the bar. Jaxon fought but eventually followed.

They stood there, in the chilly night air, breathing hard. Will said, "What the fuck was that? Jesus, do the words 'don't engage' mean anything to you, or do you always pick fights like that?"

Jaxon stamped the dusty parking lot with his foot and

growled, "He was an asshole. Why'd you pull me out of there? I wish you would've let me rearrange his face."

Will gave him a look. "Seriously? He had a foot and fifty pounds on you."

"I'm a good fighter. I could've knocked his block off and made him go screaming to his mommy."

Or you could've ended up dead. Which was more likely. But that's okay, don't thank me, Will thought, stalking across the parking lot. "It's been fun, but like I said, I've got to go. See you tomorrow for the briefing. Take it easy."

He hurried off to his pickup, unhappy about going home to his house south of Atlanta, alone, without some warm female company. Oh, well. Probably for the best. He'd have to get an early start to get back up here. There was going to be a press conference with the police to update them on the situation at the falls and on Kevin's condition, and he didn't want to miss that.

He'd left Star in the back of the car with her water dish, a few treats, and her favorite chew toy. She jumped into the front seat and nipped at his chin excitedly as he opened the door. "Hey, love you too," he said with a chuckle, pushing his overexcited pup back.

Slipping into the truck, he turned up the heat, then headed out of the gravel parking lot, onto the narrow road. He'd been to the gorge dozens of times, so he knew these roads well. As he drove, he turned on a classic rock station and tried to relax.

But he still kept thinking of Kevin. It was damn odd. They'd said the same thing about the other SAR woman, who'd been killed there. It'd been damn odd for Beez to fall, knowing all he knew about the way she'd worked.

In fact, all of it just seemed creepy.

Amy Cooper? He'd heard from one of the rangers that, before this, the park hadn't had a death in twelve years.

Now? There'd been three deaths and one near-death in a month. He couldn't shake the feeling that some dark force was at work in those mountains, trying to sabotage their rescue efforts.

Trying to sabotage them?

He laughed at himself. That was silly. The product of being overly tired.

Yes, it was a good thing he'd left early. He really needed the sleep.

He thought of his new house, which was an awesome bachelor pad. Kind of big for just him, but he knew it would impress the ladies. Unfortunately, he'd struck out with those tonight. Just as well.

The one-lane road curved up into the hills, and dark pines surrounded him on both sides. Occasionally, the trees would part, and he could almost imagine that he could see the lights of Atlanta far off in the distance. He pressed on the gas pedal, eager to get himself home.

As he did, though, a car came speeding up behind, hanging on his tail.

A glance in the rearview mirror, and Will was nearly blinded by the lights glaring back at him. Damn fool had his high beams on.

He looked back at the road, blinking away the starbursts that now clouded his vision. The car behind him swerved so dangerously back and forth and looked so damn close that Will expected to feel the tap of an impact at his bumper.

He tightened his hands around the leather-wrapped steering wheel.

He slowed, drove to the side of the road, powered down the window of his pickup, and motioned for the guy to move around him.

Just go, asshole, but don't blame me if you end up wrapped around a tree.

But the idiot didn't. He stayed there, hugging Will's bumper. Will slowed more, and so did the car behind him. Another pickup, maybe? Will couldn't tell. Maybe a large SUV. Will sped up, and the vehicle remained right on top of him. In the back seat of the truck, Star bobbed her head excitedly, thinking it was a game.

"All right, fine," Will said aloud, wrapping his hand tight around the steering wheel. He threw his truck into a higher gear and gunned it as fast as he could, creating distance between the two vehicles. "You want to play? Let's play."

It didn't last. As expected, a moment later, the other truck —Will was sure it was a truck now—sped up, only to race right up to his back tailgate.

Will cursed and looked down at his speedometer. The speed limit on this road was fifty, but he was now approaching ninety miles per hour. He knew the curves, though. Knew when he'd have to slow down. He could handle this. He just hoped no deer, which he always saw on the shoulders of the road, would dart out in front of him.

He pressed on the pedal, firing up to one-hundred miles per hour. As he did, a trickle of sweat ran down the side of his face.

What the hell is wrong with me? he thought to himself, laughing at his stupidity. He'd lost his grandfather to a road rage incident a few years ago. And what had he been thinking just a few minutes ago, when he was with Jaxon?

Don't engage.

That was the rule to live by. Just walk away.

Or in this case, drive.

After he slowed down.

Tapping his brakes, he slowed for a curve as the road crept higher into the hills. There was a guardrail as the only protection from a sharp dive down the mountain, and no shoulder to speak of. When the road opened up, he'd simply pull over to a safe place and let the asshole leave him in his dust.

He looked back at the truck, trying to see if it was the big, mean biker guy from the bar. Or any of the other enemies they'd made during their short time there. All he saw was an outline and thick hands wrapped around a steering wheel.

He gunned it, waiting for the moment when the guardrail would disappear, and he could safely pull aside. His breath came in spurts. His pupils dilated. His heart hammered in his chest.

What he didn't expect, though, was that at the minute the guardrail disappeared, the truck would swing around the driver's side and choose that exact second to ram into him, sending his truck skidding uncontrollably toward the road's edge.

Star let out a long, wolfish howl, a haunting sound she'd never made before. The impact and loud screech of the tires was such a shock that, by the time Will thought to correct himself, he was already airborne, heading straight for the tops of the dark pines illuminated in his headlights.

It was as if his truck was stretching out to meet the lights in the distance. The lights of a city he called home but would never reach.

15

Linc and Kylie had to leave early to get down to the state park, so after they made it down the hill, they stopped at Asheville Veterinary and to drop Vader off. Kylie tried to pull him out of the truck, but he dug his feet in, like a stubborn mule.

"Really?" Kylie was saying to the dog as Linc came around the side of the truck. "You're going to make a big thing out of this, aren't you?"

Linc looked at the Newf. They normally had sad eyes, but Vader's were some of the saddest he'd ever seen.

Kylie pulled on the leash again, waved a biscuit in front of him, and said, "Treat, boy? Treat?"

He didn't even look. He clearly couldn't be bribed.

"Belly rub? Ear scratching? Walk?" She groaned. "You can sleep on my side of the bed for the rest of the month?"

Nothing. The dog knew what he was doing. Kylie seemed about ready to give up.

Instead, she looked over at Linc. "Advice, Dog Whisperer?"

He shook his head, secretly enjoying watching her struggle. She was so cute whenever she got that little crinkle over her nose. But his favorite thing was when he could sweep in and save the day.

When Kylie pulled the leash again, Storm got in the way. Now, it was two against one.

"Not you too, girl! No! Come on!" she whined, her shoulders slumping. "Thick as thieves, those two are. And here I thought Storm was a good girl. Why are they ganging up on me?"

He laughed. "Go on inside and fill out the paperwork. I'll handle it," he said as she handed him the leash, glowering. He stood in the open door and gave Storm a look. "What are you doing, girl? Your boyfriend can't fight his own battles, huh? You better mind yourself."

Storm whimpered, admonished.

Then he brought Vader forth and whispered kind but firm words to him. Eventually, he jumped out of the truck without any trouble.

Dina called while he was leading Vader into the building. He answered as Kylie whirled on him and sighed.

"I hate you," she mouthed when she saw that he'd succeeded.

Grinning, he talked to Dina for a little bit, getting the update of the day. When he was finished, he handed her the leash. "It was simple...*if* you have the magic touch like I do."

She punched him in the arm. "It's a long ride down to the park, and you don't want my silent treatment."

He snorted out a laugh. "All three minutes of it?" He waved at the receptionist. "All the paperwork filled out?"

"Done!" Kylie said, handing the clipboard to the woman behind the counter as well as a bag filled with Vader's food and favorite toys. "It's all on here. We should be back in a few days."

"We'll take good care of him," the receptionist said, leaning down to take his leash. "Come on, Vader."

When the big dog whimpered, Kylie leaned down to nuzzle him while Linc patted his side. "It's all right, boy. We'll be back before you know it. You'll have so much fun here with all the other dogs, you won't even miss us."

If ever a dog could look doubtful, that was Vader. But eventually, he went into the back with the other dogs.

Linc shook his head as they went out front and piled back into Linc's truck. "Geez. You'd think that Vader was going to miss us," he said with a smile.

"Not so much us." Kylie sniffed, her eyes red from the threat of tears. She hooked a thumb behind her. "*Her*. His little partner in crime."

Linc started the engine and looked into his rearview mirror. He didn't see Storm, so he turned around quickly to find her lying down on the seat, her head on her paws. She looked up at him with sad eyes, like the world was ending. He couldn't help thinking she was pouting.

It was funny. He hadn't really thought about it too much, but now that Kylie had brought it up, he knew it was true. Storm and Vader had developed quite a friendship. He was wild, and she was sedate. They made a good couple, like yin and yang. Like...him and Kylie.

"Well. They'll be reunited soon enough."

Linc was starting to get very comfortable with the drive to the park now, but he was glad that they were going to stay at the hotel. He didn't mind the drive, but he could see, last night, how on edge Kylie had been. Her job consumed her. She never rested when there were leads to pursue. Where he was out like a light, thanks to the PTSD meds he was on, he could tell from the dark circles under her eyes that she probably hadn't slept a wink.

The morning had started out chilly, so Linc had been

blasting the heat. He lowered it now as they hopped onto the highway and said, "So, boss. What's the first order of business?"

Kylie checked her phone. "I have a bunch of places to go. But when we get there, we should head straight for the park. The police are going to update us on Kevin and conduct interviews of anyone who might have seen something in the Amy Cooper case, so we should be there. They're trying to nail down a profile of the perp."

"Yes, sir. That's what Dina said she was going to do too," he said, looking over at her. She had that intense look on her face that she only got in the middle of a heavy investigation. "You know that no one in law enforcement actually says 'perp,' right?"

She poked herself in the chest with her thumb. "Well, this girl does."

He laughed. "All right. Whatever you say."

"What did Dina say?"

"She said the autopsy came back on Amy Cooper and that she was not sexually assaulted."

"Really? That's interesting."

"Why is that interesting?"

Kylie shrugged. "You just said that the deaths of Beez and Amy Cooper were nothing alike. Well, that makes them more alike. Doesn't it?"

"I suppose."

"So…" she said, eyeing him suspiciously. He knew what that meant. She had a long line of suspects to interview, and he was the first.

"I'm innocent, I swear," he deadpanned, holding up a hand in surrender. "I have an alibi, officer, honestly."

"Har-har. Be serious." When Linc straightened his face, she went on. "Something you said yesterday was interesting.

You said you knew a lot of the other SARs from before. Have you all worked together much?"

"Yeah. The community's not that big. I've worked with a number of them. Like I said, Beez. Dina. Kevin. Will…"

Kylie held up a finger. "Yeah. You seem really close with that one."

"Will?" He nodded. "Yeah. He's an old buddy of mine, out of Atlanta."

"Hmmm. What did he say yesterday? Something about a prison break?"

Linc nodded, not sure what this had to do with anything. "Yeah, there was a jailbreak at Arrendale State Prison."

"Arrendale? Where's that?"

"About a half hour from Tallulah Gorge. It's a maximum-security penitentiary for women. It's where the women on Georgia's death row are kept."

Kylie's jaw dropped. "Women?"

He nodded. "Yeah. These three women managed to kill a guard and escape into the forest. SAR was called. Hours and hours of searching because, obviously, these three didn't want to be found. So, they kept us on our toes. When they were found, there was a standoff because they refused to give in. One of them ended up getting shot and killed by police."

Kylie stared for a moment, her mouth slightly open. "Wow. I didn't realize you went after prison inmates."

He quirked a smile at her. "We track whoever is missing, wherever we're needed. It was pretty stressful for all involved. Lasted the better part of a weekend." He yawned and drummed his hands on the steering wheel. "Beez really took it hard. She wasn't as familiar with the terrain down there and ended up doing a number on her ankle, I remember."

Kylie stared at him. "Beez was there?"

"Yeah. That was the first time I met her. It was actually

Will who set me up for the job. Told her he knew someone that could help out short notice, so I went down there. That's the problem with SARs a lot of time. Not too many people are able to drop everything and rush down at a moment's notice. But I was a loser with no life, so I was available. Now I have you."

She grinned and smacked his thigh. "Don't worry. You're still a loser."

He winked at her. "Thanks."

She rubbed her chin, thinking. "So, Storm can track a killer?"

"Well, yeah. She can track whatever you want her to track. You just need something for her to scent. In order to do that, you pretty much have to know who the subject is, in that case a killer, and that the article of clothing you have definitely belongs to that person. And that's not always easy to do." He could see the wheels turning in Kylie's head, so he quickly cut her off. "But there's no way for us to know under these circumstances. There are just too many different people going in and out of Tallulah Gorge, so we wouldn't be able to target anyone in particular. Especially since we don't have a scent."

She sighed and slumped in her seat. "When was this prison break, and how long have you known Will?"

He raised an eyebrow. "A couple years ago. And if you're asking me this because you consider Will Santos a suspect in this girl's murder, you can cross him off your list. Will's a good guy. Not some murderer."

She pressed her lips together. "I wasn't. I just think we have to look at everyone. I read somewhere that in serial killings, the murderer often returns to the scene of the crime. Gets a sick satisfaction of watching the police work to find out who did it. He might even volunteer for the search party."

"Interesting, but it doesn't apply to Will."

"Still, our killer could be close by, so we should keep our eyes and ears peeled." She rubbed her hands together, as if planning something big. "As for Will…how well do you really know him? He could—"

"No. Seriously, no. I've known him at least a decade. He's a good guy. I'm telling you, if he ends up being a murderer, I'll retire from this business and never work again."

When she opened her notebook, Linc took a peek to see where she'd written the names of all the people they'd dealt with in SAR and over the course of the past few days. She slowly drew a line through Will's name. He did a double take when he saw another name on the list.

"Wait." He was genuinely incredulous. "Seriously. You have *my* name on there?"

She shrugged. "Well, a good PI never rules anyone out." She wiggled her eyebrows at him before crossing out his name. "Fine. I mean, obviously, it's not you. I'm just trying to be thorough."

"Balance out your thoroughness with some common sense, maybe?" he suggested.

"Yeah yeah yeah," she muttered, studying the list. "I guess you're right. There are way more suspects than I have on this list. But if the person who murdered Amy also murdered Beez, then there's a good chance that he knows his way around the park and that people have seen him and would recognize his face. I bet some of the rangers and people on this list might remember him."

"Or her."

"Right. Or her."

"Because if I'm on that list, you might as well put yourself on it too."

She smacked him. "Ha."

"Even though you and I were both up in Asheville when

the murders happened, how well do I really know you? You might have snuck out at night and gone down there. You're awfully suspicious looking."

She gave him her most innocent face, batting her lashes as she did. Damn, she was adorable.

Closing the cover on her notebook, she pocketed it. "I think I should go through this list and interview everyone. Order and method. Eliminate the suspects one by one."

A sick feeling hit him. "Wait. Don't get in the police's way, though. Remember Jacob?"

She nodded. Originally, things had been kind of thorny between Kylie and his best friend, who also happened to be a Buncombe County detective, simply because Kylie kept stepping on his toes. Eventually, she'd gotten her man, so it had all worked out, but Jacob still got worried whenever he saw her coming.

"Fine. I'll wait for them to finish their work, and then I'll strike."

Linc wasn't sure if he could trust Kylie to wait for anything. She was too impetuous and had the patience of a flea. "Just…be careful. Okay?"

"What kind of trouble could I possibly get into?" she said, leaning over and kissing him on the cheek. "I have you. My warden."

"I prefer the title *bodyguard* if it's all the same to you."

They pulled into the main road heading through the park at a little before ten. A park ranger directed them to headquarters, where the parking lot was filled to the brim with cars and news vans. Kylie slid out of the truck and slammed the door, eyes wide. "Look, Linc. CNN. Does that mean this news is going national?"

Linc shrugged. "I guess we'll soon find out."

It was standing room only in the small headquarters, so Linc was forced to leave Storm outside, tied to a post. When they went in, the place was hot and stuffy with bodies, crammed so tightly into the small space that he longed for a fresh breath. It smelled like stale coffee and body odor. Linc helped Kylie to find a place to stand among the camera crews, police officers, and SAR equipment. As he did, he saw Dina near the podium at the front of the room. Dina was looking at Kylie, like she wanted to take a bite of her.

Figured. Linc had only met Dina's ex-wife once, but she was a curvy woman with long, dark hair, not unlike Kylie. Kylie stood there, tapping her pen on her chin, completely unaware.

Close by was that asshole, Jaxon, crossing his beefy, tattooed arms and looking like he'd rather be anywhere else, along with his girlfriend, who was staring at her long fingernails, looking utterly miserable. He scanned the rest of the room and nodded at Ranger Peck and the other SAR members of the team.

Except Will Santos.

That was odd. He'd said he'd be here. And what Linc had said to Kylie about Will being a good guy was truth. He was loyal. Dependable. And he cared deeply about his SAR work. It wasn't like him not to show.

He'd remembered seeing Jaxon talking to Will last night, before they started back home, so he got Jaxon's attention. "Hey. You see Will around?"

Jaxon scowled at the mention of his name. "Haven't seen him today."

"When was the last time you saw him?"

Jaxon gnawed on the side of his fingernail with clear disinterest. "At the bar last night. Pussied out on a bar fight and begged out early because he said he had to go home. Who knows? He's probably sleeping off his hangover."

That didn't sound right. Will may have been one to drink and have a good time, but he usually didn't renege on his obligations. If he said he'd be here, Linc would trust that. A kernel of worry planted itself in Linc's gut.

He lifted his phone and dialed Will's number. It rang through to voicemail.

Kylie noticed. "Are you worried about him?"

He shook his head. The last thing he wanted was for Kylie to go off on another tangent with all her wild theories. And really, Atlanta's traffic was shit. That's what Will always said. Maybe he'd been delayed by a car accident.

A police officer at the podium began to speak into the mic, introducing himself and beginning the conference. He was Officer Morgan, the chief of police. "I want to thank you all for coming. I know you have all been closely following the events involving Amy Cooper's disappearance, and many of you were on the scene for her search. For that, I thank you."

Linc looked at the door, expecting Will to show up at any moment. But he didn't.

Will wasn't one to be late.

There were probably a thousand explanations for Will not showing up. Like Linc'd said time and time again to Kylie, he wouldn't worry until there was something to worry about.

He typed in a text: *Where u at?*

Pocketing his phone, he told himself that if he didn't receive a response by the time the conference ended, *then* he'd worry.

But all the weird shit that had happened in this park had him on edge. He was already worrying. And it looked like, from the way Kylie kept checking the door and wringing her hands, so was she.

16

The room was suffocating. Cramped, crowded, and not only that. Now there was the added weight of wondering what had happened to Will Santos.

From her spot between the other sardines, Kylie could only glimpse the top of Linc's head. But she knew that Linc was worried.

He didn't have to say a word. She could tell by the way he kept checking the door, and how the muscles in his neck tensed. The veins in the side of his temple were more pronounced too. That was a dead giveaway.

Kylie stood there, sweating in the crowded room, behind a wall of a reporter for Channel 6 News who was at least six-seven, listening as the police chief droned on about the "case in question." As far as the chief was concerned, there was only one case they were actively focusing on—the murder of Amy Cooper. He said it appeared to be premeditated and asked that, if anyone had any information or had seen anything suspicious, to please come forward.

"Additionally, we feel that a homicide such as this requires special attention that is beyond our capabilities, so we're calling in the Georgia Bureau of Investigation, and if they deem necessary, the FBI."

People began to mumble amongst themselves.

Poor Kevin had really picked the wrong time to be shot at, because the police chief barely mentioned him. He did, at the very end of the press conference, say a brief thank-you to the rescuers who'd "risked life and limb to help bring Amy home," then mentioned in passing that Kevin was in stable condition at the hospital, but still unconscious.

It boiled Kylie's blood.

After that, the head ranger at the park, a tanned, hairy, muscular guy in a too-small uniform named Johnson, who reminded Kylie of Smoky Bear, said, "And of course, until the authorities have collected all the evidence they need, we've decided to close the park to visitors."

More murmuring.

They thanked everyone for coming and started to get up.

"I have a question!" Kylie demanded, nudging aside the big guy in front of her. As she did, she thought she heard Linc groan.

All heads swung in her direction. The room grew perfectly silent.

Kylie looked around, suddenly embarrassed. "Um, I'm sorry. Weren't you going to allow for questions?"

A couple of the reporters around the room nodded in agreement with her, but the two men on the podium shook their heads. "No, no questions at this present time."

Well, that blew. She had about four hundred on her pad, and she knew the authorities up there had to have the answers to at least some of them.

She couldn't hold her tongue. "But I just want to know," she blurted, "by not mentioning Beatrice Crosby and Kevin Friedman, are you considering their cases to be separate from this murder?"

Chief Morgan frowned, leaned into the microphone, and said, "That's correct. At this time, there is nothing to convince us they were anything other than unfortunate accidents."

Some of the other reporters started to speak, but Kylie spoke over them. If there was one asset she had in life, it was a voice that steamrolled over all others. "But they're both very suspicious, don't you think? Beez Crosby had decades of experience in hiking that trail and could practically do it blindfolded, and Kevin Friedman was also an experienced SAR hiking in a very populated area of the park, wearing a safety vest."

Chief Morgan exchanged a glance with Ranger Johnson. Then he leaned in and said in a *look-how-cute* voice, "We're very well aware, Miss…?"

"Hatfield." Kylie frowned at him. Why did he sound so condescending? Was it because she was young and a woman?

"Miss Hatfield. As of now, those are still considered accidents, but we're not ruling anything out. We'll lay all our evidence before the bureau and have them make the ultimate decision on how to classify those cases."

"But—" Before Kylie could say more, an arm reached forward, pulling her back behind the wall of a man. She looked over, annoyed, to see Linc.

"I think your time for questioning is up." His voice was gruff.

"But…" she tried to pull away, "I had more!"

"But you're not asking now, Lee. It's not the place."

She ripped her arm free and peeked around the massive reporter.

But it was too late. When Linc let go of her arm, and the big guy moved toward the door, Kylie saw that the podium had already been vacated. They'd probably run away to avoid answering her.

"Why did you stop me? I was making headway!" she seethed at him. She wanted to strangle him.

"You were burning bridges you haven't yet built," he muttered and shoved a hand through his hair. "Look. I know you want to get to the bottom of things. But you have to understand that they can't make connections when no evidence exists to connect the two, because they don't want to cause a panic or incriminate someone who's innocent. Calling the chief of police out in front of every news channel in the state isn't a great way to get him to cooperate with you in the future."

She sighed. Why did he always have to make so much sense? "All right. But I still think the question has to be asked."

"And I'm sure it will be," he said, smoothing her hair. "Just take a step back and watch, okay? Have patience."

Easy for him to say. But if there was a murderer out there, the longer they waited to get to the bottom of this, the more danger all of them were in. She hated having patience. She just wanted to *act*.

She grabbed her pad and pen and scribbled down *Get contact at GBI/FBI* on her long list of things to do. Then she looked at the top of the list. "I want to talk to Amy's family."

"You think that's a good idea? They're obviously distraught over—"

She blew out a long breath. She thought he knew her better than that. "You know I excel at talking to distraught people. I won't be like the police, just barreling in there and asking questions. I have tact."

"Yes. I guess," he said absently.

Kylie looked up from the pad she'd been scribbling on to see Linc staring out the window. "So, Will didn't show."

Linc lifted his phone and stared at the display. "Didn't respond to the text I sent him, either. Phone's saying he hasn't even read it," he grumbled, stalking to the door. "I have a bad feeling about this."

Kylie's mind started to spiral. "You said that you, Beez, and Will were part of the search party looking for the inmates. Who else?"

"What does it matter?" When she just stared at him, he finally humored her. "Um. Dina was there. Kevin, I think—"

Kylie's eyes widened. "Kevin Friedman?"

"Yeah, but—"

"Don't you think that's more than a coincidence? Two out of the five of you got hit, and now Will's missing?"

Linc shook his head. "Yeah. Maybe. But we've all worked on cases together before. Lots of cases. And it's dangerous work. There's no telling what any of this—"

Kylie stopped listening. Her mind was in overdrive. "You said one died being brought in. But I wonder where those other two inmates are now."

Linc held out his hands to get her to stop. "What are you saying? You really think that—"

"Well, what if? You think one of them might be the kind to hold a grudge?"

"No. And as for where they are? Probably still in prison. They killed a guard in their escape, which means they're not getting out any time soon. There're not too many options for them. Either they're dead, or still in prison. I guarantee that they're not free and prowling around the state park, looking for revenge."

She sighed. When he put it that way, it did sound kind of ridiculous.

But they'd been on cases together before. Maybe there was some other case, linking them. Some other madman on the loose, targeting them. "Do you think you can give me a list of all the cases you, Kevin, Beez, and Will worked on together?"

He gave her a disinterested look. "You think I can remember them all?"

"Well, just try. Please. For me."

"All right, all right. When we get to the hotel tonight."

"What about now?" she suggested.

He shot her the evil eye.

"Fine, fine. When we get to the hotel," she said, as in the corner of the room, that idiot Jaxon winked at her, ran his tongue over his lips, and blew her a kiss. She scowled in return and grabbed onto Linc's jacket to whisper in his ear. "That Jaxon is a total jerk. Maybe he had something to do with it."

He followed her line of sight. "What would make you say that?"

"Because he's shifty," she whispered. "He was here, helping us search. Also, he was one of the last people to see Will. I don't like the way he looks around, his eyes darting to the side like that. He's just…shifty."

"And if I had a nickel for every person I ran across who looked shifty, I'd be a millionaire."

She tapped her foot. "But he's super-shifty. I'm telling you, my spidey sense goes wild around him."

He cast a suspicious look down at her. "You sure it's not something else going wild?"

Her mind stopped reeling as what he said dawned on her. "What's that supposed to mean?"

"I'm saying that he's not an unattractive man," he said, stroking his chin and assessing him.

She let out a breath. Was he, seriously, jealous? Over that? "Ew. He's a caveman. And by the way, I have much better taste than that."

He cocked an eyebrow at her. "Do you?"

She nodded and patted his chest. "Yes. Definitely."

He smiled down at her. "All right. Just checking. But you

need to rein in your theories, Lee. People don't really take too kindly to being accused of something they didn't do."

She pouted, still furtively eyeing Jaxon. She just had a sense about him. The way he'd talked about Amy's body with no sympathy, like it'd been a piece of meat. The way he looked at Kylie's ass like it was there for his pleasure? Propositioning her, right in front of their significant others? And now, he was pawing Crystal in what looked like a high school PDA, making out with her as she sat on the ranger's counter. He was downright *creepy*.

She'd have loved to be a fly on the wall at the bar Will and Jaxon had been at. She'd have loved to have interviewed him and found out what he knew about last night, but she didn't want to get too close.

Linc was right; she shouldn't go accusing innocent people. But Jaxon Mott was far from innocent. She wouldn't tell Linc, but Jaxon was at the top of her suspect list.

As the crowd dispersed, Linc started to talk to some other SAR people he knew, so Kylie went over and took some literature from the bins the police had provided about the missing persons. As she was heading there, she saw Dina, the other SAR who Linc had said was part of the search crew looking for the inmates. Dina was also picking up literature, so Kylie decided to strike up a conversation.

"Hi, I'm Kylie," she said. "We were introduced when we were looking for Beez? Remember?"

Dina gave her a smile that Kylie couldn't quite read. "How could I forget you? You're Linc's girlfriend." She leaned forward and whispered in her ear, "What are you doing with a guy like him?"

"Actually, um, he's my fiancé, and...well," she said, a little disappointed to be known as Linc's girl instead of for her profession. And what was it about the SAR people questioning why she was with him? "What do you mean?"

She shrugged. "Don't get me wrong. He's a good guy. If you like that sort of thing."

What sort of thing? She was lost. "I do." She pulled out her business card and handed it to her. "I'm also a private investigator who was hired by Ollie Crosby to look into the death of his wife."

Wrinkles appeared on the woman's flawless brow. "Really? A PI, huh?" She scanned her, and Kylie once again had that feeling she was getting the same condescending *look-how-cute* treatment. From a woman too. "I always thought Beez's old man was a crazy old coot."

Kylie sighed in acute disappointment. "You think? I mean, he seems to think there's no way Beez could've fallen since she's been on these trails for decades and—"

"Listen, honey," Dina said, all condescension again. What the heck was with the people around here, treating her like a lap dog? "There's always something that can go wrong on the trail. It's not like it's an exact science. She slipped. It happens."

Dina stepped away, but before she could leave, Kylie quickly said, "So, you don't think there's any connection between these cases?"

She turned back to Kylie. "No. I don't." She reached out and touched her shoulder, giving Kylie a squeeze. "But it's so good of you to be exploring all the options."

"But…" Kylie suddenly felt stupid. Like the people behaving condescendingly to her were right. Maybe she was a crazy old coot, believing all these conspiracy theories. And why did Dina still have her hand on Kylie's shoulder, running her thumb over her collarbone? She stared at it, confused.

Dina noticed, then crossed her tattooed arms and said, "Okay, I'll humor you. What makes you think there's a connection?"

"Well…Beez and Kevin worked on a lot of cases together,

including the prison break. What if those inmates that you guys tracked down somehow...?" She shrugged, knowing how thin her theory was. "I don't know...it just seems too odd to be a coincidence. And now with Will missing—"

Dina's eyes narrowed. "Will? What?"

Kylie backtracked quickly. "Well, I don't technically know that he's missing, but he didn't show up today, and he isn't answering his phone."

She shrugged. "Jaxon said they had a late night. He was coming all the way from the south of Atlanta too. He's probably either in traffic or just sleeping off a hangover, knowing Will. He's quite the partier."

Kylie opened her mouth to speak. She knew there was more to her theory, but she couldn't quite articulate what she was thinking. "Maybe, but I think you should be careful. Just in case."

Dina smiled and clapped Kylie hard on the shoulder, sending pain spiraling up to her neck. "I can take care of myself. Besides, I'm getting all set to drive to California. My annual visit with the parents is this week. They're about as boring as two people can get. I really think I'll be fine."

Kylie rubbed her arm, sure she'd have a bruise there later. "Oh. Okay," she said, backing away, feeling silly.

"Thanks for your consideration," Dina said, her eyes flashing to someone behind Kylie. Kylie cringed as she added, "Your girlfriend has some pretty wild theories."

Kylie turned to see Linc standing there with an *I told you so* look on his face. He waved and tossed a, "See you," over to Dina and then took Kylie's hand. He didn't say anything, but she knew what was on the tip of his tongue.

"I just told her to be safe. There's no crime in wanting someone to be safe," she said in her defense.

"All right," he said. "What do you want to do now?"

Kylie looked at her list of questions. Right then, she

wanted to go and tell everyone to fuck off. Her cheeks blazed from embarrassment, but it was already turning into anger. Strange things were happening, and if she was the only one who believed it, fine. She'd keep the torch burning all by her lonesome. For Ollie. For the victims.

"I'd like to go and interview Amy's family," she said.

"Then let's go," Linc said, taking her hand and leading her out into the cool autumn air. "Let's go solve a crime."

17

Linc endeavored to humor Kylie and follow along on her fact-finding mission. He'd known her long enough to know that when she got an idea in her head, arguing or trying to talk her out of it was pointless. When he saw her patience growing thin, he decided to take her where she wanted to go and stay out of her way. Maybe then she'd feel like she was making some headway in the case, and she'd eventually calm down.

But as they drove back to the hotel late that afternoon, Linc deemed his plan an utter failure.

Kylie was even more annoyed than she'd been that morning. Linc had to admit, she had a good reason to be. Nobody had answered at the Cooper residence, and security at Piedmont College had nearly run them off campus when they caught the two of them asking questions to see if anyone knew the young graduate student.

They'd been all over the county trying to scrape together information and gotten absolutely nowhere.

"Well, that was a big bust," Kylie mumbled, blowing a lock of hair out of her face. "I feel like I'm on a hamster wheel."

"There has to be someone else we can talk to," Linc said, pulling out of the convenience store outside the college where they'd stopped to get sandwiches. "What does Amy's social media say?"

"Facebook and Instagram. Not much. It's private, so I can't get in. She seems like a kind of meek, quiet person, fond of books and nights home. Not one to take risks." Kylie shook her head as she picked the tomatoes off her turkey sub. "No one is willing to help get to the bottom of this. I'm afraid I'll have to go to Ollie and tell him I've run into nothing but dead ends."

He glanced at her. That didn't sound like his tenacious fiancée. Usually, when she grabbed hold of an idea, she kept plugging away at it until she found a way deeper. "Are you sure?"

She shrugged. "You have any better ideas?"

"Well…yeah. Maybe she's not the person you think she is."

She wrinkled her nose. "What does that mean?"

"Think about it. Why would a meek, quiet girl who likes to spend nights home be climbing one of the hardest trails in the park? That's got to mean something."

She listened to him, mulling it over as she blew out a breath of air that sent the stray hairs from her ponytail puffing out in front of her. "That does sound odd. I thought about that. None of the rangers had ever reported her hiking there before, and yet the first time she goes out, she's on her own, and she picks a trail that's not for newbies. You think someone put her up to it?"

"Possibly. Maybe she was planning to meet someone there. Someone who wanted her to challenge herself." Linc held up a finger. "Or…maybe she was trying to prove something to herself."

"Yeah?"

"Yeah. It's the same reason all these people who never run

more than a 5K decide they're going to go out and run a marathon. It's not because someone's egging them on. It's more for themselves. To prove that they have the mental and physical capacity to tackle an obstacle. It's empowering."

Kylie ripped a bit of her sandwich off and stuffed it in her mouth. "Okay," she said after she'd swallowed. "Maybe she suffered a bad breakup or failed a test or something, and she wanted to empower herself. So, she went on this hike to psych herself up. If I were someone in Amy's life who wanted to kill her and followed her to that spot…what does that say about me? I'd have to be in pretty good shape to navigate that trail myself."

Linc nodded. "Or the killer was already down in the gorge, and Amy had the bad luck to stumble upon him or her. Wrong place, wrong time."

Kylie tried to puzzle it together. "Why do you say that?"

"Because…" He looked at her like it was obvious, but when she gave him a blank stare in return, he figured he'd better explain. "Because yes, it has rained, but not in the last few days. Leaves have been falling pretty steadily. They're crispy. Coming that way, you can't exactly—"

"Sneak up on someone," she finished, her eyes wide. "Right! And the rangers said she went off on the hike alone, so whoever it was, the person was already down in the gorge. You're a genius."

Linc grinned. "Yep," he said, a little proud of himself.

Kylie ripped off another bite, but only stared at the food, clearly thinking. "But how can that be? The rangers specifically said that she was the first one in the park, that she was bright and early."

"Well, there are a couple options that I can think of." When Kylie leaned forward, eager to hear his theories, he smiled. They did make a good team, as insane as that idea was. "She might have been the first one in the park, but that doesn't mean she had to be the first one down. Especially being slow and not knowing the trail well, she might have spent time checking out the map before she took off. Or maybe she made multiple stops on the way."

"So, it could be the second or third person who came into the park?"

Linc moved his head in a "maybe" gesture. "Yes, but I'd imagine our killer didn't follow rules and check in at the gate."

Kylie nodded vigorously. "That's what I was thinking too. Are there many ways in?"

"It's the wilderness, Lee, and it would be easy to bypass the main entrance to the park. After all, they're already planning to break the law by killing another human. Being caught on the trail without a permit probably doesn't scare this person."

She wrinkled her nose. "Very true."

"There's also a good chance that whoever killed Amy was down there already. And that tells us that the person probably knows the trail well or maybe has been hiding in the area for some time."

She leaned over and kissed his cheek. "Wow. That's very Hercule Poirot of you. Way to use those little gray cells." She finally popped the bite of food into her mouth and chewed thoughtfully. "So, that means that whoever killed Amy was a stranger to her. Like you said, 'wrong place, wrong time.' Her death was random."

Linc nodded. "Makes sense to me."

"Which makes it all the more probable that all these incidents are connected. But the question is…why?"

Linc frowned, trying to connect the same dots that Kylie was trying to connect in her mind. "Why what?"

"Why murder? You heard the officer. Amy wasn't sexually

assaulted. She was just bonked over the head, stripped naked, and thrown in the river. So…why?"

"For the thrill? Because he could?"

"Do killers actually do that? Kill a person for the thrill of it?"

He gave her a solemn look. "Absolutely."

She shook her head and grabbed his phone from the cupholder. "I don't know if I buy it in this case. It doesn't feel right. Did Will ever text you?"

"Nope. And that's not like him."

"Hmmm," she said, flipping through his phone. "You got a text from Dina. She says that Kevin is doing well. Stable and improving. Conscious."

"That's good."

"Maybe we should go over there and question him?"

Linc shook his head. "Give the man a chance to breathe. His injury was pretty severe, and he'd had two days of dehydration. He's probably on some serious drugs."

"All right, all right. Then what?" She thought for a minute and then typed something into the phone. "You said Will lives in Atlanta?"

Linc nodded.

She pointed at his phone. "Here it is. Two-seventeen Center Street. We can go check on him."

"In Atlanta? That's two or three hours south, depending on traffic."

"Like we have anything better to do," Kylie said. "All of our other leads are total washouts. Let's go. I've never been to Atlanta, anyway."

Although a part of him just wanted to sink into a bed and crash for a few hours, it was barely four in the afternoon. They had more work to do.

And although he'd done a good job at hiding it, he really

was curious as to where Will had gone off to. Worried too. "All right," he said.

Kylie punched the address into his GPS, and they headed toward Atlanta.

Luckily, most of the traffic was going in the opposite direction, leaving the city, so they made it to his home in a minimum amount of time. The highway dissolved into nice suburban houses, and they found themselves on a pristine street lined with McMansions.

"Here it is," Kylie said, pointing out the window. "Number two-seventeen."

Linc lifted his sunglasses and checked out Will's new home. The first thing Linc noticed was that Will had done well for himself. The house was a large, spotless, stucco-walled colonial in a nice development, almost too nice for a bachelor like Will. The development was new. While his home and the houses surrounding it had green, manicured lawns, houses farther down the street were still just frames, and there were dumpsters and backhoes in the yards.

The second thing Linc noticed was that there was no truck in the driveway.

That didn't mean much. Will was the fastidious type, so he probably kept his truck in the garage. Linc unbuckled his seat belt.

"Stay here," he said to Storm as she tried to hop out with him, but it was Kylie who nodded, nose buried in his phone, probably following another lead down a rabbit hole with a dead end. She was so obsessed with whatever she was looking at, he could've been abducted by UFOs, and she wouldn't be the wiser.

Linc walked up the driveway and rang the doorbell.

The first thing he noticed was that Will's dog, Star, didn't bark. Even Storm barked when someone rang the doorbell.

He waited, hoping to hear footsteps inside. When he didn't, he rang the doorbell again.

Nothing.

Then he looked over at the mailbox. The top was open, and it was overflowing with mail and advertisements. He hadn't been home today.

He took a couple steps into the grass and peeked into the nearest window, a picture window in the front of the house. Will hadn't put up shades yet, and the room was almost completely empty of furniture. Only a large sofa and a few cardboard boxes were scattered about. Made sense if Will had just moved in.

But no sign that anyone was home.

He went back to the porch and stood there for a moment, trying to piece it together. Will had been drunk, Jaxon had said. Maybe he'd decided to go to a hotel and sleep it off. He was also a ladies' man. He could've very well picked up a girl and gone back to her place. In fact, he wouldn't have put it past him.

He turned to shrug at Kylie, but all he saw was the top of her head, the little pink tie in her ponytail. She was still buried in the phone.

To make absolute sure, he peeked into the window of the garage. No truck. He then went around to the fence. It was one of those high, white fiberglass fences that allowed absolutely no one to peek through, so that wasn't a help, but he got the definite feeling that if Star had been on the other side, she'd have been barking her head off by now.

Conclusion: Will wasn't home, and neither was his dog.

Linc jumped back into the truck and frowned at Kylie before throwing the transmission into reverse. "Well, that was a waste of time."

Kylie blinked and looked over at him, as if she was

surprised to see him. "He said he was going to be at the press conference, right? You heard him say that?"

Linc nodded. "He must've changed his mind. Maybe something came up. It happens."

"But you said that's not like him. Didn't you say he was the kind of upstanding guy that you'd trust with your life?"

"I said he didn't deserve to be on your suspect list," Linc said as they pulled out of Will's street. "Not that he was a saint. He drank a lot, partied a lot. I just know he's not a murderer."

Kylie frowned as Linc braked at an intersection. He looked both ways, trying to determine how best to get on the highway and get back to Tallulah Falls so they could resume their investigation.

Kylie looked up from her phone. "But—"

"Little help, please?" He pointed left and right.

Her head bobbed up again. "What?"

"Which way?"

"Oh!" Kylie quickly set up the GPS, and as the voice guided him through his next turn, she continued. "What do you think happened to him?"

He shrugged with a nonchalance he didn't feel. "Like I said, the guy's a little bit of a ladies' man. My guess is that he went out to that bar with Jaxon, found a girl to hook up with, and he's with her, in Tallulah Falls. Knowing him, having the time of his life."

"Would he not text you to tell you he wasn't going to make it, if that was the case?"

"I don't know. Maybe she's some really special girl."

Kylie's brow wrinkled. "Jaxon was with him last night. He didn't mention Will found a girl. Did he?"

"No, but…Will's a player. He'd go around the bar and pick up women right and left. I'm sure he's fine."

Truthfully, Linc wasn't one-hundred-percent on that. But he had to do something before Kylie's mind spiraled out of control. Sometimes, she got so obsessed and focused on certain details that she failed to see the bigger picture, which wasn't unusual, considering she'd just started investigating half a year ago.

"Will's Facebook profile is public, and he hasn't updated in two days," Kylie said.

Linc never understood the allure of Facebook or any of those social media platforms. He had no interest in knowing what the people in his circle of family and friends had for lunch. So, if someone didn't post for three days, it meant they were teetering on the brink of death?

"Okay. Well. What can I say? Maybe he had nothing to brag about."

She paged upwards. "In the past, he was updating multiple times every day. I think it's suspicious."

Wow. Linc hadn't figured Will to be a Facebook slave. "Maybe he, I don't know, forgot his password," he muttered, checking the street signs. "I should probably get gas before we go into the mountains."

They stopped at a gas station, and meanwhile, Kylie didn't remove her nose from his phone. In fact, she was now using both of their phones, comparing things on each of the screens. While he did have to admit Amy's murder was alarming, Kylie was in danger of following her right off the deep end, if she wasn't careful.

He couldn't even be sure she realized that he'd stopped and gotten out of the car, she was that obsessed. He and Storm could've very well disappeared into the night, the victims of whatever murderer she was chasing, and she'd never know.

When he finished filling the tank, he got inside the truck and pulled out onto the road, headed for Tallulah Falls.

He'd only made it a mile or so when she looked up from

the phone and yawned, big and wide. "You should probably fill up before we head into the mountains. Those gas stations up there are a little questionable."

He just stared at her.

It was fixing to be a very long night.

18

Inside, the radiator rattled like a death trap. The old Bates motel was not exactly too interested in making sure its guests had the most comfortable night of sleep of their lives.

That was two nights in a row for Kylie.

She felt like a zombie. Like she should be able to fall asleep if she simply blinked.

But every time she closed her eyes, more questions and ideas and thoughts popped into her head.

The thing was, Linc was just too blasé about these things.

Kylie couldn't understand it. A murder had been committed. Injustice had been done. In Kylie's eyes, that meant all hands on deck. No sleep until the criminal was behind bars. Work-work-work until the answers were found.

She couldn't even think about sleeping when this was on her mind.

Unfortunately, her better half had a different way of looking at these things.

She looked over at Linc, who was resting peacefully—too peacefully—next to her in the hotel bed.

What the hell was wrong with him?

Kylie was now more awake than she'd ever been. Her mind was spinning with thoughts of poor Amy Cooper and the other victims of Tallulah Gorge. Whenever she looked something up, it led her to another idea, and another, and another, until she realized she'd written fifteen pages of notes and questions.

Already, she imagined she had made more headway than the police in solving the poor girl's murder. No, she didn't have their resources, but she'd been devoting all her time to this. She felt like a crime-solving machine, ready to kick some criminal ass.

After she'd finished putting together a ton of questions about Amy Cooper's background, she began to research the theory that Linc had come up with earlier. That the killer was a homicidal maniac who could've been at the bottom of the gorge, waiting for someone, anyone to appear.

There were also two "back entrances" to the park that someone could have used to enter and come up on that side of the gorge. There was a chance someone could have used one of those, but if they had, the person had to have enough knowledge to know they even existed.

Even though so many questions surrounded Amy's death, Kylie felt fairly certain of only one thing: Amy Cooper had not known her attacker. She'd been hit from behind, surprised.

And even that, she wasn't so sure of. It was all just a bunch of conjecture. Even if she was closer than the police to answers, she had to admit, she hadn't made much progress.

Sighing, she looked at the awful seventies-style art on the paneled wall across from her. It was a cartoonish paint-by-number picture from the gorge. She rubbed her eyes, then looked at Linc, whose head was buried under a pillow.

Of all the harrowing things he'd seen in his life, especially overseas while in the service, this was probably nothing. He was on some serious medication for the PTSD, and it wiped him out during the evenings. Sometimes, she envied the way he was able to turn off his brain like that. Sometimes, she had the urge to swipe a couple of pills out from his medicine bottles.

No. Guilt flooded her. She shouldn't envy him. She was glad he'd found medication that worked for him, and his therapy was helping him to make progress. He'd spent so long a complete wreck, unable to concentrate on anything because of his PTSD. Often, he'd wake up drenched in sweat, screaming, clawing at anything—including her—that got in his way.

It was only after witnessing his nightmares several excruciating times that he confessed to her that he'd been the only one from his unit in Syria to survive a suicide bombing.

She rubbed the muscles of his back gently and smiled down at him. Sometimes it scared her, how much she'd come to love him. She couldn't imagine life without him, and with the dangerous nature of their jobs, that was always something at the front of her mind. What if something happened to him? Would she be able to go on?

Shaking those thoughts away, her mind went back to that prison escape. He'd only told her about it when she'd asked, leading her to wonder just how dangerous some of the jobs he went on were. The fact that Beez, Will, Kevin, Dina, and Linc were all on it was concerning. She still hadn't ruled out the possibility that maybe one of those inmates had escaped again and was now prowling around Tallulah Gorge, as crazy as it seemed. After all, she'd looked up Arrendale Prison, only to find out it was less than half an hour away via car. Something about it just didn't sit right with her.

Lifting her phone, she typed in *Arrendale Prison Escape* and came up with several results from just a couple years ago. The articles mentioned the three inmates, two who were incarcerated for murder, the other for attempted murder and grand theft.

She found their names and searched for additional news stories, only to find out that one of the inmates had been killed during the escape, and the other two were still safely behind bars in Arrendale.

It was a dead end.

She sighed, then looked down at Linc again, wishing she could pry open his brain and take a look around. He'd been so mum about this prison case. There may have been other dangerous cases out there that the other SARs had worked on together, but Kylie wouldn't know.

Even though she'd asked him for a list of cases he'd worked on, and he'd said he'd give them to her when they got to the hotel, he'd gone to sleep before he'd had a chance to write them down.

She'd have to get him to do that tomorrow.

She pressed her lips together. Sometimes she really felt like he was interfering with her instincts. Sometimes, he made her feel like she was stupid for chasing her hunches.

He just wanted her to stay safe, really. That was it.

But still. This was her job.

Sometimes, she had to take the risk.

As she was writing herself a note to remind Linc to make that list, her phone buzzed with the news of the day from her "local news" app. She almost closed out of it without looking. But when she swiped it open, her eyes widened as she glanced at the headline:

Man found dead when car plunges off Rte 23 curve

Hair raising on the back of her neck, she opened the article, scanning the words until she glimpsed the name of the victim.

William Santos.

Heart in her throat, she nudged Linc, who let out a growl underneath the pillow. "Huh?"

She kept nudging him, speechless. From her bed in the corner of the room, Storm raised her head and looked in concern as Kylie continued to attempt to wake her master. Finally, Kylie managed to get his name out. "Linc. Linc!"

He pulled the pillow off his head and looked up at her blearily. Still unable to formulate a coherent thought, she shoved the phone into his face, and he recoiled from the bright light of it. "What? You think I can read that?" He sat up, blinking furiously, and grabbed the phone from her. After a moment, he said quietly, "Shit."

Kylie's eyes had already started to water. "Route twenty-three. We were just there a few hours ago. Remember when we saw the police cars, ambulance, and tow truck on the side of the road, up on that hill? That must've been for him."

Linc was still scanning the article. "Jesus. Star didn't make it, either."

Kylie stared at the starburst pattern on the comforter, numb. She was thinking about how she'd met the man so recently. How alive he'd been, laughing and joking with Linc. Then she realized how funny it was that people always said, "But I just saw him!" whenever they learned someone had died. As if them just putting eyeballs on the person meant that they'd be safe from harm. Or as if people who would soon be dead should somehow know their death was coming and stay inside, away from the public eye.

"What do we do?" she asked him, fisting handfuls of the comforter.

After a moment, he raked his hand over his face, shaking his head. Shock still had its claws in him. "What do you mean?"

She pulled her legs up and sat cross-legged on the bed. "I mean, don't we have to do something?"

He scratched at the stubble on his chin. "He's originally from South Carolina. I bet they'll have the funeral there. I should go. I really want to be there."

"No!" The word came out as sharp as a blade, and she immediately placed her hand on his, giving him a *sorry* look. "I mean, doesn't this end any doubt in your head as to whether someone's targeting SAR rescuers?"

He rolled over onto his side and looked at her. "Let's not get ahead of ourselves. Yes, I'll admit that all these things happening together are odd, but Amy wasn't in SAR, and—"

"But nothing! Linc, if we don't get ahead of ourselves, you're going to end up dead."

He let out a mournful laugh and threw himself back on the pillow. "Like Will? Jesus, I just can't believe it."

She looked over at him. He wasn't one to be all emotional, but Will was his friend. He should be taking this hard. He needed time to grieve him, not sit here, playing Nancy Drew with her. She shouldn't pester him about the connection, especially not now, with Will's death so fresh.

The feeling of dread that fell over her at that moment was overpowering. "I think I want to go home," she said suddenly.

"What?" He said it like he thought she was joking. Her eyes pierced his in the darkness. "But what about the case with—"

"I'll just tell Ollie I can't help him," she said, gesturing wildly with her arms. Yes, the last thing she wanted to do was give up on a case, especially one so juicy. But if Linc's life was at stake, then it was different. "We need to get out of here before something—"

He sat up in bed. "Wait, wait, wait. Look." He grabbed her by the wrists and held them, then pulled her into his muscled arms. She had to admit, just that small action made her feel so much safer. "Kylie, sweetheart, you don't have to worry. I can take care of myself."

She snorted, but it was no more than a puff of air. "Will looked like a pretty strong guy too. A guy who probably thought the same thing. That he could take care of himself."

"Kylie, I—"

She pulled out of his arms and looked up at him. "You have to admit there is something wrong going on here. I don't want you to be next. I *can't* have you be next. You may think you can't get along without me, but *I* can't get along without you. Let's just go. Now."

He let out an incredulous laugh. "Now? You're not serious."

She stared at him. She was dead serious.

"Lee. It's three in the morning."

"Please, Linc."

He shook his head, leaned against the headboard, and crossed his solid arms in front of his ARMY t-shirt.

She intensified her pleading look.

"Come here." He beckoned her toward him, fluffed her pillow, and tucked her under the crook of his arm, where she had to admit, if she was going to sleep, this was the way to do it.

"You really want to tell Ollie you're done?"

She was still for a while. Then she nodded. "I'll call him first thing tomorrow."

"If that's what you want. It'd be more dangerous driving in the middle of the night. Just relax, try to sleep for a few hours, and we'll start back at sunrise. Okay?"

She pressed her lips together. "Promise?"

"Yeah." He held out a pinky to her, and she linked it with hers. "Now get some sleep."

She was thankful for that, at least. She expected he'd probably have a hard time falling asleep again, knowing his friend was dead, but she was wrong. His breathing steadily deepened, and a moment later, he was snoring again.

Kylie continued to stare at that ugly painting across the room. The streetlight outside slashed through the vertical blinds, putting the scene behind prison bars. She watched it, closed her eyes, opened them, wishing she could feel tired and nod off.

It didn't work.

All she could think of was the remaining SAR people. That was three out of five that had been part of that early team. And who else was in danger? She didn't like Jaxon, but she didn't want him to die. His girlfriend. Kevin. Lonnie. Forrest. Dina. Did they all have targets on their backs?

And what if they did?

A horrible thought occurred to her, suddenly.

What if Amy Cooper had been murdered simply to lure rescuers to the gorge? What if Craig Silva's suicide had been a murder too?

Her mind kept spiraling until she longed to shake Linc awake again. She wanted to discuss this with him. Even if he told her she was insane, and that she should just go back to bed.

She pulled herself out from under Linc's arm and rolled over, spying Storm, who'd gone back to sleep. She found her phone in the covers and opened it up. Then she typed in the name *Dina Avery*.

She found a number of search results. News reports regarding various rescues she and her German Shepherd, Ghost, had been on. Older articles about her honorable discharge from the army, where she'd served overseas in Afghanistan. Various times for different races all across the country. It appeared that Dina was an accomplished marathoner. She also saw that Dina's family was located in San Diego and that her father and three brothers were in the navy.

Then Kylie found a link to Dina's Facebook profile. She

clicked on it and was happy to discover it was pretty regularly updated, and not set to private.

Kylie took a deep breath. Dina had looked at her before like she was out of her mind. But maybe now that Will was dead, she'd take her seriously.

She clicked on the messenger icon and started to thumb in a message.

19

Dina Avery was actually awake when the message came in from Kylie Hatfield, though it was only four in the morning. Used to early morning drills in the army and a creature of habit, she always kept early hours. A message notification wouldn't have woken her up, even if she hadn't had her phone on vibrate.

It didn't matter, though. Because she and Kylie weren't friends, she received no notification. She only saw that a message request had come through by chance while she was taking a break from packing, this time, at nine in the morning. She was in the midst of scrolling through a bunch of messages from her brother's flaky new wife on the West Coast, who was both lonely and hysterical because of pregnancy hormones and had adopted Dina as her best friend.

Dina had absolutely nothing in common with the woman —Dina was over a decade older, had never even considered becoming pregnant, and didn't find manicures or spa appointments relaxing in the least—but that hadn't swayed her sister-in-law in the least. She'd gotten twenty messages from her in the last hour, complaining of everything from insomnia to eye wrinkles.

So, Dina really couldn't be annoyed by Kylie's message. At least it wasn't a complaint.

She read it again as she knelt on her bed, trying to zip up her duffel: *Hi, Dina, this is Kylie Hatfield, Linc's fiancée. I just want to check and make sure you're okay. By now you've probably heard about Will, and I'm worried about all of you. Please let me know everything's okay.*

She finished zipping up the bag and threw it on the floor, then laid flat on her back in bed, thinking.

Yes, she'd heard about Will. She'd gotten a number of texts before she'd gone to bed, from the police, and then the rangers at the park. Honestly, it hadn't surprised her to hear it. She didn't know Will well, but she'd worked with him often in the past few years. He'd been pretty friendly and attentive to her those first days, until he found out that her door swung the other way. After that, he'd kept his distance. She found him to be kind of surly, disingenuous, and a bit egotistical. After every search, he'd always head to the bar to blow off steam and pick up girls.

So, to Dina, it was no surprise that he'd driven off that cliff. She'd bet money they'd find it to be a DUI. Sad, but in Dina's world, you reaped what you sowed.

And now, cute little ray of sunshine Kylie Hatfield was on her butt, trying to make sure she was okay. How sweet.

Dina smiled. Obviously, the girl thought that there was some grand and sinister plan out there to destroy all the SAR workers in Georgia.

Dina didn't quite buy it. She'd seen a lot of shit in her life. Shit happened. Often.

She read the message for a third time, trying to think of something witty to say. It probably hadn't even occurred to a sweet, innocent girl like Kylie that Dina was a lesbian, even though Dina had spent far too much time unabashedly staring at Kylie's perfect heart-shaped ass in those jeans. Linc obviously noticed, from the way he was always inserting himself between the two of them, but not Kylie.

If anything, Kylie was probably jealous of *Dina*, thinking Linc had designs on her. So innocent. The world was so black and white for her, wasn't it?

Finally, she just typed in, *I'm fine. Thanks for your concern. How are you?*

A little while later, Kylie responded with: *Fine. Linc and I are headed back to Asheville.*

Well, that was probably good. Linc had probably talked some sense into her and told her there was nothing to worry about. *Heading to California in a bit. See you for the next case... hopefully not too soon.*

Although she wouldn't have minded taking Kylie aside and getting to know her, she figured it probably wasn't going to happen. She was definitely barking up the wrong tree, considering this particular tree had Linc as a guard dog tied to the trunk.

Oh, well.

Dina threw her phone on the bed and went to the kitchen to give Ghost her breakfast. When she got back, she saw her phone had lit up with a bunch of messages. They were all from Kylie:

Well, I'm still worried about you.

Do you think you could message us on occasion to let us know you're safe?

After everything that's happened with Beez, Kevin, and now Will, you can't be too careful.

You just never know. A string of smiling emojis followed.

Dina let out a little snort. Geez, Linc really had his hands full with that little firecracker. Linc was quiet and sedate.

This girl was like a shaken can of soda—ready to explode the second she was let out of her container.

Finally, she rolled her eyes and typed in: *Sure. I'll message you when I get to California in two days.*

She tucked the phone into the pocket of her jeans and dragged her duffel down to her Jeep. She stuffed it in the back and then went inside. Ghost had already finished eating. She grabbed a bottle of water and a few snacks for the trip and gave her a little pat on the side. "Ready to go, girl?"

As she straightened, the phone in her pocket buzzed.

She lifted it out and read: *Actually, I'd love it if you could check in with us every few hours before you get there. It'll really set our minds at ease.*

Her jaw dropped. Was this woman really serious? She was just supposed to pull over to the side of the road so that Linc and his uptight girlfriend could keep tabs on her? She supposed they were just trying to be helpful, but...really. What the actual hell?

She figured if she didn't agree, Kylie'd just keep hounding her, so she typed in: *Might be tough but I'll try.*

This was the reason she was still single. People were damn hard to deal with. She'd much rather have the company of dogs.

She locked up her apartment and went to her bright yellow Jeep. As she reached for the door handle, Ghost started to bark. She followed the dog's line of vision but saw nothing but all the old cars her neighbors kept. The court was always clogged up with cars. Nothing looked amiss.

Hushing the dog, she ordered Ghost to jump in to ride shotgun and climbed in beside her. As she slid into the seat, she grabbed her sunglasses from the dash and slipped them on, looking up at the deep azure sky on this beautiful, cloudless day.

Sure, the happenings at Tallulah Gorge were concerning,

as were all the strange things happening to the SARs. But most concerning of all to her was that Kevin's golden, Molly, had never been found. Neither had Beez's dog, Tiger.

SAR dogs were an expensive resource. Well-trained animals like those could fetch upwards of fifty-thousand dollars if presented to the right buyer. Someone had once offered her that much for Ghost, not that she'd ever consider selling her...ever. No, Dina liked to say she was more attached to her German Shepherd than she was to her own ears.

The thought made the skin on her neck prickle. Someone after Ghost?

Never. She'd die first, to save the good dog's life. Dina didn't know much, but she knew that for certain.

But if she allowed herself to worry about it, she'd never go anywhere or do anything. And the two of them? They were born to go on adventures. Dina had taken her practically everywhere with her and couldn't imagine not having her along.

"We have someplace to be, right, Ghost?" she said, stroking the dog's white ears.

And the dog looked back at her, licked her hand, and Dina could've sworn that she nodded.

20

It was a nice day. Perfect, really.

I felt it in my bones.

The street Dina lived on was surprising. Little more than a slum. The road was clogged with cars, many of them sitting on blocks at the curb. That was good, though. With them in the way, she couldn't see me parked in the roundabout at the end of the potholed street.

But I could see her.

I'd been in this row of shitty apartments once before. Kid I went to school with lived here, and I was invited to a birthday party that had ended with his mom and dad fighting about the cost of the cake.

They were as bad inside as out. Old as the hills. Cramped. Good for people who didn't expect much out of life and weren't really worth a hell of a lot.

Dina Avery qualified.

It was actually kind of funny in a sad, desperate sort of way. The bitch tried to pretend that she was important. Wore nice clothes, drove an expensive Jeep. It was all surface, though. A shiny veneer that covered the rot of her real life.

Disgusted, I watched as she carried a big duffel out on one shoulder. Jesus, she had bigger biceps than me. She tossed it into the back of her Jeep, pulled her phone out of her tight jeans, and glanced at the display.

I'd been watching Dina Avery for some time. I knew she was a lesbian because I'd seen her with her last girlfriend or wife or whatever. The girl was pretty cute, which pissed me off to no end. How that freak of nature could get a cute girl like that when I was still single was beyond me.

But now wasn't the time to dwell on my own inability to get laid. I had a job to do.

And from Dina's movements, it looked like I needed to move quickly.

The bitch was trying to skip town.

Dammit.

First, I'd gone to the rattrap on Route 6 to check up on Linc Coulter, only to find out that he and his girl had vacated the area. Pussies. Probably turned tail and went back up to North Carolina because they couldn't stand the heat this kitchen was pouring out. Now, Dina was leaving?

This wasn't good.

I needed to do something, and quick.

I watched as she jogged back inside, only to return a few minutes later with her dog. White German Shepherd that growled every time the damn thing saw me.

I didn't know much about dogs. In fact, the whole lot of them could just go to hell. I was only five when a big black one had nearly taken my life. I still had the scars on my belly, arms and legs as a memory of my six weeks of hospital stay. Rabies in addition to the torn muscles and broken bones. Those shots had sucked.

But none of that sucked as much as what happened after.

Clear as day, I still remembered my parents fighting over the hospital bills. Still remembered having to sell our house and move in with my grandparents. Still remembered how my uncle snuck in my room…

I slammed my hands into the steering wheel before gripping it hard and shaking…shaking…shaking. My vision dimmed as my breathing came too hard and too fast.

It'll be okay.

The sound of your voice was like drinking hot chocolate on a cold day. It warmed me. Soothed me.

For now.

I had no time to be soothed because a car door slammed, bringing me back to the present. Back to the bitch and her dog. The one taking a dump on the grass.

Stupid fucking dirty animals.

That was yet another reason that people like Dina, and Kevin, and all the others just pissed me off. They just loved those stinking animals. Treated them like family.

What a crock of shit. A dog's in your life for…what? Ten years? That was a blink in the life of a human. Most humans, anyway. The humans that weren't abandoned and left to die because the weather got too bad. The humans whose lives weren't cut short because the people who were supposed to rescue them turned chicken.

My teeth hurt from grinding them too tightly.

It was their fault. Her fault. The dog's fault that you are gone.

You couldn't replace family. Family was everything. These assholes just didn't get it.

They valued animals more than they valued human beings. They proved that with you, didn't they?

Well, I now valued the money I got from selling Beez and Kevin's mutts on the black market. Twenty-five thousand dollars each. I still couldn't believe it. Now, when I was finished with my mission, I could buy a plane ticket to Costa

Rica. I could run away from these memories, knowing I brought justice to you.

Remember how we talked about going there? Just me and you. Living on the beach, escaping this life. It was one of the reasons you wanted to be a Girl Scout, so that you would know how to live on the run when we finally escaped that house.

A sharp bark made me jump, and I sank down in my seat when I noticed the white dog staring in my direction. Dina Avery looked too, following her dog's line of sight.

Could they see me?

Feel the hate I projected in their direction?

Did my anger cause the hair to raise on the back of her neck?

I hoped so. I hoped she pissed her pants when she finally faced me, knowing that her death was imminent.

Turning her back on me, Dina shushed the dog and called for him to jump into the Jeep. I was out of time. Out of options.

I looked around. As crowded as this shit neighborhood was, there wasn't a soul around that I could see. Not another dog, or a kid going by on a tricycle...not even a squirrel.

We were alone. Mercifully alone. The luck I was having felt like a miracle. Like someone up there was trying to tell me something. *This is the time. Go for it.*

My hands tightened around the steering wheel. In two minutes, she'd be gone, and for who knew how long? I had to make a choice or lose her forever.

And that wasn't an option.

I needed to act.

Inspiration struck as I watched her look both ways from the driver's seat of her car and start to slowly back out of her driveway.

Not giving myself a chance to overthink it, I threw my car into drive and punched the gas.

I surged forward, my speed hitting thirty miles per hour when I clipped her back taillight.

Bang. Contact.

Ready to launch.

She lurched to a stop. I saw her face in the driver's side window, twisted in anger. Though my windows were closed, her words hit me, loud and full of rancor. *Watch what you're fucking doing, you asshole!*

I smiled.

Taking a cleansing breath, I stretched my shoulders before rolling and cracking my neck. As I reached down to the lever at my feet and popped the trunk, I forced a contrite look on my face before opening my door.

"Oh, my, I'm sorry," I said, running my hands through my hair.

She hopped from her Jeep, all pistons firing. She'd barely looked at me before screaming, "What the hell are you doing?" She pointed at the orange remains of her taillight shattered on the pavement. "Look at what you did! Are you insane?"

This was good. The more of an asshole she was, the less regret I'd feel later.

Oh, who was I kidding? I wasn't going to regret this in the least.

Bring it, bitch.

"You really don't know how to drive, you—" She stopped as I approached, heading not for the impact spot, but for the door of her car. I reached behind her and slammed the door to her Jeep, locking the barking dog inside. She stared at me in confusion. "What are you—"

A glimmer of recognition crossed her expression a split-second before my fist connected with her jaw. Bingo. That was it. The money shot. Hit her like a ton of bricks. She didn't even have time to put up her hands to defend herself.

She was ex-army? Seriously? With one hit she folded like a swoony, graceful little lady right into my arms. Night-night.

I scooped her up and carried her to my open trunk, dropping her inside. Slamming it shut, I looked regretfully at the dog still barking its head off. I didn't have time to take it too. Another twenty-five thousand would have come in handy, but I couldn't spend it if I was sitting in a jail cell.

I needed to move.

Jogging to the front of my car, I quickly slipped inside and scanned the neighborhood.

Not even a squirrel. Jesus, I must've been doing something right.

Pulling the cap down over my eyes and pushing the sunglasses higher up on my nose, I turned up the radio loud as I drove, out of town and to a dirt service road in the woods, near the park. As I navigated into tree cover so thick it was nearly dark as night, I thought about what to do.

This wasn't in the plan, you know? But you know how I felt about these things. Obstacles were made to be overcome. And I'd take care of her. Then I'd move on to the main attraction. It wasn't long now. I needed a great big finale. One that would knock their socks off.

When the idea came to me, I whistled the theme for Mayberry. Good old *Andy Griffith*. We loved that stupid show too. Nothing ever went wrong there that couldn't be fixed in half an hour. Nothing too bad ever happened. No death. No grief. No stupid-ass, know-it-all lesbians fucking everything up.

I slowed to a stop, then went around back and popped the

trunk again. I smiled down at a drowsy, disoriented Dina, who was struggling to come to.

"Well, what have we here?" I said with a smile, patting her cheek before leaning in to whisper, "Hello, worm. Ready to dangle?"

21

Linc walked out of the barn after feeding the animals like he always did.

One thing that was different? Kylie's face in the window. She was watching him. Again.

She held up a hand in a wave, a too-bright smile on her face. But he could see the strain etching lines on her pretty face. She was worried. About him.

Forcing a smile of his own, he waved back.

It'd been a day since they returned from Tallulah Gorge. Since then, things had gone back to normal, at least, some semblance of normal. He'd scarcely been able to go anywhere or do anything without her tracking his every move, hovering over him.

"You okay?" she called to him through the screen of the open window, where she'd been working on her computer.

He nodded and gave her a thumbs-up. His shoulder was definitely getting better, so that wasn't her concern. No, Kylie was concerned that some homicidal maniac would jump out of the bushes and carry him away. Even though he was bigger than most guys, even though they were all the way up here, practically in the heavens above Asheville, Kylie must've thought it was only a matter of time before this guy struck.

He laughed a little as she pressed her lips together. "Are you sure?"

"Seriously, I'm fine."

She stared at him, like she was trying to decide whether or not he was telling the truth. Part of him liked her attentiveness, but part of him wanted to scream, *Enough already!*

He walked to the window and looked up at her. "Let me guess. Dina hasn't replied?"

She sighed. "No, and I'm getting worried. She added me to her small friends list, so I thought she might actually update me like she promised. But…nothing. Can you believe it?"

Yeah. Linc could. Dina wasn't the type to take too kindly to being told what to do, even if she did have a little crush on his fiancée. "I'm sure she's fine."

"Yes. But I told her to text us because we were worried. You'd think she'd listen."

"She's driving to visit her family. I'm sure she's busy."

Kylie picked up her phone and studied it again. "I've sent her six texts. And nothing! Can you believe it? How rude! How blatantly, completely horribly rude!"

Linc cringed. "Six? Kylie, honey, you need to relax. I know Dina. She can easily get annoyed by that kind of thing."

Kylie scowled, but he could see the fear behind the expression. "By me caring? Really?" She crossed her arms, hugging herself tight. "Or is she like you? Remember, how you didn't even know how to text until you met me?"

Linc remembered that. They'd had quite a blowout over it, when their relationship was still in its nascent stages. It wasn't that he didn't know how to text. He simply wasn't as attached to his phone and being "social" the way she was.

Kylie lived to communicate in one form or another. She was constantly thumbing in messages to one friend or another, all day long.

Kylie fisted her hands on her hips when she caught him smiling at the thought. "What's with the stupid grin? And how do you know what she's like? What, did you two date or something, back in the day?"

He wouldn't have been able to stop the laugh from bursting from his mouth if he'd bolted his lips shut.

She stood up, her eyes on fire. "What? What does that mean? Did you...? Did you two have a hot sexual relationship that—"

He held up both hands. "Calm down. I can't talk to you with this screen between us. Why don't you take a break and come outside? It's nice out. Let's have a beer on the porch."

She didn't say a word, just shut the window against the cool air streaming in and pulled the curtains together. A minute later, she came through the screen door with two open beer bottles. The dogs came out too.

She handed one of the beers to him and sat down on the porch swing. The dogs settled at their feet. "Is this how you break to me that you and Dina once had a torrid love affair? Because I'm telling you, I saw the way she looked at you."

He snorted, took a swig of his beer, and leaned back next to her. "And how did she look at me?"

Kylie gave him a wounded look. "Like she wanted you. Obviously. And you just played all dumb about it."

He laughed. "I thought you were supposed to be good at reading people. What happened to your spidey sense?"

She shoved him. "What's that supposed to mean?"

She was obviously getting angry from his poking fun at her, but he couldn't help it. He had to admit, he liked her attentiveness, and he also liked her being jealous too. But really, she had no need to be.

He decided to put her out of her misery.

He shrugged. "What I mean is that *you're* more of Dina's type than I am."

"What…" Her eyes drifted away, then suddenly snapped to his. "You mean…she's *gay?*"

"Yeah. She was even married a couple years ago. To a *woman*. Didn't last, though," he said with a grin. "And I have to tell you that her ex-wife looked a little like you. So yeah. I was more worried she was putting the moves on *you*, when you two were speaking."

She gasped. "You mean…"

He nudged her. "Ever think of playing for the other team?"

"No!" she said, grabbing his hand. She sat back, stunned, then lifted the beer to her lips. She almost took a sip, then stopped. "So she was flirting with me back at the press conference, and I was just being a dumbass."

"Uh-huh. In a nutshell."

Her cheeks turned a rosy pink as she stretched her slippered feet out and rested them on Vader's fuzzy side. "You think I'm her type?"

He gave her a double take. "What? Are you interested?"

"No! I'm so embarrassed, though. I mean, I hope I didn't lead her on. I wouldn't hurt her feelings for the world."

"Relax." He took hold of her hand and squeezed it. "Not saying you did. You're just naturally cute, and people naturally want you. That's what I worry about."

She raised an eyebrow. "You worry about that? Seriously?"

"You know I do."

"But I only have eyes for you." She sang that part, then beeped him on the nose. "Not Jaxon, not Dina, not anyone else. You know that, right?"

He wrapped his arm around her, and they sat on the

swing, moving leisurely back and forth as they enjoyed their beers. For the end of November, it was unseasonably warm, and the snow that had fallen in the mountains recently had all but melted away. In a just over a month, it would be a brand-new year.

And then…the wedding.

They hadn't discussed it much at all. Not since the day she was supposed to go shopping for wedding dresses. With all that had happened and all that was on their minds, wedding planning had definitely fallen by the wayside.

But they had time.

Intellectually, he knew it didn't matter when it happened. Eventually, it would, whether this month or a year from now. But for some reason he couldn't explain, he wanted that ring on his finger. That paper in his hand.

Maybe it was because he'd spent so many years running from people that he wanted to stand in one place and scream…*this is my life. My wife. My future.*

And maybe he just wanted to prove to himself that he wasn't so scared anymore. That he wasn't worried so much about failing people who counted on him. Not like…

He took a sip of his beer, refusing to think of his buddies.

The therapy had helped, but there were still times when he saw that scene as if it were happening in real time, right in front of him. Maybe that would never fully go away. Maybe the sadness and guilt of being the lone survivor would never fully fade.

Kylie snuggled against him, and he breathed in the scent of her hair. The realness of her. And smiled.

She'd swept into his life like a tornado, tossing him this way and that.

He had thought he wanted quiet and peace, but he was thriving on chaos and laughter.

Thriving on Kylie.

His wife.

Some day.

But today, he had other things to think about. Other people to think about. His friend.

As if reading his mind, Kylie said, "Have you heard any more about Will?"

He took another long drink of beer. "They ruled it an accident and suspect it to be alcohol-related, though Will's body lay in the woods too long for a positive ruling. The police think he might've been spooked by a deer or a fox and was too impaired to correct his vehicle. The skid marks in the area are consistent with that."

Kylie sighed and rubbed his arm, the long up and down strokes immensely soothing. "How awful."

"Yeah. But I don't know. He was a drinker, sure. But he was careful too, when he knew he had to drive, especially since he'd gotten slapped with a DUI once before. Maybe he had something that just threw him for a loop."

"It's sad. I feel terrible for his family. His parents still alive?"

"Yes. In South Carolina. And I believe he has two sisters and a brother, all younger. I've met his brother Sam; plays ball for Clemson. The authorities are shipping him and Star back to Lake Secession, where his family lives. Like I said, that's where the funeral will be. Star's gonna be—" His voice cracked, and after a moment, he cleared his throat and tried again. "Star's going to be buried with him."

Kylie didn't say anything. When he cocked his head to look down at her, he noticed her cheeks were wet. Already crying. It was par for the course for her, but not so much for him. He stiffened his upper lip and forged ahead.

"I'm going to drive there for the funeral," he announced, enunciating the *I'm* so she wouldn't misunderstand. "I should only be gone two days. Three at the most."

He expected pushback, but he didn't get any. Her voice was gentle. "All right. By yourself? You don't want me to go with you?"

He didn't. Somehow, it felt like something he needed to do on his own.

He shook his head, still thinking about poor Star. He guessed that if he was going to go, with his dog by his side would be the way to do it. "Stay with the dogs. Vader's already been through enough. He missed you. Not just Storm. You."

"All right." She sat up and kissed his cheek. "I guess that's okay. I still have a wedding to plan. Remember?"

"Oh, right. I do seem to remember I might have proposed many moons ago." He took her hand and twisted the engagement ring gently.

"Just…" She placed her hand on his cheek, tears brimming in her eyes again.

"Be safe," he finished for her. "Got it."

She blinked the tears away, her forehead crinkling with worry. "And you better do a better job at checking in with me than Dina's doing. Big time."

He linked their fingers together. "Maybe."

She punched him. "Say yes now, or else I'm making you take me with you, and you're going to have to wear me around town like a tie because I'm not letting you shake me loose."

"All right, all right." He held up his hands in surrender. "Yes! I promise."

She sat up so quickly that the dogs straightened. "Oh. And I'm letting you go on your own on one condition."

He narrowed his eyes at her. "Right. That I check in regularly. I thought we established that."

"Nope. That's not a condition. That's a necessity. As in, if you don't do it, I'll handcuff myself to you." She stopped, chewing her bottom lip in deep thought. "Actually, two conditions. Real conditions."

He groaned. "What now?"

"The first real condition is that you don't drive. Not after Will. Don't do that to me. Just...fly. It's safer. I can drop you at the airport."

He held up a finger. "Sorry, but Lake Secession is only a couple hours away by car, tops."

She sucked in her cheeks and tapped away on her phone to double-check. "So?"

"So, it would take me twice as long to fly there by the time I had to check in early and deal with security and all that shit, then I'd still have to rent a vehicle and drive. I'll spend the night because it will probably be a two-day event."

He left out the part where he wanted to take his pistol, and if he flew, he'd have to check his luggage.

The tears were back, her nose pink from emotion. She blinked furiously, turning away as she swiped at her face. "I'm sorry. I'm just so worried."

He pulled her against him. "Hey, if it makes you feel better, I'll fly."

She sniffed hard, relief softening her features. "Really?"

He kissed her forehead. "Really. What's the second condition?"

She turned more fully to face him. "I want you to tell me about all the cases you, Will, Kevin, Dina and Beez were on."

She'd asked about this before, several times. Every time he tried to think of it, though, he just got tired. There'd been quite a few, and not all of them did he care to relive. It seemed pointless, anyway. "Still plugging away on that little theory of yours?"

She nodded. "The prison inmate one didn't pan out. The two still alive are at Arrendale, but it just makes sense. And I had a thought yesterday. What if the killer used Amy Cooper and Craig Silva to lure you guys to the park? Like bait?"

He stared at her. What a wicked theory for his sweet, sunshine-and-rainbows fiancée to come up with. Sometimes she could be so sweet that he'd forget she could be a pretty badass PI when she wanted to be. "That person would be a real deranged soul."

"Yes. But we all know those types exist. We've met them. Remember?"

He did. And he didn't want to be reminded of it. He'd come dangerously close to losing Kylie during each of those episodes. "Fine. I'll humor you. But I don't know what good it'll do."

She stared at him expectantly, as if waiting for him to give her all the details, right that second.

"Okay, okay. If you're in such a rush, I keep files of all my cases in the filing cabinet by the desk in the spare bedroom," he said. "Have at it. Just don't mess it all up. I'm trying to keep it in some sense of order."

She jumped as if she were shot from a cannon and zoomed like a bolt of lightning for the door. When it slammed, he heard her footfalls noisily rushing up the staircase.

He looked at his beer, then slowly drained it before standing. "Well, I guess I should go pack," he said to the dogs.

22

Kylie didn't have time to look through the files. She got Linc a flight, but it was one that was leaving right away. She'd barely had time to change and brush her teeth before she was driving him to the Asheville airport. She dropped him off at the curb and kissed him, feeling good that he'd be safe on a plane.

At the time, she'd told herself it would be a breeze, him being gone overnight. Less than thirty hours. She could do that.

Then she came home to the empty farmhouse and looked around, and her stomach sank.

The dogs were there to keep her company, but she couldn't shake the creepy feeling that slid up and down the length of her spine. Honestly, she hadn't expected to feel this way. She'd been so wrapped up in Linc possibly being in danger that she hadn't thought of herself.

Being alone, without Linc...sucked.

It was funny how, in the past six months, she'd come to depend on him so much. She'd once been so fearlessly independent that she hadn't even been able to consider moving in with him. Not too long ago, she'd absolutely *loved* her independence and couldn't imagine sharing a house with another person.

But in the last few months, she'd come to realize that she didn't just love him. She needed him.

It was comforting to have him, but also...scary whenever he went away.

Funny how quickly he'd turned her world completely upside down. For good? Yes, definitely.

Though it wasn't good that she had a hard time being alone like this.

Stop, she told herself, going to the fridge and getting a bottle of wine. It was only noon, but she poured herself a big glass. *You're good. You're a grown-up. You've got your guard dogs. Put on your big girl panties and deal.*

Also: PLAN THAT WEDDING.

That, at least, was what she had planned to do. She'd started home, focused on wedding planning, thinking about what needed to be done and making a checklist of all the things she'd accomplish.

But the second she thought of Linc, her mind stuck there, refusing to go back to the wedding stuff. She hoped he'd be safe. She knew how ridiculous it was to force him to fly when the actual drive would have been shorter, but she simply couldn't risk him driving on his own.

Not after Will.

The thought made her shiver. She took a sip of wine, grabbed the stack of bridal magazines she'd amassed, and laid them out before her. Taking a deep, cleansing breath, she tried to focus on the big event.

A moment later, she started wondering where in the air Linc was. She'd told him to text her the moment he landed, and he hadn't yet. Opening her phone, she checked to see that his plane wasn't due to land for another five minutes.

She looked back at the magazines. *Concentrate.*

Ten minutes later, she found herself staring at a lock of her hair and picking out the split ones. She had way too many split ends. She definitely needed a trim.

She looked back at the magazine. The bride and groom on the front of it were embracing, lost in the throes of love, but somehow, also seemed to be taunting her. *We did it. Why can't you get your fool ass together and plan it? It's only the biggest day of your life?*

She lifted a sticky note that she'd been using to mark pages from the pile and stuck it right over the couple's faces.

Then she looked at her phone. Linc's plane should have landed by now. Why hadn't he texted?

She grabbed her wine glass and took a big gulp. As she was swallowing, a text came through. She nearly pounced on her phone.

It was from Linc. *Safely on the ground.*

She smiled. It was a relief to have him out of harm's way. If there was any harm to be had. She still didn't know if he was in trouble, or if it was all just a coincidence. Still, she was glad they weren't taking chances.

Dina, the jerk, hadn't sent her a reply on Facebook. She'd gone onto her profile and noticed she hadn't updated, but Dina naturally didn't update very much—her last status was a meme about dogs, and it was from two weeks prior. Kylie could only assume that she was still on the road, driving toward California.

She'd said it would take two days. Maybe the battery in her phone had died. Maybe she'd get in contact once she arrived at her family's house.

At least, Kylie hoped.

This all sounded too much like Will's story. With Will, they'd made excuses and made excuses for him, and all the while, he'd been lying dead at the bottom of the gorge.

Kylie opened up her Facebook Messenger and looked at the last six messages she'd sent Dina. Dina hadn't read any of them yet, which yes, could've meant that Dina hadn't been able to get onto her Facebook account. She knew Linc would probably roll his eyes at her, but she couldn't help it.

As far as Kylie was concerned, there was absolutely nothing wrong with having concern for another human being. There was too little of that in the world these days.

She typed in just one more message, a quick, *Hope everything's okay,* and pressed send.

Then she set down her phone, grabbed her spiral planning notebook, and opened it to the first blank page.

A magazine article she'd read had said the first step in planning was to make a checklist of everything that she needed to make the magical day come true, from invitations to honeymoon. She picked up a pen and had only written three letters W-E-D when her phone began to ring.

It was Rhonda.

She'd been avoiding her mom's phone calls ever since she'd cancelled the dress-shopping extravaganza. There'd been at least one daily call, but Kylie had let them all go to voicemail, afraid she'd only end up feeling guilty about it.

But now, she could put it off no longer.

She lifted the phone and said, "Hi, Mom," as cheerily as she could manage.

"Don't 'hi, Mom' me," Rhonda said, accusation in her voice. "You've been avoiding me, but you can't avoid me any longer. We need to go dress shopping. Now. It's an emergency. A five-alarm dress shopping emergency!"

Kylie sighed. "Mom, dress shopping is not an emergency."

"It is this time."

Kylie pressed the heel of her hand against her eye. And her mother wondered where Kylie'd learned to be so dramatic?

"Mom," she said with as much patience as she could muster. "I haven't nailed down a date. And I've been busy. I told you about the case in Georgia."

"And you were too busy to talk to your mom for five minutes and let her know you're alive?" Rhonda Hatfield was the queen of guilt trips.

Kylie set the pen down, guilt stabbing her in her heart. "Mom, since when have our phone calls ever been only five minutes?"

"True, true." Rhonda sighed, but Kylie could hear a note of something else almost vibrating from her mother. "But you might want to pick up your phone one of these days. Because someone might have news."

She couldn't deny that. Her mother was a gossip hound to put others to shame, digging up dirt like a pro—she probably would've made a good PI herself. The only thing was, Kylie didn't care about those people's lives nearly as much as Rhonda did. "Who is it this time? A neighbor?"

"No. Someone who closely resembles your mother?"

Kylie wrinkled her nose. In all her years of phone calls with her mother, Rhonda had never been the subject of gossip. Rhonda lived a quiet, boring life, where every day was the same as the one before. It never occurred to Kylie that her mother might actually be the subject of this particular tidbit. Of course, since Jerry, Rhonda had been doing all sorts of things that were out of character...

And then it hit her.

Jerry.

"What?" she asked, proceeding cautiously.

"You're wrong! A date has been set! For us! On Valentine's Day. Mark your calendar!"

Kylie nearly choked. "Um. What?"

"The dress shopping isn't for you!" her mother shouted,

nearly bursting Kylie's eardrum. "It's for me! Jerry and I are getting married!"

Kylie held the phone away from her ear. "What?" She clapped a hand over her mouth before she shouted, *"Why?"*

She knew why. Her mother was in love and Kylie was very happy for her. But she and Jerry had just met like five minutes ago. Wasn't this a little soon?

"What? Aren't you happy for me?"

"Oh. Yes!" she corrected quickly. "Just surprised. And...surprised."

She really had no reason to be surprised. All the signs were there. The two lovebirds had scarcely been able to keep their eyes off one another since Jerry had helped Rhonda after she'd been struck by a car. All part of the crazy-stepmom fiasco.

And Jerry was as good as they came. But her mother had been single as long as she could remember, so it was easy to believe she'd always be that way. To see her suddenly engaged was...mind-boggling.

Actually, she was more mind-boggled—and a little jealous —by the fact that, though her mother had likely barely been engaged for twenty-four hours, she'd already gotten further in her wedding planning than Kylie had.

Her mother went on, babbling in a way that made it impossible to get a word in, talking about how he proposed at their favorite restaurant on a rooftop, under the moonlight, and how they weren't getting any younger, and how they were hoping to get hitched as soon as possible. Kylie tried to listen and be in the moment, but was still so stunned she went to take a sip of her wine and realized she'd drained the whole glass.

"Mom, I really am happy for you," she said when she was allowed a chance to speak. "Jerry's such an amazing guy. You're both really good for each other."

"I know, right? And like I said, I want the marriage to happen as soon as possible. So?"

"So…what?"

"Can you come? Downtown, say, be here at one-thirty?"

She checked the clock on the microwave. It didn't feel right to be engaging in frivolous things like dress-shopping when she'd just gotten back from a case where people were dying. But life had to go on, right? She figured she could spare a little time for her mom. And maybe then she could get her own dress picked out and check that off her to-do list.

She sighed as she looked at the paper in front of her with nothing but the letters W-E-D on it.

Her to-do list was still on her to-do list.

"Yes. I'll be there," she said, shoving her bridal magazines back into a pile and running upstairs. She'd been meaning to drop off her time logs to Greg anyway, and she missed his face. This would be killing a bunch of birds with one stone. "But, Mom…three hours. That's it. No more. I have to be back here by dinner, because I have to…"

Actually, she really didn't have to do anything. Plan the wedding. And did she really need to do that tonight? Probably not. She'd put it off so long, it felt like it could probably wait a little longer.

"Yes, love," Rhonda said.

But Kylie truly doubted it. After all, she'd gone prom dress shopping with her mother less than a decade before, and she still hadn't recovered from that.

23

The things we do for love.

That was what Linc was thinking as the plane finally touched down. He'd spent an hour waiting for his flight out of Asheville, which included a long security line, then another hour at a layover in busy Charlotte. Now, here he was, at his third airport of the day. He'd have to wait for his luggage, probably have to wait for his car rental too. So, a trip that could've easily been two hours tops? Six hours.

Ridiculous? Yes.

But it was what Kylie wanted, and once she got an idea into her head, nothing could sway her. Didn't matter that if there was a killer on his tail, said killer could have just as easily driven off to Lake Sucession if he really wanted to do away with Linc.

Kylie was happy and comfortable with this arrangement, and that, he felt, was all that mattered.

She was expecting a text.

Knowing her, she was staring at her phone, waiting for it.

He quickly typed in a: *Safe on the ground.* Then another: *How are you?*

As expected, a moment later his phone buzzed. *Fine. Going wedding dress shopping with my mom. Can you believe SHE'S getting married too?*

He smiled. Good news. Although it was a whirlwind romance, he liked Rhonda and got along well with Jerry. The two of them were good for each other. He got the feeling Kylie was a little weirded out about her mother actually being in love, but he knew she was happy for them too.

He replied with a: *Nice. When?*

Valentine's Day

Great news

He thought she was done, but then saw the three dots again, indicating she was adding more. Linc wasn't one to carry on conversations via text, but Kylie never met a text she didn't respond to. But the line at the front of the plane was moving. He'd have to text her later.

Standing, he grabbed his carry-on from the overhead bin and went to the luggage carousel, where he picked up the Glock he had a concealed-carry permit for, all packaged away in its safety case. At the car rental area, he was happy to discover that his car was waiting for him. Twenty minutes later, he was on the road, heading for Lake Sucession.

He'd be staying in one of the few hotels in the small town, but as he checked his watch, he realized he'd probably miss the end of the wake unless he went straight to the funeral parlor.

He pulled in at the parlor and adjusted his suit and tie. It was wrinkled from flying all over the place, and he'd really hoped to make a better impression, considering he'd never met any of Will's family. But…at least he was here.

So were slews of other people. Will was a likable guy, so this came as no surprise. Linc stood in a line that stretched out the door of people waiting to pay their respects to Will. The room was full of mourners. As he slowly inched his way to the front where the smell of flowers grew strong, he heard people murmuring the usual things: "Such a shame," "Good man," "Gone before his time," "Taken too soon." Before he got to the casket, he noticed it was closed.

Relieved, he tried to remember the last time he'd seen Will. Emotion clogged his throat as he realized that he'd never see that cocky little smirk on his face again. His jaw stiffened as he braced himself.

He knelt in front of the casket and said a quick prayer, then turned to face a woman with Will's dark hair and eyes. She was huddled between two strikingly beautiful women. He approached them. "Mrs. Santos?" he said gently.

She looked up. "Yes?"

"I'm sorry for your loss," he murmured, nodding at the rest of the family. "I'm Linc Coulter. I worked with Will during many search and rescue cases."

She took his hand and gave him a watery smile. "Thank you for coming all this way. Will always spoke so fondly of his SAR friends. Were you with him on the night that…?"

"No," Linc finished for her, seeing the pain in her eyes. "I was with him earlier in the day, though."

She shook her head. "It's hard. Hadn't seen him since the summer. He was supposed to come visit soon, but not like this."

He sat with her for a few moments, making small talk with Mrs. Santos and his younger sisters, then excused himself when other family members arrived. He walked out to the lobby and got himself a paper cup of water from the cooler, then another, sucking each one down.

Funerals were like knives to his heart.

As he was pouring out his third one, a man approached him. Linc did a double take. The man looked almost exactly like Will. "Sam?" he nearly spit out.

The guy nodded and shook his hand. "Linc Coulter. Will talked a lot about you. Said you were a legend."

Linc snorted. "Not exactly, but that was very kind of him. He spoke of you often. He was proud as hell of you. You still playing ball at Clemson, right?"

Sam nodded. "This is my senior year. One more semester then I'm heading for my master's."

"You're a running back, right?"

The kid smiled. "Yeah."

"Me too," Linc said. "Duke."

His grin broke wider. "Right! I remember Will telling me that. You were overseas too. Army?"

Linc nodded. They wound up walking together to the end of the hallway, away from the crowds and the somber mood. When they burst out into the light of the afternoon, they found themselves at a service entrance on the side of the building. They launched into a heated conversation about Clemson's chances of making the championship this year.

After a while, the conversation turned to the other thing they had in common: Will.

"He came to my last game, you know. Drove three hours straight after a long day at work just to be there," Sam said, smiling at the thought. "Geez. I can't believe he's gone."

Linc plunged his hands into his pockets and sighed. "Yeah."

Sam Santos reached into his jacket pocket and pulled out a sleeve of Marlboros, offering one on the sly to Linc. When Linc shook his head, he plucked out one and put it between his lips. "You see my mama coming, holler. She doesn't know I do this. I don't, really. Only when I'm under stress. And *dios mio*, this qualifies. Man, *mi mama's* a wreck."

Linc nodded as the kid fumbled with his lighter, then took it from his trembling hands and got the flame going.

Sam sucked in deeply, then exhaled a cloud of smoke. "You don't mind if I do this, do you?"

Linc handed him the lighter. "Nah."

The next time the kid looked up, there were tears in his eyes. "You know what? You're the reason Will stopped drinking. Did he ever tell you that?"

Linc raised an eyebrow. He'd known Will had had a problem with drinking because he'd mentioned his DUI, and he had seen him drunk off his ass quite a few times in the old days. But he didn't know that had changed. "No. I didn't know that he had stopped—"

"Oh. Yeah. You know him. Always up for a party. I think he thought it was his duty to keep everyone having a good time. When he was drinking, he was a really happy drunk. You know that."

Linc laughed. Yes, Will Santos definitely knew how to have a good time. "Yes, I do."

"Well, a few years back, my *mama* was really worried about him," he said, sucking on the end of his cigarette. "This was when he lived at home. He was always coming in, so drunk he could barely stand up straight. Every night. I was in my first year of college then, I guess, but my sisters would tell me stories of how bad he was."

This didn't surprise Linc. This was the Will he knew. Always out for a party, a pretty woman. He'd been quite the hell-raiser. "What happened?"

"Well, I was always on the horn with him, telling him that if he didn't shape up, he was gonna put our mother in an early grave. He didn't listen to me, of course. I was just his stupid younger brother." He shrugged. "But one day, he just stopped."

Linc's eyes snapped to his. "Why?"

"I asked him that too," he said, blowing out another cloud

of smoke. "And he told me he'd been out talking with you, swapping war stories, and you told him about your time overseas. And how you'd been through a lot, but when you finally got help for it, you became a changed man. Whatever you said to him really hit home because he stopped drinking then and there. He didn't even have champagne at my cousin's wedding, man. You inspired him, big time."

"Really?" Linc said. The funny thing was, he could barely recall the conversation in question. He certainly had no idea it'd had such a profound effect on his friend.

Sam's smile dissolved, and he kicked at the curb. "That's why it doesn't make any sense. That he would just drunkenly drive off the road."

Linc crossed his arms. "You don't think what the police are saying is right?"

Linc didn't think it was right either. Blood alcohol couldn't be accurately measured once a person was dead. Due to postmortem fermentation, there could be "false positive" blood alcohol levels up to 0.20 grams, which was nearly two and a half times the legal limit of 0.08 for drivers in Georgia.

"Fuck no," Sam nearly shouted. "No. He'd driven that road a hundred times. And he'd even taken one of those FBI defensive driving classes once, when he'd wanted to become a federal agent. He wasn't a dumb moron who'd overcorrect not to hit a squirrel, like some of the other guys were saying, either. He knew how to handle himself. He'd be the last person to get into an accident like that."

Linc studied him, thinking of Kylie. Oh, Kylie'd love to be here right now. She and Sam could go into their wild theories together of how a murderer was picking off the SAR people one by one. "Why'd he go to the bar then?"

"He always liked going to bars. The atmosphere. The ladies.

You know him. Loved the ladies. He'd have a beer or two, if there was something good on tap, but nothing crazy, just because he liked the taste of a really good, well-made beer. Think he liked testing his sobriety too. If there was nothing good on tap, he'd go and order a rum and coke, hold the rum. That was his big joke."

Linc started to ask if he'd had a relapse when the side door opened. In the doorway stood one of Sam's pretty sisters, glaring at her brother.

Sam quickly threw down his cigarette and stubbed it out with his dress loafer as his sister said, "Samuel, Mama's looking for you. Uncle Lucas is here from Texas."

"Be there in a sec." Sam fanned the cloud of smoke away from his face and gave Linc an apologetic look. He shook his hand again. "Really good of you to come."

Linc was still dwelling on Will's accident. "Wait, Sam. About the accident…if alcohol and user error wasn't involved, what do you think it was?"

Sam shrugged and reached for the door. "Damned if I know, but I'll tell you one thing…it kills my mama every time someone even says the word DUI. She's been through that once before. She doesn't want her oldest son to go down in the books as having lost his life that way. Our family would pay any sort of price to find out."

He went inside, leaving Linc alone. Linc took a little walk around to the front of the building, thought about going back in, but then decided to get in his rental car and go back to the hotel.

The funeral was tomorrow, and after that, he had an afternoon flight.

This had been a sad, sad day, and he needed to connect with Kylie. He lifted out his phone and stared at it, realizing that when she'd indicated she was replying, she actually hadn't replied.

He sent a message to her to tell her he was going back to the hotel, but strangely enough, didn't get yet another reply.

That wasn't like her. Knowing her, she was too busy shopping with her mother to respond. She'd respond soon.

Still, he couldn't wait to get back home.

24

Kylie got home at a little after eight in the evening.

She threw her plastic-wrapped dress over the staircase railing, then went to the recliner in the living room and collapsed on it as the dogs jumped at her feet.

"Three hours, tops" had turned into six, as her mother had tried on every dress in her size at Always Beautiful Bridal Boutique in downtown Asheville. There had to have been at least a thousand. Most brides had some idea of what kind of dress they wanted, but not Rhonda Hatfield. She was open to anything, and the stylist was only too happy to keep shuttling out dress after dress to her. Kylie helped her mother put each one on, and now the tips of her fingers ached from tying corsets and buttoning tiny silk-covered buttons.

And Kylie had tried on…precisely one dress.

The dress she'd immediately fallen in love with despite her mother's objections that she needed to shop around.

She'd seen it on the mannequin and hadn't cared one bit about the tiny little stain on the bodice. It was satiny, form-fitting with a small train, and had absolutely no fluff to it.

The stylist had told her it was a vintage gown from the 1920s.

Kylie had once seen a picture—she forgot where—a long time ago, of a woman in a similar dress. The couple had gotten married in the country, and the man had only worn a relaxed suit. The sun setting behind them had given off the most ethereal light, making Kylie sigh. That was the only wedding picture that had ever had any sort of effect on Kylie, and that bride had always stuck in Kylie's mind.

Her veil had just been a long train of tulle. It had been so romantic, the way the two of them were standing in that field, staring into each other's eyes. Kylie guessed she'd had that photograph in her head when she'd decided to buy the dress.

But now, Kylie wasn't sure if the dress was anything like that picture, or she'd look anything like that bride.

She wasn't sure about a lot of things.

One thing she was sure of? The wedding would be a disaster. With Kylie planning it, she couldn't imagine it being anything else.

Truly, her heart wasn't in the wedding planning. Not like Rhonda's was.

After the shopping, they'd gone out to dinner, but Kylie couldn't stop thinking of Linc. He'd texted her after the wake to tell her he was at the hotel and thinking of getting something to eat and then turning in early. She'd tried to get more out of him about the wake, but he was a notoriously terse texter, so she figured she'd have to wait until the following day to get the rundown.

She looked around the house in the dark, an unsettled feeling coming over her. Only one night here, alone. She could do it. Linc would be back with her in no time.

Still, Kylie poured herself another extra-big glass of wine, just for insurance.

She picked up her phone to tell him she'd gotten a dress but decided not to. Why should she be excited about something she wasn't even sure he'd like?

She just typed in: *Hope you sleep well. I love you and miss you more than I thought was possible.*

She swirled the glass of wine in her hand and took another sip. The wine was already making her feel drowsy. That was just what she needed to dull her senses to the fact that Linc's body wouldn't be next to hers.

And other things…

So many other things.

Besides missing Linc and the wedding woes, and thoughts of a possible killer targeting SAR people running around, she also had her career to think about. Before the shopping excursion from hell, she'd gone into the office to see Greg. But the office had been empty. It looked like it hadn't been open all week. As she peeked in, all those worries about Greg closing up shop and retiring came back to her.

It wasn't as simple as just taking over his business. She didn't have enough experience under her belt yet to get the license to operate on her own. She needed at least six more months of working under Greg to get that. But if he decided to retire, she'd have to find something else. There was no other way around it. Greg had been good, taking her on like that, teaching her all he knew. She imagined that most PIs didn't want to waste the time.

Not only that, she was sad. She, very simply, missed Greg. She missed his grumpiness.

Her sigh turned to a smile when Linc texted back. *You too. I love you.*

She responded with a good night, then closed out of the message and went to her Facebook. Dina's Facebook page still hadn't been updated, and she still hadn't read any of Kylie's messages. She'd said it would take two days to drive across the country. If she didn't respond by tonight, Kylie decided that she'd call someone in the morning. Find her family. Call the police. Something.

Kylie didn't even make it up to the bedroom. She fell asleep on the chair with the wine glass in her hand, having consumed about three glasses in an hour, way more than she was used to.

When she woke up, a strong light was slashing through the blinds. It felt like she'd been laying in this position for a hundred hours. The second her eyes flickered open, she had an unsettling feeling that something was totally off. She couldn't pinpoint what it was. She blinked, then felt something wet on her shirt.

"Shit!" she said, jumping up as she realized a large puddle of red wine was seeping into her favorite sweatshirt. The dogs started to bark. She grabbed a nearby napkin and dabbed at it as the wine ran down her legs, then let out a big groan. "Perfect."

She tripped over Vader as she rushed to the kitchen, grabbed some paper towels, and swabbed up the mess. As she did, she knocked over the glass, and it shattered all over the floor. "Gah!" she shouted, picking up the large pieces in her hand and carefully stepping through the minefield that she'd turned their living room into. She grabbed the vacuum and managed to clean it up, still half-asleep.

It was only when she finished that she realized she had a massive hangover.

She went into the bathroom and popped some Excedrin. When she came out, the dogs were both looking at her like, *Wow, you really can't handle yourself without Linc, can you?*

She muttered, "Exactly. Don't give me that look. Like you guys are much better without each other, Mr. Peanut Butter and Miss Jelly, over there?"

They gave her equally innocent looks.

Shaking her head, she let them out to go use the potty, and as she did, her eyes drifted to the garment bag with her wedding dress still hanging on the banister. Kylie's stomach sank. The more she thought about it, the more she was sure she'd look nothing like that photograph she'd once seen.

She decided she'd have to take the bag upstairs and stuff it deep into the closet, where Linc would never see it. As she was heading up there, thinking of Linc and wondering if he'd made out just as terribly as she had last night, it struck her. She must've been drunk. When was the last time she'd woken up and *not* grabbed for her phone first thing?

She'd also left it down in the living room. Hell, when was the last time she'd left the room without it?

Dropping her dress on the landing, she rushed back downstairs, finding it on the coffee table, right next to Linc's latest issue of *Wilderness SAR* magazine. She lifted her cell and eagerly unlocked it.

The first thing she saw was the time. It was after noon. How did that happen? When had she ever zonked out like that?

The second thing she saw was a message from Linc: *And how did my beautiful girl sleep?*

She smiled and typed in: *Are you talking about Storm?*

A moment later: *No, YOU are my beautiful girl.* Then: *Heading to the funeral now. Can't wait to see you tonight. Flight's at five so I should be in by bedtime. I'll take an Uber so I don't disturb you.*

She found herself grinning goofily at the display as she tried to think of something to tell him. She didn't want to talk about the wedding plans, or the fact that the only reason she was able to sleep was because she'd gotten herself drunk. So she just said: *I love you.*

As expected, he didn't respond.

The Excedrin had begun to kick in, so she went upstairs

to take a shower. As she was climbing into the old clawfoot tub, she remembered something else. She hadn't had a response from Dina, and she'd promised she'd address the matter this morning if she hadn't heard from her.

She quickly showered and wrapped herself in a towel, then picked up her phone again. Sure enough, there was no message from Dina.

Kylie crawled onto the bed and flopped down on her stomach, trying to decide who she should call. She looked up the name *Avery* in California, but there were too many entries, so she wasn't sure if any of them were relatives of Dina's.

Finally, she just decided to call the police in Tallulah Falls, since she knew that was where Dina lived. When she did, an operator answered. "Tallulah Falls Police. How may I direct your call?"

"Yes. I'm out of town and looking to see if someone could do a well-check on one of your residents?" she said, studying her fingernails, frowning. If she was going to get married, she really had to stop chewing them like that. "I've been trying to get in touch with her for two days, and so far, no response."

"Certainly, who is calling?"

"My name is Kylie Hatfield."

"Okay, Miss Hatfield. And the resident you've been trying to contact?"

"Her name is Dina Avery. I'm not exactly sure where she lives."

"One moment. I'll connect you with an officer who should be able to help you."

"Thank you," Kylie said, looking around the room. As she did, Vader came in and leapt onto the bed. She patted his side.

"Miss Hatfield?" a voice suddenly said. It sounded like a very young male.

"Yes?"

"I hear you're looking for a Dina Avery, is that correct?"

"Yes."

"How do you know her?"

Kylie frowned. "I don't know her well." How did she explain her spidey sense without sounding insane? "It's a long story, but—"

The officer cleared his throat. "When was the last time you spoke with her?"

Kylie rolled over and looked at the ceiling. "Two days ago. She was driving to her family's home in California. I know it's strange, she's probably fine and just busy with family, but I've been sending her messages via social media and haven't heard anything, so I was getting worried."

"Did you have any reason to believe she could be in trouble?"

She sat up. "Well…" She didn't really want to have to go into the whole thing about how she was working with SAR, and all the mysterious deaths and disappearances that had been happening lately. "I just had a feeling that—"

"Dina Avery's Jeep was found outside her house in the middle of the street. Parked but still running. Her dog was inside, but she's been missing since then, and we have no leads. If you can give us some help…"

Kylie absently shoved her thumb in her mouth and ripped a nail off jaggedly. "When was this?"

But she already knew.

"That was two days ago. She's been listed as a missing person since then, Miss Hatfield. Is there any information you can give to us regarding her disappearance?"

Disappearance. Dina had disappeared.

Dina. Had. Disappeared.

That was four out of five. The only one left, the last man standing, was...

Oh my god.

Kylie sat up so quickly that her head began to swim. Her hands were shaking, and there was a red, bloody gash right above her thumbnail. She sucked on it.

"I do...I mean, she was part of a SAR team that I was on...and..."

The words came out in an incoherent jumble. She couldn't even be sure she was speaking English. Every pore on her body was now one raging goose bump.

She wanted Linc. Badly.

She needed him. Needed to warn him. Needed to get to him, somehow.

Call him. He needs to know this.

"Miss, are you still there?" the officer asked.

"I'm sorry. I have to go," she said, hanging up and quickly punching in a call to Linc. She'd get in touch with them and give them details later.

The phone rang right to voicemail.

Right. The funeral.

Hi, it's Linc, I'm busy at the moment. You know what to do.

She wasn't used to leaving voicemail messages, but right then, she was desperate. The second she heard the beep, she exploded with, "It's me! Please call me as soon as you can!" and hung up. Then she sent him a text saying the same thing, just for added insurance.

She looked around, feeling chilled to the bone, then her eyes fell on herself. Well, that made sense. She was naked, her hair was wet, and it was November. Linc always managed the heat in the house, keeping the place toasty warm, and she didn't have a clue even *where* the thermostat was. No wonder it was freezing in the house. She ran to her dresser and grabbed some jeans and a t-shirt, slipping them on.

She had to get to Linc.

She had no doubt now that someone had to be targeting the SAR people. Someone who'd worked with them before, or perhaps a previous case? Yes, that made sense. A previous case that went badly.

She opened her phone and sent him another text as a thought hit her.

Running into the spare bedroom, she pulled open the filing cabinet that housed all his cases. She'd been going through the files, but she did so now with renewed vigor.

There were hundreds upon hundreds of files in the five-drawer cabinet, all with tabs neatly labeled at the top. Most of them were for locales in the Pisgah National Forest up near Asheville. Then she found a file that said, *Georgia/Tennessee US.* It had numerous files in it, all arranged by date, it seemed.

Kylie quickly pulled out the first stack and started to go through it. She found the case of a female hiker in the Great Smoky Mountains in Tennessee that had taken the better part of a week to find. There was a resident from a nursing home who suffered from Alzheimer's and had wandered into the forest in South Carolina. A couple of siblings who'd run away from home around the vicinity of Black Rock Mountain State Park in Georgia.

She read through each of them, not finding anything to tie them to the location of Tallulah Gorge. As she paged through, she saw that in each of these cases, the missing person or persons were located without incident.

But something was wrong.

If this file included all of the cases that he'd performed in the Southern US, then it should've contained the case of the escaped prisoners from Arrendale.

Kylie went through it again. And again, thinking she might have missed it.

No. It was most definitely not there.

Was this really all of his cases? Or did he keep some of them someplace else? Maybe he didn't keep files on all of the cases he did.

That didn't seem like Linc. Linc was methodical, thorough, exacting. He did things one way and stuck to it. He was ex-military, after all.

So where was the damn case?

Her eyes went to her phone. He definitely must've had it turned off, the jerk. He was always so careful about being courteous.

Dammit. Damn his courtesy, she needed to get in touch with him now!

How long did a funeral usually take, anyway? And when was his flight back? She grabbed her phone and sent him a few more texts.

Feeling helpless, she slumped against the foot of the bed and paged through a few more, when suddenly, Vader poked his head around the corner of the bed and stuck his wet muzzle in her ear, as if to say, *Hi, remember me? Your faithful companion WHO HAS NOT YET EATEN ALL DAY?*

"Easy, boy, just give me five more minutes," she said, nudging him away. But then, as usual, he captured her with his big, sad eyes. She gave him a pout in return. "Oh, I know what you want. I'm sorry I haven't fed you guys, but this is kind of life or death."

Vader gave her a look like, *Well, so is feeding us, dude.*

She cursed her forgetfulness. It was well past midday. Linc probably would never forgive her for starving his baby, Storm, like that. She was a bad mama. Linc wanted to marry her, why, again?

She got to her knees and climbed to her feet, dusting off the back of her jeans.

As she started to turn toward the bedroom door, she saw it, out of the corner of her eye.

It was a folder in the very back of the drawer. The only thing written on the tab was a thick, black mark.

She lifted it up.

There were only a few cases inside.

When she opened it, she immediately saw the photographs of three very mean-looking women staring back at her. Mug shots.

She flipped a page and caught the word *Arrendale.*

Here it was. The prison inmate search file.

Sure enough, she caught the names of the other SAR rescuers: *Lincoln Coulter, Dina Avery, Beatrice Crosby, Will Santos, and Kevin Friedman.*

Scanning down the rest of the page, she read a brief bio on each of the inmates. The first two were listed as *safe* while the third woman was marked as *deceased.*

Vader had begun to nose her toward the bedroom door in earnest, but Kylie simply couldn't tear herself away. She felt like she was so close, she couldn't back away now. That spidey sense of hers was giving her all kinds of warnings.

"One second. I promise!" she said to him, fending him off.

She paged through the file folder, finding some more cases. And as she did, the taste of old wine in her mouth turned bitter, and she had the sinking feeling she knew exactly what she'd stumbled upon.

This was the file of Linc's cases where at least some of the subjects had not come out of the search alive.

25

It was a myth that in order for a funeral to be really sad, it had to involve a torrential downpour.

The sky over Lake Secession was without a cloud when they laid Will Santos and Star to rest, and though Linc had been through his share of heartbreak, he didn't think he'd ever witnessed a scene quite so morose.

There were photos of Will with Star during happier times. Star as a puppy. Will and Star standing at the top of Devil's Pulpit. Will in his cap and gown from Clemson, with Star on a leash beside him, wearing his own little cap. Star's leash and orange SAR vest hung from the memorial. A couple other rescue people had shown up with their dogs, and all the dogs laid down at the grave, seeming to know they were saying goodbye to one of their friends.

And then there was Will's family. His mother cried loudly throughout the priest's speech, and even his normally stoic father's shoulders shook from the grief of his sobs. Linc wasn't one to cry, but even he felt the ends of his heartstrings being tugged, almost past the breaking point.

Linc watched as the casket was lowered into the

ground, wiping the sweat from his forehead with a hand-kerchief as the warm autumn sun beat down upon the scene. He pulled on the collar of his shirt, fighting suffocation as he stood, shoulder to shoulder, with hundreds of other onlookers.

Then, it was time to pass the casket and say one final goodbye. He waited for at least an hour for his turn, then proceeded up to the casket, and nodded one last time at his friend.

After that was done, he paid his final respects to Santos' parents, then started to walk to his car, which he'd parked on the street in the cemetery among those belonging to a long line of mourners. As he did, pulling on his tie to loosen it, dying to get out of this monkey suit, someone clapped him on the back.

It was Sam Santos, Will's younger brother. The two men shook hands. "You heading to the house, Linc? We're having some people over for food. Come join us."

"Can't. I already told your parents that I've got a five o'clock flight I'll already be cutting close to make." He reached into his pocket and turned on his phone, which he'd silenced. It took a moment to power up. He put a hand on this kid's arm in a brotherly way. "You do good at Clemson. I'll be watching. If you need anything from me, Sam, don't hesitate to ask. Okay?"

Sam nodded. "You have a safe trip. It was good of you to come all this way."

"Wouldn't have missed it. Your brother was one of the best," Linc said honestly as his phone finished powering up. He stared at the display. He had...what? An actual voicemail from Kylie? Since when did she leave him voicemails?

He waved goodbye to Sam and continued to his car, looking down at his phone.

He pressed on the voicemail icon and immediately heard

her panicked voice: "It's me! Please call me as soon as you can!"

A glimmer of worry struck him, but it didn't capture him completely. Kylie was known to get completely carried away at times. She used a similar tone when she couldn't get Vader to follow her commands. Maybe he was just being a bad boy without Linc there. He always seemed to misbehave when Linc wasn't around, and he thought he could take over as the alpha of the house.

He started to put in a call to her when he realized he also had a number of texts from her. Twelve, to be exact.

That was bizarre. Yes, she was a textaholic for sure. But twelve? That was pushing it, even for her.

He opened the messages as he finally made it across the green to his rental car. Sliding behind the steering wheel, he read the last one:

PLEASE. I'M SO WORRIED.

Whoa. He needed to back up.

He scrolled up to the first message she'd sent, after the "I love you" she'd sent him before he'd gone into the funeral. He started from there.

Call me as soon as you get this.

Dina's car has been found with Ghost inside. It was abandoned. She never went to California. She's missing.

Now, do you believe me that someone is going after SAR people? Please call me.

Linc. Call me.

I'm worried.

I think it may be one of the cases you all worked on together so I'm going through your files.

I don't know. I can't find anything yet. Just call me. Let me know you're okay.

?

??

???

PLEASE. I'M SO WORRIED.

Jesus. It was almost too much for his eyes to take in. For a good ten seconds, he just stared at the screen. Holy shit. Dina, missing?

He looked up. Looked around, noticing things around him he hadn't noticed before. Had that old van always been there? Who was that suspicious guy smoking near the mausoleum? For the first time, something thick and constricting wrapped around him. Try as he could to shake it off, it only wormed its way tighter, pressing against his chest.

He'd made fun of Kylie's weird theories, but he had to admit, there was definitely some merit to them. Especially now that he was the last man standing.

Right now, he imagined Kylie sitting at the kitchen island, going through all his cases with a fine-tooth comb, trying to find something that connected the five of them. She'd been so wrapped up in the prison inmate case, but he'd thought that was a long shot.

He hadn't wanted to tell her then, because he knew how her mind inflated things, but there were other cases she knew nothing about that could be more likely.

As he sat in the car, he mentally sifted through those other cases. Cases that had happened in the vicinity of Tallulah Gorge. Cases that hadn't had happy endings. The team had never done any cases together in Tallulah Gorge before Beez, so his mind wandered to other locations nearby, in Georgia. He hadn't done a whole lot of those, and most of them, the subject had been found safe.

Funny, he'd had many more successes than failures. About ninety-five percent of his endeavors had ended happily, with no loss to life nor limb. But it was those few failures that always managed to stick in his head.

The Smithgall Woods State Park case was pretty much

cemented in the front of his mind and had been there for the past twenty-two months.

Smithgall Woods State Park was located in Helen, Georgia, about thirty miles away from Tallulah Gorge. Linc had gotten the call one evening that a girl scout junior—only nine years old—had gotten separated from her troop during a camping trip. The troop leader reported that they'd gone on a hike, and the girl had somehow disappeared during the easy one mile walk from their campsite to the visitor's center.

The sun had been setting when Linc got the call, but he and Storm hopped in the truck immediately and made the two-hour drive down to the park. When they'd gotten there, it was dark, and it had started to pour, so the search was difficult.

To all of their dismay, they'd eventually been forced to call it off when Beez's dog and Kevin nearly killed themselves navigating some of the steeper trails in the slippery mud. The fact was, the park was small, and none of them, except Beez, had been very well-versed in the terrain. One SAR, who was supposed to be an expert on the trails, hadn't been able to make it due to illness.

They'd waited in the ranger's station, drinking coffee and twiddling their thumbs until daylight broke and the sky cleared. That kind of inaction, when he knew someone was suffering, was the worst. Especially a little kid, so helpless and scared. He hated being powerless like that. So the second the sun came up, they went out again, looking for the little girl.

Jill. That was her name.

Pretty little girl. Big thick glasses that amplified her big blue eyes. Freckles. He'd tried to avoid looking at the pictures of her that had been plastered all over the news afterward. It was too damn haunting.

Linc had found her little body, pale and motionless in a swollen, stagnant pond beneath a steep cliff. She was still wearing her little green vest with all its carefully sewn-on badges. Sometime during the dark of night, while wandering and trying to find her way back to the camp, she'd slipped on the path, fell from the cliff, and broken her neck when she landed in shallow water.

Linc swallowed the bitter taste in his mouth as he recalled it. It was one of those cases he'd worked hard to block out. She'd been such a little, helpless child. Every time he thought of it, his chest ached as he imagined just how frightened and alone she must've been during her last moments.

Even now, the thought tore him up from the inside. He closed his mouth and fought the urge to gag.

How long ago was that? Maybe it was more than twenty-two months. Not one of his brightest moments in SAR. Certainly, one he didn't care to relive. In fact, it was one that made him question why he didn't just go and get a boring desk job. Become a blood-sucking lawyer like his father and brothers. Losing an adult was painful enough, but a kid? Those losses were definitely the most agonizing. He hadn't had many, but they stuck with him hard, haunting him sometimes, just like Syria did.

He flashed back to the parents. Small, frail couple made smaller by the loss of their child. He'd had to break the news to them, and they'd been beside themselves with grief. They'd fallen down into a huddle and screamed their daughter's name, again and again. Every time they said it, "Jill, Jill, Jill," it was like an arrow to his heart.

Could one of them be holding a grudge?

No. They'd been distraught, but even in their profound grief, they'd thanked the team for everything they'd done. They'd been grateful. The whole team had shown up at the funeral, and the parents had been glad that they were there to express their sympathies. Now, *that* had been a sad funeral. Sunny, too, he remembered.

But time had a way of changing things. And now, he knew not to dismiss Kylie and her theories so easily. So, possibly...

He looked up, feeling like a sitting duck staying still like this. He started up the rental car, wondering if he was being watched from afar. From what he was able to hypothesize, both Will and Dina had been followed while in their cars.

He engaged the locks, just in case, and punched in a call to Kylie.

As it started to ring, another call came through. He went to put that one to voicemail when the name appeared on his screen.

Holy shit.

It was Dina Avery.

He ended the call to Kylie. He had to. This was one call he definitely had to take.

26

Kylie grabbed the "dead" folder, as she called it, and rushed downstairs, the two dogs at her heels.

Didn't matter how important her research was. She couldn't put this off any longer. The dogs had all but turned on her and were about to eat her alive.

"Okay, okay, guys," she said to them, pretty sure they were conspiring against her. "I'm delivering."

She went into the bin under the kitchen cabinets and brought out their bag of dog food. She gave them each two healthy scoops in their bowls. They dug in at once, like hungry wolves devouring their prey.

"Go ahead, pigs," she muttered, changing out their water bowls.

Once she'd done that, she headed to the barn to take care of the other chores before all the animals gathered together to lynch her. She was especially careful around the llamas, who looked like they were close to taking her head off with great big balls of spit.

Back in the house, she settled on a stool at the island with the file open in front of her.

Linc was fortunate, really. Of all the cases he'd been on, relatively few had ended up with the subject being deceased. There was a reason the SAR community called Linc the best in the business.

She felt a surge of pride for him as she flipped away from the file with the prison inmates. That one didn't really even count. He'd located them as required; it was the inmate's own fault for pulling the gun on the police officer.

She swallowed as she looked at the next case. It was for an inexperienced solo hiker on the Appalachian Trail. Found dead from hypothermia after wandering off the trail. The profile photo was that of a grandmotherly woman.

Kylie's heart ached. Knowing Linc, he probably took every one of these deaths personally. Hell, he probably even felt guilty about the inmate. That was him. He was just so *good,* so selfless. Wired to be the hero, every single time, as unrealistic as that was.

Because really, no one, not even Superman, was the hero *every* time.

Her eyes went to her phone. No text or call from him.

That seriously had to have been the longest funeral in the history of funerals. What were they doing over there? Burying him twice?

She felt guilty, thinking something so bad about a good man like Will. But god, this was driving her crazy. Where was Linc, and why hadn't he called her yet?

What if the killer had gotten to him already? What if he was already dead?

She shook those thoughts away, lifted up the phone, and sent him another text. This time, in all caps. That made an even twelve. Then she told herself that she wouldn't send him another text, even if she had to chop her thumbs off.

She read a little more about the grandmother who'd died, then lost interest when she realized it had happened north of

Asheville, in Pisgah. If she was looking for a killer, she expected the murderer to have some connection to the Tallulah Gorge area.

She flipped through the next few—another in North Carolina, two in Tennessee. All very sad cases. One of a pretty woman with a perfect smile who'd disappeared while hiking with her new husband, another of an autistic teenager who'd wandered away from his family during a camping trip. She paged through them, sickness blooming in her stomach.

So much death. And she hadn't even been a part of the SAR crew for these.

She flipped the page and froze when she came to the picture of a tiny young girl in a pink unicorn sweatshirt, with thick glasses, bright blue eyes, freckles, and stringy red hair.

Kylie's heart squeezed at the sight of such a vivacious little girl with the wide smile and the two missing eye teeth, in this file...this file of death.

Jill Peck. That was her name.

Kylie stared at the picture, wondering why it was that Linc had never mentioned this child. It had to have been one of his more memorable cases. Just glancing at the beautiful, innocent face of the little girl, Kylie felt hard-pressed to forget little Jill. In fact, she knew she'd probably dream of her at night.

She read the location. Someplace called Smithgall Woods State Park in Helen, Georgia. She wasn't quite sure where that was, so she picked up her phone and searched for it on her maps app. It was in the northeast corner of Georgia, just like Tallulah Gorge. Not more than thirty miles away.

She read the names of the SAR team. Linc Coulter, Dina Avery, Will Santos, Kevin Friedman, and Beez Crosby.

The fabulous five. The same five who were now all either dead or injured.

All except for Linc.

Her spidey sense leapt into overdrive. *This is it, this is it, this is it,* it seemed to whisper to her.

Kylie shifted on her seat, hugging herself, reading on, her eyes quickly absorbing all the information. The little girl, Jill, had been on a scouting trip and had gotten separated from her troop. She read the account, written in Linc's own words, her heart tightening as she imagined him trying to put the heart-wrenching details down on paper:

Arrived at SWSP after 2200 hours. Met with DA, WS, KF, and BC for briefing. Regular SAR familiar with terrain unable to make it to site due to illness, received briefing from ranger instead. Heavy downpours in the area. Ranger stated most trails would be unsafe and to use extreme caution. Upon studying map, advised BC to take VCT, DA to take ACT, WS to take MMT, and KF to take CET, I took LRT. Set out at 2245.

Visibility poor. Fog and rain. Upon radio calls from BC and KF indicating difficulties navigating trails and extreme dangers pulled back SAR team. Advised to begin search at 0600 hours.

Set out at 0600 hours, same trails as above. Approximately 1.2 MM of LRT Storm located scent. Followed to a steep drop-off. Upon looking over the edge of the drop found subject facedown, submerged in pond. Efforts to resuscitate were attempted but failed. Time 0632.

Kylie looked up, tears clouding her eyes. Linc had been through a lot, but she knew, without a doubt, that this would have been the most difficult thing that he'd ever gone through. Linc loved kids. During family get-togethers, he loved playing with his nieces and nephews so much more than he cared to converse with the adults. Everywhere they went, he always seemed to gravitate to the dogs and the kids…and they to him.

It suddenly hit her, why he never talked about it. It was why he never talked about his time in Syria, until she'd dragged it out of him. It was just too hard. Linc buried the things that hurt him the most.

She wiped at her eyes as Vader nudged her knee, sensing her pain. She patted him gently, noticing the two dogs had handily finished all of their food. She reached into a drawer and tossed them each a couple of treats.

Then she looked back at the poor little girl. Jill Peck looked back at her with those big blue eyes. What a tiny, innocent little thing. Only nine years old.

Her death had doubtlessly been painful to so many people. Not just Linc.

Was this the case that all the other murders hinged on? If so…who was responsible?

She turned the page, reading on about the parents, who'd been notified of the death. They'd both been understandably distraught. Was one of them the culprit?

Grabbing her phone, she quickly typed in the words: *Jill Peck death GA*

The first thing she saw was an article from a year after the case. It mentioned the suicide of John Peck, the father of Jill Peck. He'd died from a single gunshot wound to the head. Kylie read on and saw a quote from a neighbor: *He never was the same after the death of his little girl.*

Kylie wiped a tear from her eye.

Then she typed in: *Jill Peck obituary GA*

The first result was from a local funeral home in Helen, GA. She quickly opened it and scanned the names of her relatives: *Mother, Anna Law Peck, father, John Peck, loving brother, Tanner Peck, paternal grandmother, Violet…*

Kylie froze. Tanner Peck. Now, why did that name sound so familiar? Not only that, why did it seem to have a very strong connection to the Tallulah Gorge area?

She vised her head in her hands, trying to think. Slowly, it came to her. That first day they'd arrived at Tallulah Gorge

State Park. It was pouring out, and that young, barely legal looking park ranger with the acne scars had been there. He'd said he was new to the place, thanked them for coming out, and had given them maps…

The hair raised on the back of Kylie's neck.

And he was a killer.

Kylie jumped straight up, knocking into the low-hanging lamp with her forehead, making both dogs jump too. "Oh my god!" she said aloud, ignoring the pain screaming through the sore spot on her hairline. "Of course! Jill Peck's brother is a ranger at Tallulah Gorge State Park."

She grabbed for her phone, not sure who she was going to call—the police or the ranger's office—when it began to ring in her hands. Her heart leapt when Linc's name popped up on the display.

She couldn't pick it up fast enough. "Linc!"

"Yeah, it's me," he said quickly. "Listen."

She heard the rush of air in the background and guessed he must've been driving somewhere.

"No! You have to listen! I found something out!" she said, looking at the clock on the microwave. It was after seven by now, and the sun was sinking down. It suddenly hit her as he began to talk over her that his flight wasn't even supposed to land until eight. "Wait, why are you not on your flight? Did it get in early?"

"That's what I'm trying to tell you. I'm driving the rental. To Tallulah Gorge."

Her mouth opened. That was the absolute last place she wanted him to be. "The gorge? Why? No!"

"Listen to me. I got a call from Dina. She's in trouble. I need to get there right away."

"What? How do you know you're not walking into a trap?" Her heart was pounding in her chest. "You can't go there, Linc! It's not safe. I know who's doing this! That little girl, the scout. Jill Peck. Her brother is Tanner Peck, the ranger at the park. He's going to kill you and Dina."

A pause. "Well, then, I guarantee I am walking into a trap."

"Linc," she begged. "Don't do this. You can't—"

"I have to." He sounded remarkably calm. "I'm not just going to let Dina die."

She knew that about him. In his mind, better they both die than for his fellow SAR to die and Linc do absolutely nothing. "If you are going there, I'm going too!"

"Hell no. Did you hear me, Kylie? Hell. No. And I mean it. You stay put. And don't call the police. She said that if anyone else shows up, he'll kill her. So just let me do this alone. All right? I'll call you when I can."

"No!" Kylie shouted. "No! This is crazy. Please, Linc. Don't go. Please, just come home to me. Please."

"I can't, Kylie. Just...remember," he said, his voice shifting from calm to strained. "I love you."

And then he hung up.

Kylie stood up and screamed at the phone, stunned by what he'd just said. No. This couldn't be happening. She grabbed hold of it and called him, but it went right to voice-mail. She dialed again. Voicemail again. Voicemail, voicemail, voicemail, for each one of the ten times she called afterward.

Slamming the phone on the counter, she gave it the finger. "You bastard!" she screamed.

Then she sank down onto the stool and started to sob.

Vader came by a moment later and laid his head on her knee. A second after that, Storm came and did the same thing. Peanut butter and jelly.

She looked up. "You're exactly right, you guys. I don't care what he says. Peanut butter without jelly is pretty useless."

And she jumped up and ran for her car keys.

27

Slipping his tie from around his collar, Linc made it to the park at a little after nine. Didn't matter that the park had closed at 8:30, and now, it was deserted. Clouds covered the moon, threatening rain.

He had a flashback to that dark, hopeless night, looking for Jill, and quickly squelched it.

Night searches were not his favorite thing, especially considering all the death this park had seen lately. Not to mention that the thick foliage made it sometimes look like night, even in the day. It was damn dark. The headlights of Linc's rental car, cutting through the blackness, felt like the only lights for miles.

And in his rental car, he didn't have a flashlight.

On a trail, like this, in the dark of night? This could be a problem.

There was a metal gate across the main road into the park, with a sign that said *Park Closes at Sunset.* Linc stopped there, recalling the phone call he'd had with Dina. She wasn't one to wear her emotions on her sleeve, but this ordeal had gotten the better of her. Dina had been sobbing.

"Come to the bridge or he'll kill me. Bring no one else. Please!"

"The bridge?" he'd said, having a good idea of which bridge she meant. There was a slim suspension bridge on the Hurricane Falls Trail Loop at Tallulah Gorge. He'd wanted to stall for time so he could make sure he understood what he needed to do.

"Yes! Please hurry! He's going to kill me!"

"I'm in South Carolina right now. It'll take me—"

Dina screamed, and a rustling sound came over the line before a male voice. "Listen, asshole. You'd better drive ninety the whole way. Get here now, or I'll slit her throat. You understand? I left the door open for you."

And then he hung up.

Linc pulled to the side of the road and got out quickly, checking to make sure no one was coming. He went to the gate and tested it. Sure enough, though it was closed, it hadn't been padlocked. He pushed it open and went to the back of the car, taking out his knife, which he slipped into the pocket of his slacks, before loading his Glock. He hopped back into the car, put the gun on the passenger seat, continuing down the winding road to the visitor's center.

When he pulled into the parking lot near the North Rim trailhead, he saw one vehicle there—appropriately, a white serial-killer van. He tore open the glove compartment and found a small flashlight. He turned it on and tested the light. It emitted only a dim gray glow. Pretty useless.

He reached over and took his gun. As he opened the door, the clouds overhead parted, and a full November moon lit the way.

It felt like a miracle.

He just hoped that miracle would last for the next hour, so he could find his way down to the bridge. A glance at the night sky was evidence that his miracle probably wouldn't be happening tonight. But he'd take advantage of the moments of moonlight as they came.

He jumped out of the car, popped the trunk, and pulled his hiking boots out of his bag, glad he'd brought them with him. Slipping out of his dress shoes, he stepped into the comfort of his boots. At least he had those. He rolled up the cuffs on his dress shirt and hurried for the trail, holding the gun in both hands as he made his way across the uneven terrain.

Two thousand. That's how many steps he'd have to take down to the suspension bridge overlooking Hurricane Falls.

A nice hike, in the day. He'd done it many times before.

But as he thought of his conversation with Kylie, his chest tightened. She was right. It was a trap. Tanner Peck, the ranger from the station, was obviously holding a grudge against them. And he didn't just want Dina's blood. He wanted Linc's too.

So walking down into the gorge right now, unarmed, in absolute blackness? It felt like a death sentence.

He tried to concentrate on the job at hand—one step at a time, that's what his therapist said. *Don't get too far ahead of yourself. Take it little by little.* Making sure Dina was safe. That was step one.

But his thoughts kept going to Kylie. How frantic she'd been on the phone.

He didn't trust her to stay home, no matter what he said.

Knowing her, she was on her way here, right now.

Then he thought of Storm. His other girl. Couldn't have asked for a better companion for all the shit he'd been through.

He knew what he'd said. And he meant it. Better that Kylie and Storm stayed safe.

But still, it would've been nice to see them again, just one more time.

KYLIE LOOKED in her rearview mirror at Storm as she drove her bright yellow Jeep like a bat out of hell down the rural streets of Georgia, heading for Linc.

"Okay, yes," she said in response to Storm's reproachful glare. "I know this is ignoring a direct order from an army officer. *But...*I am not in the army, so it's fine."

Storm whimpered at her.

"Oh, who are you kidding?" she said to the dog. "You want to go help your man too. What? You want me to go faster? Good."

She pushed on the gas, and the powerful vehicle surged ahead.

Making light of it and joking with her pups was the only way that Kylie could stop her teeth from chattering. She kept thinking of the way Linc had sounded. He had been remark-ably calm, like he'd already been resigned to his fate.

Hell no. She refused to lose him now.

She was not going to just sit at home and sob and wonder what was going on. This was *their* case, together. She was in it as much as he was. And she refused to let him down.

She checked her GPS on the way, discovering he actually had a shorter drive from Lake Sucession than she had from Asheville, but she hoped that by putting the pedal to the metal, she could get there around the same time. When she reached the welcome sign for Tallulah Gorge State Park, she saw that the gate, which had a sign that said *Park Closes at Sunset,* was open.

She'd parked at a couple of lots in the place, but wasn't sure exactly which one Linc had gone to. The first one she came to was the South Rim parking lot, and because that was the easy trail they'd done that first time when they'd been looking for Beez, she decided to take that one.

She grabbed her flashlight and backpack from the floor of the car, and as she was sitting up, her lights illuminated the NO DOGS sign.

That made sense. The park had an awful lot of steps and steep inclines, too difficult for an ordinary dog to manage. Storm would have no problem, but...

She looked back at Vader. Oh, he would howl. And moan. And complain. And she probably could kiss her headrests goodbye.

But it'd be for her own safety. She couldn't manage two dogs on the trail, that was for sure. "I'm sorry, boy," she said, giving him a quick hug.

She clipped the leash onto Storm's collar, led her out of the car, and closed the door, trying to ignore the mournful howl and bark that Vader let out as she led his best friend toward the trailhead.

"Come on, Storm," she said to the dog, giving her Linc's hat to sniff. "Find. Let's go find your master."

28

Linc Coulter thought he was something special, didn't he, Jill?

Just like Dina Avery, Mr. Lincoln Coulter lived a façade of a life too.

On the surface, he was strong and brave, but I knew—and *you* knew most of all—that he was a coward underneath.

He'd been given all kinds of awards, been asked to talk and teach at all kinds of seminars. One of the dumbass newspapers actually called him the best rescue guy in the business, or some shit like that. The way he strutted about with his dirty mutt clearly meant he thought a lot of himself.

And I was here to bring him down a peg or two.

I couldn't wait. Jill, you'd be proud of me.

All the others had been fine. Too easy, actually. Except Kevin. Well, he was a blip. He should've died, but my arrow missed his heart by a millimeter at most. With any luck, he'd die of sepsis one day. But the others? They weren't even a challenge. Almost too easy.

Sure, the first one had gotten my heart rate pumping. For a moment I had wondered if I could actually do it. Could I fulfill my promise of making them pay? Could I actually step up to the plate and end another person's life like they did yours?

I still feel a little bad for pushing that lovesick suicide jumper. The bastard had chickened out and was backing away from the cliff's edge when I gave him a little nudge. In the long run, I think I saved him a lot of pain, though. He was probably grateful that I could do what he could not.

Beez was totally different. When I shoved her, the pure adrenaline and joy that surged through me was unlike anything I'd ever felt before.

And then you know how I felt, Jill?

I felt like God.

Like I could do nothing wrong.

Over the hours and days that followed, I waited for that feeling to wear off. To feel something like guilt take its place.

I should have, I know. I took away a life. I ended that little granny's life and took away everything she had on this earth. I should've felt something. But you know what I felt?

I felt glad. Happy. Like I'd done this world a favor.

And after that? It got easier.

Amy? What was she? A sad girl searching for a purpose. What she really needed was to stop being a little slut and sleeping with her professor to get her grades up. Okay, I didn't know about that at the time. Hell, I didn't even know of her existence until she showed up at my station that morning, bright and early, before anyone else had come out.

The shy little thing wanted a permit for the Sliding Rock Trail. I'd flirted with her, told her that she could get hurt on a trail like that, but she'd told me she could handle herself. She told me how she needed to prove to herself that she could do it. She told me everything.

Sleeping with her professor? That was when I knew for sure that she needed to be put out of her misery.

She'd been so easy to follow. So easy to sneak up on. One hit and she was down. Rock meets head, easy as cracking an egg. She didn't even see it coming, which was probably the only thing I regretted.

I wished I could have told her why she had to die and let her know her death wasn't in vain. That she was bait being used to take out the cowards of the world.

Kevin? His little snot-nosed kids would probably be better off without him. Maybe it'd help them grow a set of balls. When I'd gone to the hospital to see if I could end him, the way they cried and clung to their mother made me sick, especially the one who looked like he was your age.

Bet you hadn't cried.

Bet you would have been brave.

I closed my eyes, trying to force the image of your face away. Not the smiling, happy face, but the face that had been devoured by little fish.

Anger replaced sadness as I refocused on my mission.

I wished I could have seen Will's face as he plunged down that ravine. Even if he hadn't been part of the failed search party, a man like him needed to be wiped off the face of this earth. He thought he was something special. Treated women like commodities. He was over.

Everything was almost over now.

Leaning against the tree above the South Rim Trail, I cocked my rifle, embracing the sound of metal on metal.

I didn't believe in god, but I felt like, if one existed, he'd be nodding at me. He'd be saying, *Right on, man. Remove those errors from my world. They were my mistake. Thanks for cleaning up for me.*

Wasn't that what Dad always said? Try to make your mark on the world. So here it was, my mark. A big X right over the face of the search and rescue team that'd destroyed my family.

Jesus, I had to piss.

That was the one negative about this place. The sound of constantly rushing water left me with a consistent need to relieve myself. I'd been here three hours already, waiting for prick boy. Prick boy who was such a damn *saint*, who had to go and pay his last respects to the man-whore over in South Carolina.

Setting the rifle on a branch, I unzipped my cargo pants and did my thing, pissing between the branches, letting it hit the leaves below. I wished my stream was long enough to splatter Dina in the face.

As I palmed my cock, images of Linc Coulter's hot girl-friend flashed through my mind. She'd probably be devastated by her loss. She'd probably need someone to step in and comfort her. Kiss her. Stroke her. Make love to her.

A scream rent the air, and adrenaline flooded into my system before I realized what it was. A bobcat made a number of sounds, one of which sounded like a crying child.

Was that you?

Warning me? Scolding me?

I dropped my cock and zipped up, immediately ashamed. You're right. Not the time for that. I needed to focus.

Taking a deep breath to calm my racing heart, I lifted the rifle again and looked through the scope. Drew a bead on that long, winding staircase cut into the side of the gorge. From here, I'd have a good vantage point for anyone coming down the North Trail. I adjusted the lens, focusing on Dina.

Oh, yeah. I had the last two team members right where I wanted them.

Dina whimpered again. Poor little butch went all girly the second I started to drag her across the suspension bridge. She must have been thinking I was going to toss her off.

What fun would that have been?

I was way more imaginative than that. I had class. Style.

It'd probably be totally underappreciated by most assholes, how much work I'd put into this little gig.

But it was a work of art. My magnum opus.

And god, it looked good. I couldn't stop staring at it. I had her tied up like a Thanksgiving Day turkey, right in the center of the suspension bridge. She couldn't move a muscle, Jill, because you know I'm a knot expert. Did a couple constrictor knots and double fisherman's, so she wasn't ever going to get out of there. In fact, all that moving and sobbing she was doing was only making the knots tighter, making the bridge sway more.

You knew knots too, Jill. I'm sure you would've been proud.

Mom and Dad would have been proud too. Dad taught me everything I knew. He was a good guy to have around in a pinch. Well…before you…

He took it hard when you died. Thought he hadn't taught us enough, which was wrong. Damn wrong. I would've told him that if I'd known he was going to put that gun barrel in his mouth. Mom too. But she was too interested in her booze by then.

Well, now it was just me.

And why?

Because there were assholes like these guys. Called themselves rescuers. Knew shit about tackling the wild. Not a damn thing. They had blood all over their hands.

And I knew you'd agree with me, Jill. They deserved to die for what they did.

I leaned back, thinking of my little sister, thinking of how we used to laze inside, tying knots while watching old television shows on TV Land. I felt kind of like I was at the end of my run. You know, when everything's been done in a show, and there's nothing else left to do? The only thing that's left, after that, was cancellation. The end. Goodbye.

What would happen after today, after I finished?

Would I feel something? Or would I go back to feeling how I'd felt since the moment you left?

Empty.

Just…nothing.

That would suck.

I couldn't think about that right now. I had a job to do.

My hands tightened around the rifle, a gift from my dad on my ninth birthday. He was going to get you one, Jill, when you turned ten, because you were quite a shot too. Did you know that? Of course you didn't. I hope you know that now.

Across the gorge from here, I saw the first glimpse of a flashlight and smiled.

It was almost over now.

After I was finished with these two, I'd run. Or not. Maybe I'd just take a dive and say *goodbye world*.

Cancel myself.

See you in the reruns.

29

L inc slowly wound his way down the trail, using the meager flashlight and holding his gun in his hand. Despite the cool breeze, sweat streamed from his temples, and his chest tightened more with every step he took deeper into the gorge.

When he reached the stairs, he stopped. He could hear the falls in the distance. Overhead, an owl hooted.

He scanned the darkness around him, looking for unnatural shapes and shadows among the trees. Quietly, he listened, trying to pick out sounds from the rushing water and the breeze rustling the leaves. Nothing out of the ordinary.

Still, he had the distinct sensation that he was being watched, and under the circumstances, he knew the instinct was correct.

At that moment, he thought of Kylie and how she'd climbed down those steps so carefully. That'd been broad daylight. If she were out here on this night, she'd never make it down to the gorge. There was no way. He pictured her, lying in bed, thinking of him, and hoped that was where she was.

God, he wanted to be there too. In her arms. He loved the outdoors. Lived for it.

But he'd come to live for her more.

That fact had never been clearer to him than at that very moment. As it occurred to him, a chill snaked its way up his spine. He stiffened his back and shook it loose.

From here, the moonlight was nearly enough, so he cut the flashlight and shoved it into the pocket of his pants. Then he began to pick down the steps, one by one, clutching the handle of his pistol in both hands.

As he stepped down farther, he began to hear a different sound.

A human sound. The sound of someone sobbing.

Dina.

He cleared the tree branches, and the suspension bridge came into view. There, in the center of the long bridge, he saw Dina's shape, and the moonlight illuminating her spiked platinum hair. She let out a muffled cry, and he made out a dark line cutting into her mouth. It had to be a gag.

Squinting, he saw the ties binding her to the ropes of the narrow bridge, like a sacrificial offering. Peck had spread out her arms and legs, leaving her vulnerable to attack.

Beyond her form was nothing but darkness. Everywhere else he looked, he saw no signs of life. Like all of it was hiding away from him.

Tanner Peck, where are you? Show yourself.

He took a deep breath, and another step.

And another.

There was no other choice.

He needed to get down to her to free her, and she was in the middle of the bridge, exposed. Easily picked off by anyone with a gun. That meant if he went to try to free her, he would be exposed too.

But there was nothing else he could do.

Listening hard, he gazed into every shadow, searching for anything that didn't belong. He narrowed his focus, moving his eyes from one tree to the next as the moon slid behind a cloud.

Dammit.

Step by agonizing step, he made it down, holding his gun cocked and ready. When he reached the last step, even with the suspension bridge, he made up his mind to give up his position.

"Tanner Peck," he called, as Dina swung her head to him. She shrieked his name, then hung her head, sobbing, as it echoed around the gorge. "I know you're out here. Show yourself."

He held out a hand to calm her and waited for a response, scanning the area.

Only the wind answered back.

He took a step forward and called louder, "Tanner Peck. I know you're listening."

Just when he thought he'd get no response, a voice said, "So you know who I am. Good for you. I wasn't hiding it. I was waiting for you to figure it out. Took you forever."

Linc scanned the area, trying to get an idea of where it had come from. It sounded like it'd come from across the gorge, but he couldn't be sure with the way sounds always echoed around the place, bouncing off the rocks.

"Look. I know why you're doing this," he called out. "And I'm sorry about Jill. We all are. We went to the funeral. We took it really hard too."

He stopped, listened. Nothing.

"You have to believe that not a day goes by that I don't think of your sister. If it was that bad for me, for all of us, I can't even imagine how rough it has been for you. And I'm sorry. But killing other people won't bring her back. Listen to me."

Nothing, this time. Nothing except Dina, who was still sobbing loudly.

He took a step closer.

"Think about this. Come on out and let's talk this over," he called, lifting his foot to take another step.

As he did, he felt the force of a rifle shot hitting the ground just inches from him, and stopped where he was. "Don't move," came the reply. "Or the next one will be right between your eyes."

So, it turned out, Linc realized, that Tanner Peck, the bumbling kid from the ranger's station, wasn't without his talents.

He was actually a pretty damn good shot with a rifle.

30

H *ow do I get myself into these things?*
Kylie kept repeating that to herself as she made it down the trail, feeling about as graceful as a cow with a gun. She'd thought walking these trails before was a nightmare. She'd obviously had no idea what a nightmare was.

She couldn't see a damn thing and was terrified to use a flashlight, afraid of giving herself away and taking away the only advantage she had—the element of surprise. She'd flick it on for just seconds at a time, giving her enough visibility to traverse the worst parts of the trail.

Everything beyond the little orb of light was so dark—edge-of-the-known-universe dark. She felt like a sitting duck and like her fear was a beacon, guiding every bear and cougar in the area right to her.

"Um, Storm," she asked, her voice trembling, "are their bears and cougars in these woods?"

The dog ignored her and took another sure-footed step in front of her, pulling the leash taut, urging her to go faster. Kylie's teeth chattered. Of course there were bears and cougars and other wild animals here. That's why they called it the wilderness. This was not fit for civilized people.

As she imagined herself being shredded to death by predators or falling hundreds of feet to her death, an animal screeched overhead.

Kylie almost shrieked along with it but managed to clap a hand over her mouth.

Some giant, weird winged insect flew in front of her face, flittering in her eyelashes.

She squeezed her eyes closed, willing herself to be still.

A frog or some other close-to-the-ground creature that seemed entirely too near let out a noise that sounded like, *YOU DIE.*

She nearly dropped the leash, turned tail, and ran back to the car, screaming bloody murder.

Then she thought of Linc out there, somewhere, needing her desperately.

Even she had to admit it...if she was his last hope, he was probably well and truly screwed.

She pulled Storm's leash and took a deep breath, trying to regroup. Tucking the flashlight under her arm, she fanned her face, which was sweaty despite the chill in the air.

Calm, she told herself. *Remember, to some people like Linc, nature is beauty. People love this. It's actually quite wonderful, America's natural splendor. Be at one with it.*

Somewhere, an animal howled. Storm's ears perked up.

"I hope you're going to protect me, girl," she whispered to the dog, "because nature's splendor can go kiss my ass. There are wild animals out here that can rip my throat out. This is not a place for a human being."

Storm just looked up at her the way Linc sometimes did; like she wasn't sure they could still be friends.

She took another cleansing breath and let out the leash.

"Okay. I'm ready," she said to Storm. "Lead the way. Slow. Don't get me killed."

The trail turned into a staircase, a steep one without a railing. Storm humored her, going undoubtedly slower than she went with Linc, but it felt too fast. More animal noises seemed to come from everywhere—buzzes, growls, shrieks— she kept craning her neck in the direction of each new sound until she felt whiplashed. These woods were definitely bigger and darker and scarier than the ones in Asheville.

At one point, she stubbed her toe on a rock or a protruding root and went flying, only catching herself when she grabbed onto a hanging tree branch. "Why didn't you warn me, Storm?" she whispered at the dog. "I thought you were here to—"

She stopped when she suddenly heard it.

Not the sound of rushing waters or the wind blowing or an animal finding its way through the night.

This was something so much more familiar.

A human voice.

A human sob.

And then another voice. This one she knew in an instant.

Because it was Linc's voice.

She stilled, listening for it. Nothing.

Maybe she was mistaken. Hallucinating because that's what she so desperately wanted to hear. Or maybe he was dead, a ghost now, and haunting her.

She took another small step down when she heard it again. Soft enough to be a whisper.

But it was definitely Linc. She'd know his voice anywhere.

Storm heard it too. Her ears pricked up, and she took a few steps forward, tightening the leash, urging Kylie on.

Kylie kept listening, trying to make out what he was saying. With all the noises all around her, she couldn't,

couldn't even make out the tone of his voice. It was something she could use to her advantage, the noise, because even
though she was trying to be quiet, every dried leaf she
stepped on, every stick, felt enormously loud in her ears.

Taking a calming breath, she fed Storm more leash and
crept a few steps down. Kept navigating the stairs, a little
faster now.

*Go...go...go...*became her mantra.

Storm jumped ahead, and Kylie followed, trying not to be
so careful. She hit a step too hard and felt her ankle give way,
and then she was slipping. As she tried to right herself, Storm
let out a guttural growl and yanked the leash. Kylie felt it slip
through her fingers, and then the dog wrenched itself free
and took off fearlessly down the trail.

"Storm!" she whisper-shouted as she watched the dog's
dark rump disappear from view. The moon slid behind a
cloud, making everything even darker.

Perfect.

She was already stooped over from her almost-fall, so she
took the last little bit and let her butt fall onto the step
behind her. Sitting there, she lifted the flashlight, tempted to
arc it into the darkness while she tried to decide what to do.
But she knew the meager flashlight wouldn't help much, and
would only give her location away.

The moon was back, and her breath caught in her throat.
She was still high above the water.

High above everything. High enough that falling and
breaking one's neck was a definite possibility.

Linc's voice still seemed way off. She listened to it, hoping
it would calm her, but it didn't.

She had to do this. Face her fears and get closer, at least so
she could try to figure out where Linc was and what he was
saying.

Come on, Kylie. Be fearless. Be like your fiancé. Hell, be like your fiancé's dog. Show them you're a Coulter too.

Fisting her hands, she tucked the flashlight in her pocket and started back down the steps, one at a time. That's what Linc had said to her once—if an obstacle or job seemed too big, break it into little pieces, take it one step at a time. Hearing his voice in her head, she concentrated on the first step in front of her, and then the next one, and the next one.

Before long, she heard Linc speak, and she made out his voice clearly. "Look, Tanner. I know you don't want to do this."

He sounded calm, as usual. Calm, direct, and in control. But he was also pleading, and on the edge of exasperation.

She was shocked when somewhere, much closer by, a voice growled, "Don't tell me what I want to do. I know what I'm doing."

Her heart caught in her throat. That was Tanner Peck. The murderer. And he was very near. Closer than Linc. Maybe just down the path. And where was Storm?

Heart beating triple time in her chest, she peered into the darkness. Oh, this was a dream come true. Lost, in the dark, on a cliff edge. If she managed not to break her neck here, she vowed to herself that she would never, ever put herself in nature again. This was the last straw.

She blinked, frozen on the staircase, clinging to it as her eyes adjusted even more to the darkness. Moonlight streamed down upon the open space of the gorge, and in the distance, she could make out the suspension bridge. She craned her neck. Was that…

Was that Dina, tied up on the very center of the bridge?

She swallowed the gasp that wanted to escape.

Linc's voice again. Now, she was pretty sure where it was coming from. He was across the bridge, on the other side of the gorge. He said, his tone becoming firmer, "Fine. Why don't you show yourself? Come on out of wherever you're hiding and face me like a man?"

The response was so near, it made her jump. "You're not a man. A man would've been able to save a little girl."

She froze and let out a shaky breath. The voice sounded like it was floating among the trees, just slightly ahead of her.

So she'd established that Linc was on the other side of the bridge.

But Tanner? The killer?

He was on this side, with her.

Very, very close.

And where was Storm? She was alone, in the dark, with a killer. Doing what? Biding her time? Stalking the man? Or had she fallen, silently to her death and this was truly a nightmare?

Kylie tried to think like Linc. He had such a cool head under pressure. What would he do?

Probably something macho and badass. Rip his arm off and beat Tanner Peck into submission. He was good like that.

Kylie, however? No.

"We tried, Tanner. You know that. Come on down. Let's have a talk. Man to man."

"You're a baby killer!" Tanner screamed, and suddenly, what few leaves were still on the trees were rustling, and she saw a shape jumping out of the tree below, not twenty yards in front of her.

Her breath caught in her throat as the moonlight glistened on the shiny barrel of the rifle in his hand.

He started to walk toward the bridge. He didn't know she was there, behind him. Watching. Waiting.

She *definitely* knew what Linc would do now. He'd take advantage of the element of surprise and tackle the sucker from behind.

Not with her bare hands. Kylie'd get herself killed if she did that.

Tanner started to make his way toward the bridge, away from her, taking the steps as surely as if it were daylight.

Kylie crouched to the ground, feeling for a weapon. All she felt were piles of dried leaves. *Sure, you can just autumn him to death.*

Frantically, she watched Tanner's big form near the opening of the bridge. He stopped, cocking his gun and getting it into position. Lifting it. Taking aim.

Hurry! You're going to lose your chance!

Just as her hand wrapped tightly around the flashlight, another form bolted out of the woods. It leapt into the air, poised to tackle the young man to the ground.

A single gunshot went off.

A strangled yelp followed.

She'd never heard such a heart-wrenching sound, but she knew the animal that had made it. She could see its body slide to the ground, motionless.

It was Storm.

"No," she gritted out. She wasn't sure how she made it the rest of the way down the steps, but it was like she was flying, because a second later, she was coming up fast behind him with her makeshift weapon. She held it, poised to strike, when Tanner swung around, striking her across the face with the barrel of his gun.

She fell backward, stunned, sliding across the hard rock surface as he leveled the rifle toward her. "What the—?" he shouted, his finger moving to the trigger. "Where'd you—"

A snarl came from above them, and Tanner stopped, looking up.

Kylie scrambled to her feet and backed away, sure it was some bear or cougar about to do away with them all. In her terror, she turned on her flashlight, more afraid of the wild animal than the vengeance-filled ranger.

She gasped when she made out Vader's uncoordinated, fluffy body, galumphing his way down the stairs, his big black eyes trained right on Tanner Peck.

There was something Kylie'd never seen before in them.

It was dark, so she couldn't be sure.

But it looked like vengeance.

31

L‍inc's heart nearly stopped.

He leveled the gun, stopped, leveled it again.

It was too risky.

Too dark, and everything he loved was on the other side of that bridge.

He'd seen Kylie, her face illuminated by her flashlight, and he willed her to turn it off. She had no idea what she was walking into. He'd also seen Storm, storming into the situation—that was how she'd gotten her name, after all—ready to take no prisoners.

He'd also heard the yelp she emitted, a sound he never wanted to hear again, and he raced to the edge of the suspension bridge, consequences be damned. When he got there, he realized Tanner was facing away from him. Kylie had proved to be the perfect distraction.

He lifted his gun and aimed, ready to take a shot.

But from his vantage point, he noticed something tumbling down the stairs on the other side—something big and lumbering, like a black bear.

When it dove for Tanner, he knew what it was. "Vader!" he shouted.

As he watched, Tanner disappeared, and dread filled Linc with its icy claws. He took off, rocketing across the swaying bridge, willing himself to go faster. He stopped long enough to check on Dina.

"You hurt?"

Her face and eyelids were swollen, two crooked trails of dried blood leaked from her nose. She shook her head. "No. I'm okay. Go get him."

He reached into his pocket, pulled out the penknife, and cut the binding on her arms loose, then handed the tool to her so she could cut herself free. He looked up at the edge of the gorge, where Tanner had fallen. He couldn't make anything out.

"Kylie!" he shouted, stumbling around Dina on the planks that creaked and moved under him like an undulating funhouse ride.

Nothing at first. Then, a moment after he'd broken into a run, a breathless voice shouted, "I've got his gun!"

Kylie. He ran the rest of the way across the swaying bridge, hope flooding every cell.

His feet hit solid ground. The second they did, Kylie screamed, "No!"

Fear like he'd never experienced raced through his veins like ice. "Kylie!" he yelled. His echo was his only reply.

No. She couldn't be gone. He refused to believe it.

"Kylie!" he screamed again, the word ripping from his throat.

He listened for her reply. He listened for the dogs. Anything.

"Linc."

His name was close to a sob, but it was the sweetest sound he'd ever heard. Her voice fueled him, and he ran to her, grabbing the flashlight from her hand. She sat cross-legged on the rocks, Storm's head on her lap.

The dog wasn't moving.

No. Please, God. No.

A fresh flood of adrenaline competed with the pain and grief of seeing his beloved partner so still. Beside Kylie, Vader whimpered, pushing his nose into Storm's face. The big dog looked up at him, his expression practically shouting, *do something, you idiot.*

Kylie was crying harder now, her hands stroking over Storm's bloody fur.

Linc heaved in an unsteady breath, his whole body feeling like it would explode. He crawled closer and took the dog's body onto his own lap. Her fur felt warm. He couldn't detect a pulse, though.

He ran his hand down her side and felt the sticky viscosity of blood. There was so much of it that he couldn't tell where the wound was.

This couldn't be happening.

Not after all the time he'd known Storm. First, as barely a puppy in Syria, then through hundreds of SAR missions. And now…

Not now. Not here. He wasn't ready for this.

He brought his hand to her muzzle and touched her face, and as he did, she opened her jaws and licked his hand.

Linc let out a sigh of relief. He tilted his head, encouraged. "What are you doing, Storm? Taking a break?"

The dog's eyes fell on him, and she licked his hand again. Then she lifted her head and put it up on his knee, as if to say, "Adore me?"

"That's okay, you deserve it."

He laughed as Kylie suddenly flipped on her flashlight, shedding some much-needed light on the situation.

He saw the problem at once. Storm's front leg had taken

the brunt of a bullet. He touched it gingerly, frowning. Then he looked up at Kylie. "You have anything up there I can use for a bandage?"

She reached into the bag, and a moment later, pulled out a red bandanna.

He wrapped it around the wound carefully, then patted the dog's head. "Good girl," he whispered in her ear, then reached over and hugged a trembling Kylie. Then he pulled Vader into the mix. "Good boy, hero dog."

Kylie gave a shaky laugh, wrapping her arm around the big dog too. "Yeah. You saved us, boy."

"Are you okay?" he asked her as she crouched into his side, shivering.

She gave him a watery smile. "Fine. But what about Storm?"

He patted the dog's side. "She'll come through. She's a tough old girl, right, Storm?"

She looked up at him with love in her eyes. He wondered if she knew what he knew. They might have called Linc one of the best in the business. That was because he was part of a tremendous duo, a crackerjack SAR team with some of the best rescue rates in the country.

But Linc knew it, and there was something in Storm's eyes that said she knew it too. That crackerjack team, sadly, would never work together again.

32

Six months later...

It was such a beautiful day. A winner, as Rhonda was fond of saying, a perfect ten. Especially for May in the mountains, where one day it could be hot and sunny and the next, almost frigid.

But today was gorgeous. The temperature perfect. The birds were singing in the trees, and the bulbs Linc and Kylie had planted had transformed into a rainbow of tulips.

It was like everything was saying to her, *We're perfect for you...so now, you have to be too.*

And it made the knot in Kylie's stomach twist tighter.

Kylie looked down at herself, then back at the mirror in the hallway, and then at her mother. She tucked her grandmother's handkerchief in her bouquet for the tears she'd undoubtedly shed, swished her thighs together to make sure she was wearing her "something blue" garter and checked to make sure her "girls" weren't overexposed or flushed. "Am I ready?"

Rhonda nodded. "As you'll ever be."

"What does that mean? I have to look perfect. I have everything, right?"

Rhonda swirled the skirt on her lemon-yellow mother-of-the-bride dress. "Except the husband. Yes. Go on and get that man."

She gnawed on her lower lip. "But do I look okay? I'm supposed to be perfect."

"Nothing's ever perfect. Find perfection in the imperfect," her mother said cryptically.

Kylie's head swam. "What does that mean?"

Her mother leaned over and kissed her on the cheek. "Yes. You look perfect. Perfectly beautiful. Now stop worrying, my little flower. Linc is going to flip when he sees you."

She sucked in a breath. She wasn't sure she'd ever been this nervous before in her entire life. "All right. Then let's do this."

The months had flown by, faster than she thought time could move. Who knew that when she met him, almost a full year ago, that that stoic, grumpy stick in the mud actually had a beautiful, romantic heart?

He'd actually been gung-ho about the whole thing. Once she confessed to him that she was having trouble with all the preparations and was too overwhelmed by the sheer volume of plans that had to be ironed out, he'd said, "Why didn't you say so? I thought you wanted to plan it yourself. I'd love to help you. Team effort, right? That's what marriage is, anyway."

And he had. He'd taken over every last detail that she'd been fretting over, making all the planning as easy as pie. They'd agreed on so much, it was a wonder she hadn't asked him sooner.

He'd done good too. She had to admit that so far, everything was going like a dream.

And now, all that was left was to get married, relax, and have a good time.

If only.

She opened the screen door and walked out onto the porch. Cars were parked everywhere, in the place Linc loved so much for its peace and quiet. He didn't mind, though. The last time she'd seen him, before they'd been separated to get ready, he'd practically been bouncing up and down on his feet, he couldn't sit still. He'd reminded her of Vader.

She closed the door and wobbled a little in her fancy heels. On the field to her left, a giant tent had been set up. With her mother's help, she lifted her train and walked across the grassy field, to the tent, with its flaps open and waiting for her.

Time to get this show on the road.

The guests stood in unison and turned toward her, waiting for her to make the trip. The trip that would change her entire life and make her a wife.

She looked over at her mom once more. "You're not lying to me?"

Rhonda laughed and hugged her arm tighter, almost like she was afraid she might run away. "Don't tell me you're getting cold feet now."

"Not about the man. Heck, not even about the event anymore. Linc planned most of it, so I'm sure it'll be fine. It's mostly about the dress. It's the one thing on the checklist Linc didn't have a hand in."

Rhonda's smile almost brought tears to Kylie's eyes, she looked so proud. "That dress is so *you*, Kylie. Linc will love it, I promise."

She hoped. She'd gotten the stain on the bodice out, and then she'd spent a long time thinking of the jewelry and accessories she wanted to wear with it. She'd selected a pearl choker, and she'd decided to wear her hair long, with that long, romantic piece of tulle for the veil. Just like that photograph.

"All right. I'm ready."

She looked over and nodded at Erik Coulter, one of Linc's older brothers, who was handling Vader, the ring bearer. He dipped his head to go into the tent and walked the dog down the aisle. A moment later, she heard a commotion as someone shrieked. She peered in in time to see Vader streak down the aisle, tackling the priest like a football player stopping a first down.

Kylie grabbed her bouquet tightly and clenched her teeth. "This is going to be a disaster, isn't it?"

Her mother craned her neck as the shrieks and gasps turned into laughter. The priest was laughing too. She patted her daughter's hand. "Even if the whole world ends today, it'll be just perfect. Imperfectly perfect. *You're* perfect. Because you two are finally together, and today you become Mrs. Linc Coulter."

She smiled at her mom. Yes, that was true. In the grand scheme of things, what did Vader's excited antics or the flowers or the tent or the dress really mean?

All that mattered was that she was in love with Linc, and today they would become each other's forever.

"Okay," she said again. "I'm ready."

At her nod, a violin quartet began to play the wedding march, and they proceeded to walk down the aisle.

She'd promised herself she wouldn't cry.

But since when did anything happen to her, and she didn't cry?

So, of course, she cried.

The second she saw Linc, all the love she felt for the man slid down her face, mussing her waterproof makeup. But none of that mattered. All that mattered was the look on

Linc's face. It was a look of awe, of such powerful love, that it took her breath away.

And what was that?

Was he crying a little too?

She couldn't stop smiling, and it wasn't one that she'd put on for the photographer or the video cameras. It was because, for the first time, she finally felt like she was where she was meant to be. And she loved him so much she felt like her heart was going to explode.

When she reached the front of the aisle, Rhonda kissed her and helped her arrange her train and veil. Then she put Linc's hand in hers and moved aside.

Kylie gazed into Linc's eyes.

Yep, definitely tears. He couldn't hide it this close.

"You look beautiful," he murmured to her, his smile so wide, she'd never seen him smile like that before.

The rest of the ceremony was a bit of a blur. Vader disappeared with the rings to go canoodle with his girlfriend, Storm, who was resting on the side aisle next to Greg. Kylie got so excited for the kiss that she jumped into Linc's arms before they were officially announced as man and wife. She tripped on her train a little when they turned to face their guests.

But none of that mattered.

"Presenting to you, Mr. And Mrs. Lincoln Coulter," the priest said, as the whole tent—fifty-five of their closest friends and family—burst into applause.

Linc wrapped his arm around her, lifting his chin proudly, and walked her back up the aisle. "That dress is really something," he said to her.

"You like it?"

"Hell yes. You look like an old-time movie actress. That's right up my alley. What can I say? I have a hot wife."

Her face hurt from smiling so much as they made their way to the end of the aisle. As they did, she finally noticed people she hadn't when her eyes were focused at Linc. There was Jerry, her new stepfather. Jacob Dean, Linc's best friend, along with his girlfriend, Faith. Annie, her best friend growing up, and her husband. Linc's brothers and their kids, and his parents. All of them wishing them well on their marriage.

It was growing chilly outdoors, so another tent had been set up for the reception. Before that, she and Linc went out to the field behind the house as the sun finished setting to have their photos taken.

Holding her hand, they walked together, alone, into the sunset, the photographer following at a considerable distance. He leaned into her and kissed her cheek. "Are you happy?"

"More than I could ever imagine," she said to him, feeling like she was going to cry all over again. "This is like a dream. I never thought I could feel this way."

He took both of her hands in his and gazed into her eyes, his warm chocolate-brown eyes melting her, body and soul. "Good. I'm going to do everything possible to make sure you stay that way. That's my mission in life."

He leaned over and kissed her as the sun began to disappear, painting the sky with a palette of color.

Kylie got just the exact recreation of the photo she was hoping for when they paused in the field to kiss—with one addition. Storm had limped out to join them, and of course, wherever Storm went, Vader was never far behind. It was their first family photograph.

When the photographs were done, they went in to the reception, to more applause. The DJ announced them as man and wife, and then they went onto the dance floor for their first dance. As "Can't Help Falling in Love" by Elvis Presley began, she smiled as Linc waltzed her around the floor, astonished. She didn't even know he could dance this well.

"Do you approve?" he asked her.

"Yes, I do, but...how is this our song? What made you choose it?"

He grinned. "It was playing in the vet's office the first time I met you. Remember?"

She raised an eyebrow. "Was it? How did you...?"

"Because when your world gets flipped around, you tend to remember everything, even the most insignificant details. I remember all of it," he said, kissing her.

After the toast from Linc's father, they walked around, thanking all the guests for coming. Because it was intimate, she'd met most of the people before, and she felt the love swelling in the room. They went around as a couple, kissing a lot of people, fielding congratulations. When they stopped in front of Greg, he kissed her. "So, you're taking a week off. What's the honeymoon looking like?"

She shrugged. "We're going to the beach in a few weeks. Just for a long weekend. We need to be somewhere with the dogs, because of Storm. We didn't know when she was going to have her babies. She's about to give birth any moment now."

After the excitement at Tallulah Gorge, they'd taken Storm to the vet for emergency surgery. They'd had to amputate her front leg, but during the surgery, they learned she was pregnant. Both dog parents had been floored.

Linc had never gotten her spayed, planning on letting her have a couple litters of puppies he could one day grow into SAR dogs. One day. And to a male dog of his choosing.

But it appeared that nature, and Vader, had made other plans.

Kylie and Linc strongly suspected that any day now, there'd be little Newfoundland/German Shepherd mix puppies running around the house. Yes, ten or so little Vaders...the horror. Kylie wasn't worried, though, because thankfully, she'd have the Dog Whisperer around to train them.

Though they both knew, as their old sofa and the broken handle on her new Jeep could attest, Vader sometimes defied even the best dog trainer's directions.

This was going to be an adventure.

That was okay. Kylie felt ready. Ready for the next step in her life. Even if it meant not becoming a PI. They'd talked about it before, and since Linc seemed eager for kids, she admitted that it wouldn't be the worst thing in the world to have to give up on being a private investigator and maybe start working for Linc full-time.

No, she wasn't a Dog Whisperer, but she could help him with his SAR videos and website, and around the farm.

Though she hated giving up being a PI, which she loved, she was ready to do what she needed to do, because it felt like anything with Linc was the right choice.

"Well," Greg said. "Don't think you need to rush back into work anytime soon. I know how you hate taking those vacation days, but you deserve them. Both of you need a little time off."

"Thanks," she said, stroking his hand fondly. For a man who'd been such a grump when they first met, she couldn't believe how much she'd come to love him.

He straightened his tie. "So, tell me...don't I get to dance with the bride?"

She gave him a look. He was always so, well, grouchy, and he'd always harrumphed at her, whenever she'd tried to liven things up by dancing around the office. "You want to? I mean, you even know how to?"

"Hell yes. And I know how you like to dance."

Linc grinned at the two of them. "Knock yourself out."

"Well, all right then. Let's cut a rug," she said, taking his hand.

She led him out to the floor, where a slow song was playing. He twirled her around, and she followed his lead. For a big grouch, he was surprisingly graceful and light on his feet.

"Now that you're an old married woman, are you expecting to be barefoot and pregnant right away with that dreamy man of yours?"

She laughed. Way to be direct. "What, are you trying to get rid of me? Actually, I thought it was *you* that would be barefoot soon, on an island, or your retirement yacht, or something."

He nodded. "Oh, that's an idea that's been batted around. But when you came on, I decided I had to do something first."

She wrinkled her nose. "Me? What?"

"Get you enough time under your belt so you can get your PI license and take the business over from me."

She blinked. "What?"

"You heard me. You ever think of owning your own business?"

"Yes, but…when did you decide that?"

"About fifteen seconds after I hired you and realized you wanted to do everything *but* what you'd been hired to do. I looked at you and thought, this is just the tenacious little thing this broken-down business needs to keep it going. Up until then, I'd planned to get the filing squared away, clean up the office, pull the shingle off the front door, and call it a day."

"Really? But…" She trailed off, just trying to imagine it. She was so shocked, she let him dip her. Right then, a feather could've knocked her down.

When she looked back into his eyes, he was smiling. "Yeah. Tell me you haven't thought about it."

"No, I have. I just…I mean, Linc keeps saying I could stay home if I want and work for him."

He raised an eyebrow. "Hmmm. You want that?"

She glanced over at Linc, who was dancing with her mother. "Well, that's beside the point. We're a team now. He has enough money to support us with his grandparents' inheritance, and he wants me safe. He wants kids, and he thinks the business of private investigations is a little dangerous."

"Kylie, kid. You've been shot. Kidnapped. Nearly bitten by a poisonous snake. Had your car torched. Nearly had your fiancé murdered. I'd say Linc's right. It's been a *lot* dangerous for you. And knowing you, that's not likely to change."

She nodded. "True."

"But I can tell you love it."

She nodded again, a small smile appearing on her lips.

"What's more, you're damn good at it. So I guess it's up to you, what you want out of life. I don't think you can go wrong either way. But will you really be happy if you give it all up for good?"

When he said it like that, she knew she'd be sad if she gave it up. It was something she'd need to give enormous thought to. "Okay, I'll think about it. How would it work?"

He shrugged. "Any way you want it to. I could stay on as a consultant until you have your license. The building's a lease, so you can operate out of anywhere, but we can work out a deal and I'll transfer everything else over to your name. The accounts, the assets, everything else. I don't need it, and the business means more than money to me." He gave her a wink. "Would be nice to see it live on."

She hardly knew what to say. They finished out the dance with her having a bit of an out-of-body experience, imagining what it would be like to run her very own business. For a girl who barely a year ago had been waffling around trying to decide on her future, this was a massive step.

Kylie Hatfield, a business owner.

Er…Kylie *Coulter*, a business owner.

She practically shivered with excitement at the thought.

She hugged him as the song came to an end, her mind still dwelling on the opportunity. In another six or so months, she could have her license, and the entire business could be hers.

Theirs. She'd share it, of course, with her husband.

All the goods, all the bads. The profitable clients, and all the danger that went along with it.

She kissed Greg's cheek. "Thank you. This is so much better than business cards. It's like a dream."

He laughed. "Just don't make it a deadly dream."

When the dance was over, she walked back to their sweetheart table in a daze. Linc was sitting there, having just said goodbye to his little nephew, finishing the last of his strawberry champagne. He noticed something was up right away. "You okay?"

"Well…yeah. But I guess…" She stopped. It was silly to have a deep conversation like this, when the name of tonight was to celebrate their love. That was what she wanted to concentrate on. "It's nothing."

He grabbed her hand and kissed it. "It's something. Just tell me. If Greg is closing up shop, it's not a big deal. I told you that. You can stay home, I can support us, and we can get started on that family right away. No problem. So—"

"It's not that," she said breathlessly. "No. He *is* planning to retire soon, but he wants to leave his business to me."

Linc's eyes bulged. "To you?"

She nodded. "All of it. The accounts, the name, the assets. The building is just a lease but…everything else." Even as she said it, she realized what a tremendous opportunity it was.

One that was impossible to turn down. But she saw the worry in Linc's eyes. She squeezed his hand. "I didn't tell him yes. We obviously have to discuss it."

"Yeah. It's dangerous. Especially if we have a family."

"You think your job is free of peril? After what we just went through with Tanner Peck? *Both* our jobs are dangerous," she reminded him, cupping his face with her hand. "I wish there was a way we could combine them. You know, that way, we could keep an eye on each other."

He nodded, thinking.

She waved the idea away. "Oh, but you're going to be so busy soon. Training a new litter of SAR dogs? You probably won't even have time to breathe."

"Now, wait a minute," he said, his forehead wrinkling in thought. "It wouldn't be a terrible idea."

Her heart jumped. He was thinking about it? Seriously?

But then she realized they were both frowning when only five minutes ago, they'd had ear-to-ear grins on their faces. They had to stay in this moment. That's what everyone always said to her: *Your wedding day goes by so fast. Enjoy every last minute of it.*

Right now, that's what she wanted to do. She didn't want to think about the future.

She shook her head. "Maybe not. But we don't have to decide anything right now, husband. Right now, I want to enjoy my wedding reception. And then my wedding night." She bobbed her eyebrows. "Come on, let's dance."

Kylie Jane Hatfield Coulter took her husband's hand and led him to the center of the floor. "Oh What a Night" was playing, and when she stepped into his arms, nothing else mattered.

33

Spring bled into summer, and soon, Kylie had her brand-new PI license. Greg was still in the picture as a permanent consultant, but since he was semi-retired and living in a waterfront condo on Lake Norman further east in the state, she didn't see or hear from him as much as she'd like.

Still, business was booming. Because she and Linc had decided to combine the two ventures, she'd moved the investigations business up to the farmhouse, and worked out of there with Linc. Greg had given them the blessing to change the company's name to Coulter Confidential, so the two of them had set up an office in the front living area, two desks butting up to one another.

They had a very comfortable setup in what had once been the unused dining room of the house, with state-of-the-art computers, and of course, a Keurig.

What they didn't have was downtime.

"Great, Ollie," she said with a smile as she cradled her phone between her cheek and shoulder. She reached for some of the papers she'd printed and tripped over a tail. Then she went back, feeling for the back of her chair, and tripped over a furry head. "I'm so glad to hear things are good for you. Thanks for checking in. Talk again soon?"

Kylie hung up and absently sat down on her chair and rolled up under her desk, stapling a report together. As she started to reread it, she felt a wet sensation on her butt.

She frowned. "All right," she called out loud to nobody in particular, "who was drooling on my chair?"

As she rolled out, she almost kicked one of the other puppies. All ten of them were now big, adorable, and rambunctious—so rambunctious they were even giving Linc a run for his money. They were always, absolutely always, underfoot, always drooling, always hungry, always playing and being mischievous. And when Linc and Kylie tried to go to bed? Forget it. Their bed had been consumed by twelve dog bodies.

The humans were definitely the underdogs in this house.

"Ollie's got a girlfriend," Kylie said out loud to Linc, though she really wasn't sure where he was. "He just called to check in and tell me that he really appreciated all that we did."

Linc came over with coffee for her in the I HEART NEWFS mug Greg had gotten her for Christmas. He set it down on the desk and kissed her on the top of the head. "Again?"

She laughed. Beez's widower had called about five times to say that. The old man had really appreciated what they'd done. He'd sent them flowers and chocolates and had spoken highly of Kylie to Greg. And now, he was checking in all the time, like their best friend. "He met a woman at Bingo. Says she's not Beez, but she'll do. He's so funny."

Linc shook his head. "Leave it to you to become his best friend."

"Well, he is an old man. He needed a friend. I like being friendly."

Linc nodded. "You sure do. So guess what?"

She looked up at him. "What?"

"Fixed the handle on your door."

"Really? No kidding? Thank you," she said, blowing him a kiss as he went to sit at his own desk. It'd only been eight months of her having to wrestle with the chewed-up door handle or else use the passenger's side door and jump over the console. Vader had really done a number on the handle—not the headrests—that night at the gorge. "You did it yourself?"

He nodded. "Wasn't so hard."

"Then I don't know why it took you eight freaking months." She smiled at him sweetly.

He blew on his fingernails and pretended to polish them on his chest. "Pure genius takes time. How's work in here going?"

She looked around at the accumulating pile of papers on her desk. Maybe *she* needed to hire a filer. "It's going. The monsters are at it, though, as usual."

He shrugged and put his hand down to pet one of the pups. That was the good thing about living in this house—there was no shortage of cute faces to pet. "That's nothing new."

"Did you train them at all today?"

"Best I can. Puppies are hard. They're coming along, though. Slowly. But I can tell they're smart. They just got a hell of a lot of energy. They'll make good SARs, though, one day."

Because of the summer heat, he'd been walking around in nothing but gym shorts all day, and she had to admit, looking mighty fine doing it. They'd just celebrated their three-month anniversary, and she was still as excited to look at him as she ever had been. She laid a hand on her stomach to quell the butterflies.

Or maybe that was something else.

"You feeling all right?"

She looked up to find him gazing at her with worry. "Oh. Fine. Why?"

He pointed to her face. "You just look a little...flushed. You okay?"

She swallowed. Flushed? Or was it a glow? She'd been having feelings lately...feelings that both excited and terrified her. And she wasn't quite sure how to articulate them to Linc. She knew he'd be thrilled, but still...what if she wasn't ready?

"I'm perfect..." she said, forcing a smile as a couple of puppies started to nip at each other behind Linc. He spun on his chair to break it up, and as he did, she fanned her face.

Body, stop acting so weird!

She sipped her coffee, trying to concentrate on the report. On work. That was the name of the game. Getting Coulter Confidential on solid footing. Yes, they'd taken over all of Greg's accounts, including the one with his biggest client, Impact Insurance, but that didn't mean they could just take it easy. Greg had been very complacent with his business. Kylie was a go-getter. She didn't want Coulter Confidential to survive—she wanted it to thrive. To grow.

To do that, she'd been working on advertising to drum up business, and Linc had been helping her with a new plan to possibly expand into other markets in the next five years. It was an exciting time, and now, with the wedding behind them, she had all the time and resources to really pour into making it work.

Of course, in order to do that, she'd told Linc that she wanted to put off having kids. Just for a little while. At least the next two years. He'd been supportive. After all, she was still young. They had plenty of time.

Or...maybe no time at all.

A bit of nausea climbed its way up her throat, growing more intense as she tried to swallow it down.

She pushed away from the desk and stood up. "I'm just going to…" She pointed to the bathroom.

Linc, too busy looking at his computer, just waved at her.

As he clicked away at his computer, she fought the now-overpowering urge to vomit until she made it to the bathroom. Behind the closed door, she dry-heaved over the toilet, trying to keep the sound of her gagging down.

Well, that was new.

She took a breath as she hung over the toilet. She couldn't put this off any longer.

When she was done, she wiped her mouth with a bit of toilet paper, opened the drawer and pulled out the wand from the back of the cabinet where she'd stashed it. She'd gotten it a week ago at the drugstore when she'd realized she was a few days late. She hadn't really noticed until then, because her periods had been somewhat irregular; she'd been forced to go off the pill because they were giving her headaches. They'd lately been practicing the rhythm method of birth control and using condoms…usually. It should have been fine. But now…

She read the instructions, which told her that once she provided a sample, she'd have her answer in less than three minutes.

Three minutes. Moment of truth.

Taking another deep breath, she squatted on the toilet. No pee.

Of course, she'd suffer from performance anxiety during her moment of truth. She closed her eyes. Squeezed.

Nothing.

She tried to focus on waterfalls. Oceans. Then she reached over and turned on the faucet.

Eventually, she was able to concentrate enough to get a

few drops of pee on the stick. As she was hitting full stream, her phone rang. Linc picked it up. She heard him say, "Coulter Confidential, this is Linc."

She got up from her squat and stared at the stick. "Kylie, you need to take this. Almost done in there, or do you want me to ask them to call back?"

He sounded pretty urgent, like he didn't want to lose the call.

They had a pretty well-delineated division of responsibility. Linc was good on the SAR matters, but any PI cases were her jurisdiction. He was often calling her in to take down notes on these cases, because she knew how to ask all the right questions.

"Yeah, I'll be right there!" she said through the door, quickly rolling up the garbage and stuffing it into the garbage can, then tucking the wand back into the bottom drawer.

After washing her hands, she stepped out and walked to her desk as he held the phone out to her.

"Who is it?" she asked. "One of Greg's clients?"

He smiled and shook his head. "New one. Saw our ad online. Sounds like a pretty big deal. Something about investigating a phony adoption agency."

She sucked in a breath. Greg's clients were all well and good, albeit it was always dull day-to-day grunt work, conducting background checks and workers' comp surveillance. Nothing too exciting. It was those big crimes that really got Kylie's heart pumping. And this sounded like one of them. The opportunity they were waiting for, maybe.

"Seriously? That does sound big." She picked up the phone. "Hello. Coulter Confidential. This is Kylie Coulter." She never got tired of saying that name. "Who am I speaking with?"

She took down the information as professionally as she

could. But even though something like this would've had her dancing around the office, unable to keep still, her mind was focused on what was waiting for her in the bathroom. She'd have to look as soon as she got off the phone. She didn't want Linc finding it before she even had a chance to process it.

Whatever it was, it'd be okay. They'd deal with it. If kids came now, they'd find a way to make it work.

At least, she hoped.

She hung up and looked over at Linc, who was watching her expectantly, waiting for some information. "Well?"

She smiled at him cautiously. "I have a feeling we are in for a very interesting few months."

Linc raised an eyebrow. "Big case, huh?"

She leaned down to pet the sea of puppies around her chair and sighed. Actually, for the first time in a long time, she wasn't even thinking about a case.

The End
To be continued...

Find all of the Kylie Hatfield books on Amazon.

ACKNOWLEDGMENTS

How does one properly thank everyone involved in taking a dream and making it a reality? Here goes.

In addition to our families, whose unending support provided the foundation for us to find the time and energy to put these thoughts on paper, we want to thank the editors who polished our words and made them shine.

Many thanks to our publisher for risking taking on two newbies and giving us the confidence to become bona fide authors.

More than anyone, we want to thank you, our readers, for clicking on a couple of nobodies and sharing your most important asset, your time, with this book. We hope with all our hearts we made it worthwhile.

Much love,
Mary & Bella

ABOUT THE AUTHOR

Mary Stone lives among the majestic Blue Ridge Mountains of East Tennessee with her two dogs, four cats, a couple of energetic boys, and a very patient husband.

As a young girl, she would go to bed every night, wondering what type of creature might be lurking underneath. It wasn't until she was older that she learned that the creatures she needed to most fear were human.

Today, she creates vivid stories with courageous, strong heroines and dastardly villains. She invites you to enter her world of serial killers, FBI agents but never damsels in distress. Her female characters can handle themselves, going toe-to-toe with any male character, protagonist or antagonist.

Discover more about Mary Stone on her website.
www.authormarystone.com

Bella Cross spent the past fifteen years teaching bored teenagers all about the Dewey Decimal System while inhaling the dust from the library books she loves so much. With each book she read, a little voice in her head would say, "You can do that too." So, she did.

A thousand heart palpitations later, she is thrilled to release her first novel with the support of her husband, twin girls, and the gigantic Newfoundland she rescued warming her feet.

facebook.com/authormarystone

instagram.com/marystone_author

bookbub.com/profile/3378576590

goodreads.com/AuthorMaryStone

pinterest.com/MaryStoneAuthor

Made in the USA
Coppell, TX
08 January 2021

47769098R10168